Books by Niki Livingston

Theia's Moons Series

Eyes Wide Shut

Enyo's Warrior

Protectors of the Stars

Guardian

The Chaos Awakened Saga

Marked Chaos

Expanded Chaos

Transformed Chaos – coming February 2021

Novels

Be My Leprechaun

Novellas

Wrong Side of the Mirror

Novelettes

A Web Through Time

Wicked Heart

Wicked Soul

Jolly Old Monster

Unable to Wake

EXPANDED CHAOS

Blood ties could be their undoing

NIKI LIVINGSTON

Expanded Chaos

ISBN: 978-1-952537-08-0

Publisher: Unbound Wonders Press

Editor: Novel Nurse Editing

Cover Artist: Niki Ellis Designs

To connect: www.NikiLivingston.com

To Chandler.

I hope the winds take you to the highest heights of your dreams.

My mind rages with a whirlwind of chaos and madness.

A fragmented heart of piercing beauty.

Guarded, but fierce.

Heartbroken with the strength of a warrior.

A powerful tempest that evil fears.

CHAPTER ONE
Family

KIA LYNN

I stared dumbfounded at Jax and Alex, then scrunched up my nose in distaste.

"We are family?" I asked, my gaze shifting between the two as I pointed at myself and then at each of them.

Jax nodded with a hopeful eyes. "I would be considered your uncle, and Alex is your cousin."

I tilted my head. Rafael was Zoe Dawn's cousin and they hated one another. But I had always believed family was what mattered, even though the ones who were not blood seemed far more loyal than the ones who were. Mama was blood, and supposedly her brother was standing in front of me. How was it possible I never knew he existed? Why would she have kept that from me?

"No," I snapped, unable to wrap my mind around what they were telling me. "Mama would not keep you from me."

Jax's brows lifted and Alex released a heavy sigh.

"Your mother was not the most honest woman," Alex whispered, averting her eyes.

"Your aunt and my mama are not the same person," I hissed between clenched teeth. My hands tightened into fists and a gust of wind wrapped its way around us, pushing them closer together.

Jax steadied Alex and held his other hand out toward me. "Kia Lynn, you have every right to not trust me, but do you really believe Alex would be lying to you?"

I inhaled a long breath and looked past them at the butterfly swarm. The air softened as the sharp winds dissipated. "No, I do not believe Alex would lie to me." I swallowed back the fear pounding in my chest and returned my focus to Alex and Jax. "She is my mother. Why would she not tell me about her family?"

"Because I betrayed her." Jax hung his head in shame. "When her anaman traits began to recede, I was embarrassed of her. I let her fall into the hands of tormenters, never once protecting her like I should."

"And what about Alex?"

"She did not know Alex existed until after she left you," Jax replied as he wrapped a protective arm around Alex's shoulders. "In the end, Kia Lynn, we want to be your family. I want to make amends for the transgressions I committed against your mother by having a solid presence in your life."

I pressed my lips together, still unsure if I could trust him.

Alex stepped forward and grabbed my arm. "No matter what you decide, I am your sister. Connected for life. I can be your cousin as well, but we are family either way."

My shoulders relaxed from her touch. She was right. I grasped her hand in mine and squeezed it. "Then we are all family. Now"—I rubbed my palms together—"if my mother is really alive, how do I find her?"

Alex's jaw twitched as she dropped my hand and turned away from me. She was hiding something. I turned toward Jax and lifted my brows in waiting.

"We don't know if it is possible to find your mother," Jax said, his hand resting protectively on Alex's shoulder. "Tallisa's offensive behavior forced us to separate before we arrived to your world, and we have not seen her since."

I shook my head, frustration crawling up my spine. "We never leave family behind."

"But she left you behind," Alex whispered, her eyes still turned toward the rising sun.

"Alex, please don't," Jax muttered, squeezing her shoulder. "This is not the time."

Alex whipped around and glared at Jax, then turned her narrowed eyes toward me. "Kia Lynn, I am most definitely your family. After what we just went through, I will forever be joined with you and Zoe Dawn." Her gaze dropped to the flowers below our feet. "But I cannot help you find your mother."

She then pivoted on her heel and trudged toward Malcolm's small city, which was nestled between the cliffs of the red mountains he called Zion. The landslide that now covered the giant tunnel, the one Tatum and his people had dug to infiltrate Malcolm's protective shield, was a new feature to the city, and it marked the graves of many enemies to me, but those who were friends of my mother.

The entire situation was overwhelming and confusing.

My newfound bond with Alex was enough to question Mama's actions. Two days earlier we had revived Mother Gaia to her full beauty, releasing the vibrancy back into the vegetation, along with the insect and animal life that had long been forgotten. I had learned magic really did exist. It now surrounded us, but even the mystical elements did not have the power to force a person to reveal their secrets.

I stared after Alex as she disappeared into the orchard of fruit trees. I would speak to her later.

My gaze drifted toward Jax. "What do I need to do to find my mother?" Papa always told me I had received my stubborn streak from Mama.

He sighed. Mama had inflicted much grief upon him and his daughter. I could see the agony bubbling up in his eyes, but it did not change the fact I wanted to see her again. Touch her face. Smell her hair. The thought of wrapping my arms around her neck, just like I had when I was a child, nearly made me giddy inside. But I held back my sudden elation and focused on Alex's father.

"I will look into it, Kia Lynn. But no promises."

I threw my arms around his neck and squeezed him tightly. He tensed from my embrace, but then relaxed and wrapped his arms around me.

"Thank you!" I dropped to be flat on my feet again and stepped away from the large anaman. "Wait, this makes me part anaman, correct?" The realization swept over me like a raging whirlwind, sending goose bumps up and down my arms.

His eyes widened, as he must have seen the disappointment in my expression. "It is not all that bad to have anaman blood in your veins. Ask Alex." He leaned forward and wrapped my hands in his. "We are family, and family takes care of one another. Anaman or human, it does not matter in our world."

"It just seems strange is all," I said with a small smile. "Anamans have always been the enemy in my life. It is odd to know I am one of you. And even more bizarre that Mama was able to hide that information from the Doyen."

"Your mother is only half anaman and barely has any features resembling our kind." Jax released my hands and straightened. "Tallisa appeared more like an anaman as a child, but the color of her skin lightened as she aged and freckled from the sun, just like yours. Any sign of her anaman skin disappeared by the time she reached your age, but she still possessed a heightened ability to sense other people's intentions. She is also unfazed by the wind, so it makes sense that air is your elemental gift."

I nodded slowly, faded memories popping into my mind. "Mama's mystical tendencies either impressed the Doyen or frightened them," I replied, remembering how Mama would glide just above the ground at times. I had thought it was normal. It was not until after she disappeared when I realized not all adults could do it.

Zoe Dawn waved from the top of the hill, right outside the umbrella of the orchard trees. "The ship is ready, Kia Lynn. They are taking us home." She leapt into the air, clapping her hands with excitement.

I grinned and waved.

"It is time we all returned to our homes." Jax beckoned for me to lead the way. "We can always talk about this more at a later time."

I stopped and glanced back at him. "Not too much later."

He nodded and I continued up the hill, smiling to myself. A whisper of my young life danced on the edges of my memories. Mama's voice carried as she belted out her melody on our long strolls through the forest surrounding our village. Then she would twirl me under her arm and lift me high above her head, laughing as if she did not have a care in the world.

"Sugar Plum," she had called me. "My sweet, sweet Sugar Plum."

Her words had held power and were a force not many challenged in the village. She saved her gentle nature for only me. I knew I was her one love, and she had been mine. She was a beauty with her vibrant auburn hair cascading over her shoulders like a waterfall of fire. I idolized her when I was a child and had placed her on a pedestal after her disappearance.

Zoe Dawn met me half way down the trail and dragged me at a jog the rest of the way. Covyn was waiting just outside the bay door. She had decided to join us in our village until Jax and his people ensured Beck was no longer hiding in her little ancient town. Once she saw how we lived, she would not want to stay long. I was positive of that.

Alex ran toward me and threw her arms around my neck. "If you really need to see her again, I will help you," she whispered in my ear.

I pulled back. There were tears shining in her eyes. I reached up and wiped away the ones from her cheek, then grasped both of her arms.

"We will talk soon, cousin—sister." I corrected myself with a smile, tightening my hold on her. "Whatever my mother has done, she will answer for, but first I must see her. Then we will judge her for her crimes."

Alex's chin quivered, but she nodded in reply.

"We will see you soon," Zoe Dawn said, squishing us both in her embrace.

I wiggled my nose as her fuzzy, inky-black hair pressed against it. She squeezed us tighter, and I blew out a laugh as I tried to turn away from all her curls, but she only held me closer.

"Zoe Dawn, I will jab you with my fist if you do not let go," I muttered behind her veil of hair.

She dropped her arms and stepped back with a wide grin plastered across her face. "I dare you, sister," she jested, putting her fists up in front of her face and bouncing on her toes.

Tiordan whisked around the corner with a smile gracing the edges of his lips. "My three favorite elementals," he gushed, holding out his hands toward us.

I took one and Zoe Dawn took the other.

"Are we not the only elementals?" I asked, realizing I had never even thought there could be more.

Alex's palms pressed together, and she held her thumbs against her chest. "Are there more of us, Tiordan?"

"Possibly," he replied, glancing at each of our faces. "But if there are more, your connection with them will only be apparent when they are needed." He dropped his arms to his sides, then clasped his hands behind his back. His eyes held a quizzical look. "I wonder..." He paused and stared off behind us.

"What do you wonder?" Zoe Dawn asked, after several silent moments. Her lips pursed as she waited for him to answer.

He scratched his chin. "You are about to see your creation from up there and the moment will be one you will never forget." He jabbed his thumb toward the sky.

"But I do not believe this is the end."

My smile faded.

His arms folded in an X over his chest and he shook his head as if he was shaking away a thought. He did not notice our troubled gazes. "The beauty that has unfolded across our Earth is astounding, but there is more to come." He finally focused on our faces. "I sense another."

"Really? Like another elemental?" Alex's fingers wrapped over my shoulder.

"Yes." He nodded, then he quickly shook his head. "No." His eyes closed and he tapped his fingers against his forehead. "Maybe. I cannot see it just yet, but I feel there is more to come."

My heart leapt in my throat. I did not want another battle. Beck. Jacko. Tatum. Nikita. None of them.

Tiordan opened his eyes. "I am rambling." He grasped my hand and smiled. "I could be wrong. The stories tell of a shift and in my mind I had an idea of what that would be. I thought it would be physical, a movement through space perhaps, but maybe it is more of mental shift in our consciousness."

Malcolm moved out of the shadows of a nearby tree. "Tiordan, it is time." He nodded toward the three of us. "Goodbye for now. We will stay in touch."

Tiordan nodded and one by one touched us on the right shoulders. "Do not mind me. You three were astounding. Perfectly splendid." His palms met together at his lips and he bowed his head. "Until we meet again. May Mother Gaia shower you with all the love and abundance you deserve."

"Cheers to that notion," Zoe Dawn replied, glancing at me.

Alex and I both nodded in agreement as he and Malcolm turned and walked away. I noticed Tiordan lean in to Malcolm and whispered something before throwing us one last glance. Did he really believe we had not completed our duties to Mother Gaia?

"Time to go, my new friends," Covyn said. Her fingers circled over Zoe Dawn's arm and drew her in close so she could plant a soft kiss on Zoe Dawn's cheek. Then she turned her smile toward me. "Are you ready to introduce me to your family?"

I eyed Covyn suspiciously. Zoe Dawn only let me and Aly close like that. And now Alex.

"The real question, is Zoe Dawn prepared for you to meet her mum?" I asked, raising my brows at Zoe Dawn. I held back a laugh as her eyes widened. I knew it. "This day is just about to get interesting."

I skipped past the two, waving at Alex and my new

family before I disappeared inside the bay door. Alarix was waiting for me. I stopped in front of him and circled my arms around his neck.

"Hello, mate," I whispered and kissed him softly on his lips. My eyes searched his as he locked us in an embrace, his lips pressing hard against mine.

When he broke away, a concerned expression had replaced his smile. "What will your people think about us? Your father in particular."

"He will be happy I found a suitable partner," I replied, lacing my fingers with his and pulling him into the interior of the ship. "We will make it official as soon as we can."

Malcolm and Aly both glanced up when we stepped into the main room. The lights from their machines glared back at me and my heart leapt into my throat. I dug my heels into the ground. It looked nearly identical to Beck's ship.

"The resemblance is spooky, isn't it?" Covyn muttered. She stopped next to me and folded her arms over her chest. "I'm not sure this is a great idea. Crash-landing a ship is not an easy memory to forget."

I shook away the cobwebs gathering in my mind and patted Covyn's shoulder. "Beck does not get that power over us. We fly again to drive out those horrifying memories." I nudged her with my elbow and then pulled her farther into the room.

"You have more courage than I do." She settled into the chair between me and Zoe Dawn.

Zoe Dawn grinned at us both. "Don't ruin my first *real* spaceship ride, sisters. I have been waiting my entire life for this moment." She patted both of her armrests like a small child.

Malcolm and Aly glanced at one another and I wondered what Zoe Dawn meant by *real* spaceship ride. She had been in this ship before, hadn't she?

I didn't have time to ask as we lifted off the ground and slowly rose above one structure after another, followed by the red mountains. It was a smoother ride than Beck's, so I released my held breath. The view from here was enchanting. Mother Gaia was most definitely awake in all her glory.

Alarix leaned forward in his chair, and Covyn's sigh sent goose bumps up my arms. Our view was like nothing I had seen before. The ground was covered in the brightest green trees I had ever seen, with a rainbow of blossoms spread out as far as the eye could see. The land sparkled like fresh rain had washed it clean. I was mesmerized.

"We did that?" Zoe Dawn asked, her voice barely a

whisper.

Aly turned our way. "I always knew you had greatness in you. Both of you."

"Was this what the planet looked like before the stars struck Her?" Covyn asked as her fingers absentmindedly found Zoe Dawn's. Her eyes never left the outside world.

Malcolm shrugged, his attention remaining on the controls around him. "It is possible, but I believe even then it was not this stunning."

Malcolm moved the ship forward, then sped up gradually, allowing us to take in the view around us. Taking a slight detour, we sped past the sunken hole that Tatum's excavator had dug to Malcolm's city. The machine was gone, along with their ship. I thought they were all buried underneath the mountain, but Tiordan claimed their energy still lingers nearby. To me, that just meant they have chosen to not pass on and nothing else. The few who had survived, cleaned up and left. Good riddance.

But what about their friendship to Mama? The question pounded at the back of my mind. With all the memories I have of my childhood, I would have never placed myself in this situation today. My mother danced, played, and showered her child with love and affection, then one day used men and women, anaman and human, to hunt and hurt that child who'd grown into a woman.

The thought consumed me, nearly broke me inside to face it. I pressed it away, doing my best to focus on the upcoming outside scenery.

Malcolm slowed as we neared Beck's ship. The ground cover had completely changed. The massive ancient's pole I had been tied to was now overtaken by vibrant green vines, and the vegetation crept along the ground in every direction.

We circled around the ship, which was being cleaned, and Alex's people were preparing it to be taken to their village. They wanted their belongings returned, but more so, they were hoping to find out where Beck was hiding.

We hovered nearby for a few moments. Zoe Dawn turned my way, and I shot her a tight smile. I was stronger than my experiences, and I was most definitely better than the man who had believed he could use me to take control of our world. As for the news of Mama's possible return—that would be kept between me and my new family. For now, at least. It would only worry Zoe Dawn and I needed to find out what Papa knew before I set out to find the one woman I loved most.

My attention returned to the view just beyond the glass. After turning the ship toward home, Malcolm zipped through the sky. My breath caught in my throat for a brief second, but when the black mountains came into view in front of us, I pried my fingers from the armrest and relaxed my shoulders.

CHAPTER TWO
Lindon

ZOE DAWN

I stretched my legs out, then leaned forward against my safety belt and watched the villagers gather near the Doyen temple. We were home. It was a changed place; I could see so from my vantage point. The vegetation had always been an issue, but now the trees and gardens were filled with fruits and vegetables. The abundance was breathtaking.

Planting my feet back on the ground, I undid my restraints and wiggled to the edge of my seat. This was by far the best way to travel. The most exciting part was that Mum was going to be livid.

My cheeks warmed from the thought of seeing Mum again, even though she wanted me banished from the village. She was still my mother.

Covyn leapt to her feet once Malcolm set the ship on the ground. She reached over and hauled me up, then pulled me next to her.

"Are you sure this is a good idea?" she asked, whispering in my ear.

I rubbed my forehead. "Yes, of course." I snaked my arm around her waist.

My instant attraction had been a surprise. I'd been bound and determined to remain single the rest of my life, but Covyn had thrown me off guard. Her dimpled cheeks, chestnut eyes, and black, spunky hair pulled me in the moment I laid eyes on her. And now I had to break the news to Mum—another reason for her to want me banished, as I never follow their ludicrous traditions.

Kia Lynn raised her brows at me before following Alarix and Aly to the bay door. I grabbed Covyn's hand. My heart thudded against my ribs, and I could not tell if it was because of excitement or worry.

"Do you think they will like me?" Covyn asked, interrupting my thoughts.

I nodded my head and smiled. "Of course they will. Come on." I tugged her forward. "My mum is going to love you just like one of her own." It was a lie but worth comforting her.

We hurried after Malcolm, who was waiting just inside the bay doors for us. He waved us forward. The sun warmed my face when I stepped from the shadows. Returning home after all I had been through was the most comforting feeling I had experienced in a long time, aside from our moment with Mother Gaia. Nothing would ever compare to that.

My gaze swept over the crowd, searching for Mum, until I met Rafael's sullen expression. He lifted his hand at me. I could not help but glare in return, but then I focused on the glistening tears on his cheeks. Something was wrong.

I dropped Covyn's hand and raced toward him. "Where is Mum?" My tone was dark and accusing.

He sniffed and wiped the back of his hand across his cheek. "She has fallen ill," he whispered. He hung his head. "I could not protect her, Zoe Dawn."

"What do you mean you could not protect her?" I cried, squeezing my hands into fists. Then I pushed him. "What do you mean, cousin?"

"Nikita brought an anaman into our village." He glanced at Kia Lynn, who was listening from a few feet away with Alarix next to her. His eyes widened for a split second, then his gaze fell to the ground. "Ask Kia Lynn. He wanted her to leave with them."

My eyes narrowed. He was acting strange. "I know about the anaman, Rafael. What does he have to do with Mum?" Flames of anger shot through me as I stared at his keefie face.

19

"He did something to her. To a few of our people." Rafael lifted his chin and held out his hand toward me. "I will take you to her and explain more."

Covyn's fingers wrapped over my shoulder. "I will wait with Kia Lynn. Go to your mum."

I shoved my curls out of my eyes and stomped past Rafael. I knew my way to the infirmary. He was quiet as we hurried toward the building and remained a few feet behind.

Why did he look at Kia Lynn that way? As if he were disappointed. Surprised. Maybe even hurt. I could not tell, but I would find out later.

I threw open the door to the infirmary. The air was stale, and I wiggled my nose from the strong herbal scent swirling around me. The curtains were closed around several beds and I could not see Mum.

"Where is she?" I asked as I leaned over and tried to peek underneath the nearest curtain.

Rafael squeezed around me. Three beds down, he pushed aside the fabric. "She is in here. Sleeping."

I pressed him away with the tips of my fingers as if any more contact would disgust me, then slid the curtain until I saw Mum's face. She was pale with a blue hue peppering the edges of her lips. I tiptoed closer. Her eyes twitched but remained closed. She drew in a choppy breath as I sank to my knees in front of her.

"Mum, I am here," I whispered, placing my hand over her aged fingers.

Her eyelids fluttered, then closed again and she blew out a long breath.

I pressed my lips together and twisted to see Rafael.

He sighed. "She has not awakened for over a day."

"And you believe this anaman did something to her?" My teeth gnashed together at the thought. For his own good, Tatum better be buried under the red mountains.

"Who else would do this to her? To any of our people?" He jabbed his thumb back at the other beds. "An anaman infiltrates our village, turns Sister Nikita against us, and banishes the other members of the Doyen. He had an agenda."

"Nikita was already plotting against us long before Tatum arrived," I snapped, rising to my feet and pushing past him. I yanked the curtain closed. "Is the only reason you believe he did this is because he is anaman?"

"The anamans want us dead," he snarled as his face reddened. "Stop questioning me."

"You are a fool, cousin," I muttered. I could see the outline of the ship through one of the obscured windows. "We need help. The anamans' help."

I raced from the building. Rafael grabbed my

shoulder just as I tried to blow through the doorway, and he pulled me to a stop.

"You know his name? The anaman's name?" He stepped in front of me and blocked my view. "I want to know what you know. And why would you ever ask the anamans for help? That is against everything the Doyen have taught us."

"Did you go soft while I was away?" My hatred for Rafael was poisoning my veins.

"Rafael is the reason I could save you," Kia Lynn said, walking up behind him. "He helped me escape when Tatum and Nikita were keeping me prisoner." She reached over and patted his arm.

Rafael flinched at her touch. "Not sure it was worth it right now."

She drew her hand back as a crimson flush crept up her neck. "Rafael, we will fill you in on everything we know." She avoided my gaze. Instead she glanced behind her as if searching for someone. "What is wrong with your mum?"

"Malcolm has a healing station in his ship," I said, making a mental note to speak with her later. "Mum is dying."

Kia Lynn's gaze snapped to mine. "What? How?"

"Rafael believes Tatum has something to do with it."

A deep sense of dread wormed its way through my stomach. "If he did and he's not dead already, I will strangle him with my bare hands. Please excuse me. I need to find Malcolm."

I left them there, annoyed they had been keeping a secret from me, but even more so that Kia Lynn defended Rafael. If he had helped her escape, he had a motive. An agenda of his own. Rafael was nothing but a snake.

I saw Malcolm's big head towering above everyone else's as I rounded the side of the ship. Most of the villagers were still there. I waved at him and he nodded in reply as he made his way toward me.

"Yes, Zoe Dawn?"

"Mum is ill. Can your healing station help her?" I asked, bouncing impatiently on my toes as I spoke.

He ran his fingers across his whiskers, which had grown nearly an inch over the past few days. "Possibly. It depends on her sickness. Regardless, we can monitor her and, if nothing else, at least know what we are up against." He snapped his fingers, and two of his guards jumped up from their seats just inside the bay door. "We need to bring Zoe Dawn's mother into the ship for a medical evaluation."

"Yes, sir," they said in unison.

Within a few minutes, they were entering the ship,

one of them cradling Mum. Malcolm led the way to the lower floor where I had been secured on my flight to the red mountains, except we turned down the opposite corridor. The first room we came to, Malcolm opened the door and the guards followed him inside. A large object stood in the center, shaped like an oval with a glass shell over the top.

Malcolm pressed several buttons, then the shell lifted and leaned to the far side. His guard laid Mum on the lightly padded surface. A few more clicks on the screen and the glass shell lowered back into place.

"It will take some time to run all the tests," Malcolm said, strolling toward the doorway. "You can wait here or come back later."

"What if she wakes and no one is around?" I asked, staring at Mum cocooned inside the glass bed. I would not want to wake inside there, especially alone.

"She won't," he replied, wrapping his fingers around the doorframe as he leaned back into the room. "I programmed it to keep her unconscious until the diagnosis is complete. Then it will notify me."

I shot Mum one last glance before following Malcolm back outside. As we neared the exit, a tall, white-haired man came into view. He stuck out like a sore thumb, and I recognized him immediately. My brain exploded with fury. Why was he here?

Memories of the botched mating ceremony flooded through my mind. He had been the man the Doyen had instructed me to select as my life partner. One of Sister Nikita's ideas to make sure I was out of the way when they infiltrated the village and held Kia Lynn prisoner.

He glanced my way, and a delighted smile blossomed across his face. He waved as if we were old friends. I scrunched up my nose while I stomped toward him.

"What are you doing here?" I barked, resting my hands on my hips when I stopped in front of him. I was fairly certain flames of rage were dancing in my eyes.

He backed up a few steps, holding his hands above his shoulders. "We were supposed to be mated. I was allowed to enter your village to find out why you had been removed from the mating ceremony. My people are waiting for our return."

"Arranging mates is against our laws," I snapped at him. I knew my nostrils were flaring, but I could not calm my rage. "We are not mated. You may leave now." I whirled around.

"Your mum insisted that our union continue, for the sake of our agreement," he said, raising his voice so several others turned our way.

He was a bold one. I drew in a shaky breath as my

gaze met Covyn's. I turned back to face the stranger, then crept closer to him, never breaking eye contact. I signaled for him to lean toward me. When he did, I turned and pointed at Covyn.

"Do you see that stunning woman over there? The one with the short, black hair."

He nodded slowly and stood straight. "Yes."

"She is who I want for my mate."

He laughed as if I was telling him joke. "You cannot produce a child with another woman," he scoffed, plucking a leaf from his arm and letting it go to flutter to the dirt. "The Doyen will not allow this."

"Good thing I do not answer to the Doyen any longer." I pursed my lips, then kissed my fingers and pressed them to the kenaz rune on my chest. "I only follow the Goddess—an independent and fierce force of the Divine." I looked him up and down with a smirk raising the edges of my lips. "And I take after her as well."

I shot him one last glance before I skipped away. A smile rose on Covyn's cheeks when she saw me coming, and she held out her hands toward me. I took them both as I planted a kiss on the tip of her nose. Let them all stare at my affection for this woman. I no longer cared to be discreet.

"How is your mum?" she asked, concern etched in the lines around her eyes.

"Malcolm's healing machine is checking on her," I said, waving my hand dismissively as if it were a normal occurrence around here. "When she is well, it will be a delight to finally introduce you to her."

She reached forward and toyed with a lock of my hair. "Who was that man you were speaking to? He did not seem thrilled by your words."

"He is nobody," I muttered, throwing a look at him.

He was speaking to Rafael, and they were both watching us. Rafael nodded, then strode toward me.

"Here comes my nosy cousin." My hand tightened around Covyn's. "Watch him try to tell me what to do." I could feel Covyn's eyes on me, but I avoided them as I tugged her away from Rafael.

"Zoe Dawn, may I speak with you?" Rafael called.

I shook my head and continued toward Mum's home.

His fingers curled over my shoulder, and he pulled me to a stop. "We must talk about Lindon."

"Is that his name? I would not know, as he is not my concern." I shoved his hand off my shoulder.

"The Doyen traded you to his family," Rafael said, the words sliding off his tongue as if they burned him.

I flinched. As I twisted to face him, Covyn's hands

clung to my right arm, holding me back. "They did what?" I hissed, my brain exploding with fury.

"It was arranged by Nikita." He must have seen the flames in my eyes because he took several steps back and held up his hands. "To create an alliance, she told them. It was all planned two seasons ago as they knew you would break the Doyen's rule to stay within the village boundaries."

The heat in my body was rising, and I feared I would not be able to control it. I raised my hands. The tips of my fingers were turning a bright red. When we united with Mother Gaia, our elemental gifts had nearly been drained from our bodies, but as my fury roiled through me, I felt fire energy building within me once again.

I shoved Rafael to the side and stumbled forward several steps, my focus locking onto Lindon. When the flames erupted on my hands, I raised them and with a flick of my wrist, flung them at the pale man. Then I watched in horror as the vegetation around him burst into an inferno.

CHAPTER THREE
Missing

ALEX

I breathed a sigh of relief at the sight of our village. The electric fence was standing and Mom pointed at our now-completed home as we flew past it.

The trees surrounding the house were now taller and fuller, and their greens sparkled almost like emeralds. Colors were no longer muted, and a clear sky stretched on for as far as the eye could see. I grinned as a clean energy filled my chest.

I never imagined my presence in this world would be an intricate piece to awakening its beauty. Even after our explosion of energy and connection with Mother Gaia, I was still pinching myself. Me—an elemental and included in a prophecy. It was blowing my mind.

My smile only widened when I noticed the cleared piece of the land just outside the boundaries of the village and behind our home—a spot for our ship to land. The new cloaking device would keep it safe, and in the next few days, we would wrap the fencing around it as well.

After we landed, I followed Uncle Henry into the back room where he had moved his time machine.

My elated mood dampened slightly. "How will you find her?" I asked. The thought of Tallisa entering this dimension terrified me more than Jako and Beck combined, but I had to know the plan.

Uncle Henry raised his brows as he tinkered with his machine. "It will take me a few hours before it is up and running again, but once it is, I hope I can pinpoint the chip in her arm. If she hasn't removed it, and it has not been disabled, I believe I can still find her whereabouts, even if she is in another dimension."

I leaned my elbows on the platform encasing the machine and propped my chin on my hands. "Can I stay with you?"

Mom popped her head through the doorway. "Why not spend the night home? Then tomorrow morning, you can check in on Henry. Sleep in your own room for a change."

I was torn. I really wanted to be here when Uncle Henry found Tallisa, if only for my mental health. But I wanted to see everyone in town and curl up on my new bed that Mom had the factory on the large ship build for me.

Expanded Chaos

"You win," I said to Mom. She held out her hand, and I took it. "If you find her, please send me a message. Or better yet, keep calling me until I wake up."

"Come see me in the morning, Alex," Uncle Henry said, his voice muffled from behind the machine. "I will set this baby up, then let it run all night while I sleep. I need my beauty sleep more than you do." His head rose just above the flashing lights and gadgets. He winked at me and ducked back down.

Mom dragged me from the room. Eshah was waiting at the other end of the corridor with Dad. They waved for us to follow them. Moments later, we were outdoors and entering the boundaries of our fence. I glanced back, but the ship was now blocked from my view. It was only one night—one night before I will know if the woman who'd tortured me had followed us to our new world.

My home was beautiful. The wood beams gleamed as if someone had scrubbed every inch of the home. My fingers trailed across the railing that separated the entryway and discussion room. The kitchen faced the back and the french doors led to the jungle that was our backyard.

"Do you want to see your room?" Mom asked, pinching the bridge of her nose as if to stop a sneeze.

"Yes, please," I replied.

I reached up and rubbed both my shoulders as I followed Mom and Dad to the other side of the house. I needed to find a way to let go of my worry. Even though I knew my connection to Mother Gaia was the most powerful gift in this world, Tallisa's cruelty continued to overpower it. And with Kia Lynn being her daughter, my life was becoming far more complicated than I knew how to manage.

We entered a short hallway and passed by one door. Then the second door, Mom opened.

"Lights on," she said and beckoned for me to follow as the room filled with light.

What looked like a four-poster, queen-size bed stood on the far end of the room. Black silky drapes hung from the beams at the top, flowing down and nearly kissing the floor.

Mom opened the closet door. It was filled with my clothes from the large ship in low orbit. I was not sure where I would wear them, but I was delighted I finally had more options.

"And this door leads to the bathroom," Mom said, opening the third door. "It is all yours."

I reached my arms toward her and wrapped my arms around her shoulders, squeezing her tight. "Thank you, Mom. I can't wait to crawl into bed tonight."

"Do you really love it?" Dad asked, his body filling up the doorframe.

I grinned at him. "Definitely. I never, in a million years, thought I would live in a home like this."

"You are not alone in that," Dad said, glancing around before he ducked back out into the hallway. "Now, let's discuss this boy, Dax."

I groaned but followed him back into the front room where they had inserted a recessed couch. Dad stepped down using the three steps, but I leapt over the back of the couch and was sitting before he realized what I had done.

"When will Dax be allowed to visit me?" I asked, leaning back and folding my arms over my chest.

"When we know he really isn't in contact with Beck," Dad replied, sinking onto the cushion next to me. He reached over and squeezed my knee. "How much do you really like this kid?"

I laughed, but it came out as a snort. "He's not a kid, Dad. Geez. I'm not a kid either."

"He's a kid to me, and if he wants to see my daughter again, he better learn some manners." Dad crossed his arms over his chest as well.

Mom patted him on the head as she joined us. "He did save her life, Jax. Give him a little credit for that."

"Or a lot," I said, piping up as I threw my hands in the air. "He saved my life more than once and he helped me get to Mom and Uncle Henry when you decided to play hero on your own."

Dad's cheeks reddened. "He also drugged and abducted you. If he hadn't, he would not have had to save your life so many times."

I groaned. He had a point, but I was not giving up. I already missed Dax.

"Then tell me what he has to do," I replied, crossing one leg over another and bouncing my foot in the air.

Dad reached over and rested his hand on my bouncing leg. "I will think about it."

I looked at Mom with pleading eyes, but she shrugged in reply.

"Your father needs some time to get used to the idea that his daughter likes a boy," Mom said. She leaned my way and planted a kiss on my forehead. "All this travel and the excitement of the last week has done me in. How about dinner and a movie? We can discuss this further tomorrow."

I sighed but nodded. "I am an adult. Don't forget that when you two talk about this privately."

"We are aware of your age, but this is our sanctuary, and we intend to protect it at all costs." Dad rose to his feet and hauled me up beside him. "Especially after all that has happened. We don't know what Tallisa has asked Tatum to do."

"There is no way Tatum made it out of that tunnel. He has to be dead, right?" I asked, following both of them into the kitchen.

Mom and Dad glanced at one another, then turned toward me.

"We thought so," Mom said as she tied her hair back into a ponytail. "But it would not be the first time he has slipped through our fingers. He has a history of performing Tallisa's dirty work and then disappearing, even though your dad and he were longtime friends."

"More on that at a later time." Dad swiped at the screen of the preparation oven. "What should we have for dinner tonight?"

I stretched my arms above my head and yawned. The ceiling in my room had been painted black with sparkles that shone in the dark. It looked like the stars were above me. Everything was perfect. Too perfect. Which meant the other shoe would drop any moment now.

I rolled over and stared at the curtained window that stretched across most of the far side of the bedroom. The edges were lighting up. My cheeks warmed with a smile. It was time to check on Uncle Henry. I really hoped he had discovered Tallisa's whereabouts and she was nowhere near our dimension.

I opened my messages. Uncle Henry had called after all. I wonder why I hadn't heard it. I activated my com connection with him. It beeped several times, but he didn't answer.

"Sleeping, I'm sure," I muttered, rolling to the edge of my bed.

My feet hit the floor, and I wiggled my toes against the soft carpet. The fine texture felt like silk against my skin. If I wasn't in such a hurry, I would have melted to the floor and spent the rest of the morning watching movies on my wall-generated television. This place really was a dream come true.

Instead, I shuffled to the bathroom. After a quick shower—the water supply and filtration was still a work in process—I dressed in denim jeans and a plain black tank top. I tugged on my black combat boots, then twirled around in front of the mirror before hurrying to the kitchen to grab a quick bite to eat.

Mom and Dad were still sleeping when I slipped out

the back door. Thank God they had not hidden how to open the section of the electrical fence near the ship.

God—the idea of a deity was never one I had felt drawn to, but now I was reconsidering. After my experience with Mother Gaia and finally understanding my elemental gift, my awareness of the divine was shifting drastically. Experiencing a connection to everyone and everything was changing my reality. There was more to this life than what I had been taught by all those nuns back in 2025.

I entered the code to deactivate the electric current in this section of the fence. It had been built with two metal beams close together, like a wide doorway, allowing the rest of the current to remain active while the entryway was in use. Giving it only thirty seconds to turn back on, I hurried over the threshold and jogged toward the ship.

As I drew closer to the launch pad, a trail of wires scattered down the shadowed path to my right caught my eyes. I stopped short in my tracks and gulped. My blood ran cold. Without thinking it through, I broke into a run toward the uncloaked ship.

I leapt onto the launch pad and squinted at it. The bay door was open, and from where I was standing, it looked like the inside had been torn apart. My feet started moving before I could rationalize the decision. I raced inside and flew through the first set of doors, then turned down the corridor toward Uncle Henry's room. The door was closed. I pounded on it, but there was no answer. Using my override code, I tried to open his door, but it did not budge.

I scooted to the next door, which held the time machine behind it. "Uncle Henry!" I shouted, pressing my hand against the scanner. It opened nearly halfway, then jolted as if something or someone was in its way. I pushed at it, but it would not dislodge. "Uncle Henry, are you in here?"

Silence hit me like icy water. I sucked in and squeezed through the doorway. The motion sensor light snapped on, flooding the room and my eyes. Stepping back, I examined every inch of the room. My breath shook as a cold sweat broke out across my brow. The time machine was gone.

I twisted to see what had blocked the door, but nothing was there. At closer inspection, I realized the doorframe had been kicked in. It must have been damaged when they ransacked the room.

My fingers trembled as I swept my right thumb down my left wrist, activating my com and tracking device. I squeezed back through the doorway and raced toward the surveillance room.

I pressed the connection to my parents, initiating the chip near my ear. "Mom. Dad. Are you awake?"

There was no reply. I slid to a halt just outside the surveillance room. It was trashed. The monitors were torn from the walls, and the glass keyboard was smashed to pieces, but it looked like they did not find the hidden wall with all our weapons.

"Mom. Dad. Please wake up. We have a problem," I said again, whirling around to take in the rest of the damage of the ship.

"Alex, what is wrong?" Mom replied, her voice muffled. "Wake up Jax."

"Mom. Someone gained access to the ship. Uncle Henry is gone." My words rushed out so quickly, I wasn't sure they made sense.

"Slow down," Mom demanded. She was awake now. "How do you know he is really gone and not back in the village?"

I gasped in a lungful of air. "The ship has been ransacked. If he is in the village, then great, but the time machine is gone and the surveillance equipment is destroyed." I sagged against the wall and leaned forward as I slid to the floor. "Mom, please come now. Something is really wrong here."

"We are already on our way," Dad replied, his breath

coming in short as if he was running.

The light in the room flickered, chilling me to the bones. My gaze flashed around, noticing it looked like someone had been thrown against the metal closet at the far end of the room. Hard. It was indented, either by a giant fist or a body.

I nearly choked on my anger and fear as it thrashed inside me like violent waves in a hurricane. If Uncle Henry was hurt, I didn't know what I would do. He had saved me when Tallisa held me prisoner and was intent on murdering me in front of our entire civilization. Thinking of him suffering at all drowned me in turmoil.

I shook out the cramps in my legs, hoping Mom and Dad would arrive soon, when something shattered in the corridor. I leapt to my feet and balled my hands into fists. The weight of a body slammed against the wall, and I jumped back a few feet. Terror had every muscle in my body tightened. My fingernails dug into my palms as I squeezed my fists.

"Dad, is that you?" I managed to croak out.

A moan drifted into the room, and another bang against the wall nearly sent me to my knees.

"Who's out there?" I screamed, wiping my fists furiously at a few tears that had escaped my eyes.

I could hear a pin drop as silence greeted me. The

seconds ticked on by, and just when I was about to venture toward the door, the sound of shuffling feet drew nearer. I yelped and crammed my fist against my mouth.

The room's temperature dropped and a thin frost swept across the walls. I stared in disbelief at the growing ice cycles dangling from the ceiling. My fists loosened, and I snuck a peek at my chilled fingers just as a bloody and beaten Dax stumbled into the room.

CHAPTER FOUR
Two Choices

KIA LYNN

"What needs to be done to heal our village?" I asked Aly as I scanned over the worried faces of my people. "If they banished the other four members of the Doyen, who will lead them?"

"We will send out scouts to find our Brothers and Sisters, then give them the option—" Aly's gaze darted over my shoulder, and her eyes widened as her hand reached past me. "Zoe Dawn, no!" she screamed, knocking me in the shoulder as she pushed by me.

I whipped around. The brush near one of the smaller homes was ablaze. Malcolm tore across the pathway as well, catching up to Aly in only a few strides. The villagers jumped into action as flames danced up one of the larger trees and spread across its branches before the dire situation even registered on my mind. I let out a harsh breath as my mood plummeted.

Racing toward Zoe Dawn, I tried to piece together the

circumstances. The white-haired man was backing away from the fire, which seemed to nearly surround him. Had she aimed at him? Zoe Dawn's horrified expression told me she had not meant to set a fire, but he must have been the target.

"What did he do that required instant justice?" I asked Zoe Dawn as I slid up beside her.

She hiccupped, still staring wide-eyed at the fire tearing through the vegetation and veering in the direction of another home.

Her bloodshot eyes turned my way and she opened her mouth to speak, then closed it again. She blinked several times and finally drew in a long breath. "He traded with Nikita for my hand as a mate," Zoe Dawn cried, biting down on her trembling lip. "My mum allowed Nikita to treat me as an object."

I froze when I heard her words, and a deep sense of contempt trembled down my spine.

Malcolm was back at the ship, pulling a long snake-like object from the bay door. He stretched it to as close as he could get it to the fire and turned back toward the ship.

"Turn it on!" he yelled. He wrapped his arm around the thick snake-like object and pointed it at the nearest home on fire.

Seconds later, a fountain of water shot out and doused the flames, making the meager buckets of water useless. The villagers dropped their arms and stepped away as they watched Malcolm.

After several long moments of us watching with held breath, the flames sizzled, then died out completely. Malcolm's shoulders dropped and he let out a long sigh of relief. I related to how he was feeling as my breath emptied from my lungs.

I turned back to face Zoe Dawn. "What do you mean he traded you?"

"Nikita traded me to Lindon in order to create an alliance with his family." Her hands shook as she reached up and pressed her tight curls away from her face. "And Mum allowed it to happen."

"Who told you this?" My fingers found hers, and I squeezed her hand.

"Rafael," she replied, jerking her shoulder back at him.

Lindon circled around the blackened homes and vegetation and was heading our way.

"Rafael!" I yelled.

He glanced my way. I wanted to be angry with him, but I had seen the hurt in his eyes when he saw me with Alarix. I did not know how to address it right now. Our moment had been brief, and I did not realize how much it had meant to both of us—until now. But first, I needed to know how this had happened with Zoe Dawn. I beckoned for him to come over, tucking away my feelings for him in the far recesses of my mind.

As Rafael made his way through the crowd that had gathered, I noticed Papa hobbling down the pathway from our home. My heart swelled as I lifted up on my toes and waved at him. He was a sight for sore eyes. The few days away from him had been too many.

I stepped his way, but Zoe Dawn tugged me back toward her. "Don't leave me yet."

"But it is Papa," I said, pointing at him, desperate to have his comforting arms around me.

Tears gathered in her eyes. "Please, Kia Lynn."

Covyn wrapped her arm around Zoe Dawn's waist. "I'm here with you. Let Kia Lynn go to her father."

"You do not have a choice, Zoe Dawn," Lindon barked as he closed in on us, a crimson flush speckled across his cheeks.

My gaze flashed between Papa and Zoe Dawn. I sighed and turned to face the quickly approaching white-haired man.

Rafael picked up his speed. "Hold on, Lindon. We can negotiate another deal," he said, placing himself between Zoe Dawn and Lindon.

"No," Lindon said. He looked over Rafael's shoulder at Zoe Dawn. "This is a sealed deal. You must return home with me."

"What do you mean a sealed deal?" I asked, blocking his view of Zoe Dawn.

More of the villagers crowded around, their curiosity outweighing their fear of Zoe Dawn's inferno abilities.

"It means Nikita was given tools and gifts for your village in order for this union to take place, as well as a signed alliance for your safety." He tried to circle around Rafael, but one of the village's men stepped in front of him, preventing him from advancing on Zoe Dawn. Lindon's arrogant expression regarded the man for a brief moment, then his gaze flitted to Zoe Dawn's. "We fulfilled our side of the bargain. If you do not comply, my people will have no choice but to come for you."

"Why is my cousin so important to you that you would not be willing to negotiate a new deal?" Rafael asked, setting his hand on Lindon's shoulder.

Lindon glanced at Rafael's hand, raising his brows at it as if it was a pesky insect. He shrugged it off. "We do not live by the same rules as the Black Mountain People."

"You are not a member of the Black Mountain

Clans?" Aly asked. She stepped into view and drew closer to me. The fine lines around her eyes deepened with her look of disdain. "Only our people are allowed to participate in the mating ceremony."

This argument was ludicrous. "You do not belong here, Lindon!" I shouted, fury rolling through me. My teeth gnashed together as I fought of the urge to strike him with my fist.

A burst of wind shot through the crowd, and the ends of my hair hovered around my face. After Zoe Dawn's fire episode and now my ability to control the air had returned, it was becoming more obvious that our roles as the elementals had not ended in Zion. What more could we possibly do for Mother Gaia?

Lindon was not fazed by the wind. His eye narrowed and his lips pressed into a hard line as he stared at me with clear disdain. Any warmth he had portrayed toward Zoe Dawn had disappeared.

"We want the woman who can create fire," Lindon hissed between clenched teeth. "Our seer had foreordained that my mate is Zoe Dawn, and I will not accept anything or anyone less. We are not interested in any more wind walkers within our masses." His eyes snapped to Zoe Dawn. "You were promised to me."

He talked about wind walkers as if he knew them.

Was there really more wind elementals? I opened my mouth to respond.

"I am not your property." Zoe Dawn screamed, launching herself at the obstinate man.

Covyn held Zoe Dawn back and I grasped her arm. "Do not allow him to take your power, sister. We will not let him take you." I tightened my grip to get her attention.

She glared at Lindon, then blinked and met my gaze. "Nikita will pay for what she has done."

"You will regret your defiance," Lindon hollered over the crowd that had gathered between us and him.

I twisted to see his face. Throwing up his arm in defeat, he whirled around and stomped toward the village center.

"Make no mistake!" he shouted, waving his arms around. "There will not be peace if Zoe Dawn is not surrendered within two days' time."

I forced down a sick feeling swirling in my gut. Zoe Dawn's fingers found mine, and I turned back to face her.

"What now?" she asked, sadness clouding her features. "Mum wanted this to happen. I cannot remain here. Once again, I will have to leave home." She hung her head and rubbed her eyes with the palms of her hands.

"Tonight we will unwind from our travels," I replied, seeing Papa over Zoe Dawn's shoulder. He looked feeble and exhausted. "Then tomorrow we decide how we will respond to Lindon and his people. Do not fret, sister. He is powerless against us."

I squeezed her arm as I stepped around her. The crowd was dispersing, and I had other issues to deal with besides Zoe Dawn. Papa held his arms out toward me as I approached. Sinking into his embrace, I nestled my face against his chest. Despite his weak body, he held me tightly, running his fingers over my hair.

"I heard the mating ceremony did not end well for you or Zoe Dawn. I am grateful you made it home and can start over," he whispered in my ear, patting my back as if I was a small child. "You can do better than mating with a man you do not love and living your life by his rules."

I squeezed him tighter. He had no idea what I had been through these past few days. "I missed you, Papa."

His grip loosened, and I felt the tremble of his limbs against my arms. He was still not well, despite his reassurances before I had left for the mating ceremony. Leaving him was the worst thing I could have done.

"Let's go home, Papa." I wrapped my arm around his

waist, then threw a glance at Alarix.

He smiled in return and waved, before turning back to Aly and Malcolm. Discussing my love life with Papa was not the most comfortable subject, but he needed to know I had picked a mate.

We walked slowly down the wide pathway, the branches of the largest trees creating an umbrella above us. The vegetation had changed here as well, and I was still familiarizing myself with the alterations across our land. The vibrant colors were enchanting, but I feared they would not last, as malicious people still existed in the world. One in particular—Beck. And even though it had only been two days since our unification with Mother Gaia, the memory was already fading.

Our home was the same as when I had left it, but the garden surrounding it was flourishing at a rapid speed. My fingers skimmed over the wooden fence as we walked around its corner. At the far end, my small greenhouse stood tall. I drew in a long breath at the sight of it. My herbs were safe.

Papa led the way into the home and sank onto the nearest chair. "I fear my health is deteriorating quicker than I thought." He leaned his head back against the wall behind him.

"Malcolm's ship has a machine that can possibly heal

you," I said, wrapping my hand around his as I knelt in front of him. "Attica is in there now, but Malcolm will make time for your recovery as well."

He shook his head. "I do not want to be controlled by the anamans' technology."

My heart leapt into my throat. He had to know I was one of them. "What about Mama?" I asked, hoping he would admit to the secret he had kept from me.

His eyes snapped open. "What about her?"

My pulse quickened. "Did you know?"

He pursed his lips and straightened in his chair. I could tell it hurt him to move. If there was a way for him to heal, why would he not take the chance?

"Your mother was many things." His leg twitched, then the other did as well. "I carry her secrets because she asked that I did. She was the love of my life and the mother of my lovely and brave daughter. Why would I ever reveal what she asked to be hidden?"

"Because *I am* your daughter." My shoulders tensed as I rose to my feet and raked my fingers through my hair. "We do not keep secrets. Remember? I have mourned Mama's disappearance for nine years, and I am beginning to finally understand the person she truly is. And I deserve to know who I am. I ask again, did you know?"

He kneaded his upper thigh with his knuckles and avoided my eyes, but I could tell he was thinking. Keeping myself busy, I cleaned the food preparation area and wiped out the wooden dishes. It was strange to have experienced a life rich with abundance and fine objects, then return to these meager belongings.

"Are you asking about Mama's origins?"

I turned back to face him. "I am asking about it all."

Papa was not old, but in this moment, his frailty gave the illusion he had aged twenty years. Even with his diminishing health, he had always seemed young to me, but not now. The wrinkles in his face deepened even more as a haunted expression swept down his features.

"You do not like the anamans," I said, breaking the silence. "But you mated with one. Why would you keep that from me? You had to know."

He nodded slowly. "I did. But she is only half, which makes you even less of an anaman."

"But they are my people too." My skin prickled with annoyance. "If you can love her and me, why not them as well?"

His eyes closed again, and I noticed the weariness flood down his expression. "Mama was different." A single tear slipped from his eyelid.

There was a knock at the door. I jumped slightly, and

Papa's eyes flashed open.

"I will see who it is," I said, waving for him to stay seated. "But we are not done with this conversation."

He nodded in response.

Opening the door, I blew out an exasperated breath when I met Rafael's gaze.

"I won't take much of your time," he said, shuffling his feet and glancing over my shoulder at Papa. "I just need to speak with you in private for a moment."

"Papa, I will not be long," I said, before slipping across the threshold and shutting the door. I followed Rafael to the edge of our garden. "Is this about Zoe Dawn?"

He shook his head and turned toward me. "It is about me." He gulped. "And you."

Memories of his kindness, his touch, and his gentleness when he had burned the rune from my skin came swirling back into my mind. I grasped his hand.

"What is it, Rafael?"

He gritted his teeth and avoided my eyes. "It is difficult for me to put my thoughts into words." His gaze drifted to the side, and the tension in his neck and shoulders caused his muscles press against his shirt.

I reached for his chin and forced him to look at me. "What is wrong? We are friends now. You can talk to me."

His face fell when I mentioned we were friends, and a bell rang in my mind. All the muscles in my body tightened. I was not ready for this. Not after devoting myself to Alarix.

"I do not want to just be your friend, Kia Lynn," he said before I could stop him.

"Rafael, I—"

"Please, let me finish, before I lose my nerve," he said, interrupting me. He grabbed my other hand and pulled me closer. "I think about you every waking moment. What we shared in the caves was a connection I have never experienced before, and I regret all those wasted moments where I allowed my selfish arrogance to rule my heart. Even before the mating ceremony, I knew I wanted to know you more, but after our history, I was afraid you would mock me for the feelings I have for you."

"I would never." I shook my head and tried to step backward, afraid if I stayed close I would not be able to think clearly. He held on tight and inched closer. I inhaled the tobacco and mint on his breath. It was mixed with the honeysuckle that stuck to his clothes.

"My keefie manners were inexcusable, but I am asking for your forgiveness." His eyes searched mine.

"You and are capable to moving mountains together. I know it in my heart." He released one of my hands and tapped his chest, then tugged my other hand up to his lips and gently kissed my knuckles. "Would you consider being my mate?"

The temperature rose several degrees inside my chest, and I held my breath, unable to reply.

He stepped in close, resting his hands on my sides, and without thinking, I leaned closer. His breath was hot on my cheek. All I could hear was the beat of my heart against my skull as I wrapped my arms around his neck. That was all the encouragement he needed. His lips pressed against mine, and he parted them with his tongue and dove in for a kiss that held so much passion, I knew it would be easy for me to lose myself in him.

A heat in my core swelled and I went in for more, digging my fingernails into the back of his neck.

A chill ran down my spine and I gasped when I stumbled backward. I lifted my gaze and stared at Rafael in shock, but the figure on the other side of the fence made my heart stop mid beat. Shame coiled around me as I stared at Alarix's copper eyes.

CHAPTER FIVE
Strangers From Above

ZOE DAWN

"What is your favorite childhood memory?" I asked Covyn, pressing my toe into her side.

Covyn tore her gaze away from the stars and turned toward me. It was early in the morning and we had not been able to sleep after I had woken her from all my thrashing in the bed. It was the same dreams I have always had. They made no sense, but in my heart, the people in my dreams felt like family.

Instead of lying in Mum's house, we headed for the orchard, climbed one of the larger trees and were cradled in the twisted branches of one of the nearby trees.

"One time, my mom snuck me out of our village on a night like this one," Covyn said, tucking her hands behind her head and looking at the stars again. "We walked for what seemed like forever. She took me to a small meadow, tucked away from everything else. It seemed to be untouched by anyone, except the animals.

When she took my hand, I noticed she was trembling. At first I thought she was afraid, but when I looked at her, she was grinning wide with excitement. We crept into the middle of the meadow where a large boulder stood. She lifted me on top and we laid and watched the stars until morning. When the animals arrived, it was the first time I believed in magic. I finally saw what she had been dying to show me. There were beasts I had never seen before— tiny ones and larger ones all grazing in the meadow and undisturbed by our presence."

"Sounds amazing," I said, smiling at the thought of being surrounded by the furry creatures. "Were you worried the bears would attack?"

She shook her head. "The bears were not that scary." A laugh bubbled across her lips. "They are definitely adorable from afar, at least. They stayed on the far side of the meadow and did not disturb the other foraging animals. It really was so peaceful."

I turned back to view the stars, imagining how wonderful it would be to be surrounded by beautiful animals. We were quiet for several breaths and I actually enjoyed the stillness.

"May I ask you a personal question?" Covyn asked, breaking the silence.

I glanced at her and poked her side with my finger.

"Of course. I may or may not answer, but you can always ask."

Her cheeks lifted in a soft smile, showing off her one dimple. "Fair enough. Why is the symbol etched on your chest different from the rest of your people? Kia Lynn's matches, but I noticed no one else has one like yours."

I pursed my lips and stared at the stars. "I do not know." My fingers instinctively drifted to my chest, and I ran them over the kenaz rune. "Mum once told me my symbol meant I would be a beacon of light to our people in the future. Maybe since my gift is fire that is what she meant."

"Maybe that is how it was supposed to be." Covyn reached over and squeezed my arm. "Your flame is your light."

I shrugged my shoulders. "Kia Lynn has a birthmark on her leg that matches my rune. When we were children, we convinced one another that we were bonded because of our unique markings." I tapped my fingers against the rune. "This etching on my chest is colored differently as well. I don't know if I was born with it, like Kia Lynn, but the raised red hue seems more natural then the flat black tattooed on everyone else."

"Then you two knew you were bonded long before Alex arrived?" Covyn's fingers were still wrapped around my arm.

I patted her hand. "We were children. It was all a game back then."

She pulled her arm back and rested it on her chest, turning her eyes back to the night sky.

"I am grateful you came home with me," I said, changing the subject. "Malcolm believes Mum will be healed by morning. Whatever poisons Nikita gave her will be detoxed from her system, then you will finally meet her."

She scratched her chin, but did not turn to look at me. "It will be nice to finally meet her so my nerves will calm down. Speaking of nerves, I really hope Malcolm finds Beck and Jako soon…" Her voice trailed off as she bolted upright and pointed at the sky. "Look, Zoe Dawn."

I followed her arm and nearly shot off the branch when another anaman ship passed over our heads. It continued to the mountain peaks on the other side of our village and disappeared. I exhaled a withheld breath, clawing the bark of the branch I was sitting on.

"Who was that? Alex, maybe?" Covyn asked as she slid down the branch and dangled her feet over one side. Her arms shook, and I realized she was probably thinking of Beck. He had really done a number on her.

"Possibly. Hopefully. But why would Alex and her parents be out so early in the morning?" I searched the sky to make sure they were gone, just when the ship crept back into view. I pointed. "They have returned."

It hovered above the mountain peaks, fully in view from where I sat. After a few long moments, it slowly moved toward us, circled the entire village, and then stopped above Malcolm's ship.

"I don't think they are friendly. We need to warn everyone!" I shouted, sliding down the branch and leaping to the ground.

I heard Covyn's feet crunch against the sticks and rocks as she followed me. Racing toward the village center, I yelled at the top of my lungs. "*Intruders! Intruders!*"

The warning bell rang from the tree tower. Whoever was on watch must have finally noticed the ship. I bolted down a pathway behind the infirmary and slid to a walk. Tiptoeing around the corner, I zeroed in on the ship as it eased down next to Malcolm's near the village center. I glanced back at Covyn and pressed my finger to my lips.

Quiet whispers and shuffling from the nearby homes brought my attention to them. The village people were rising from their sleep. Brushing my palms down my trousers to wipe away the sweat, I crept forward, watching the ship like a hawk. It had to be Alex. No one else would be bold enough to enter our village uninvited. And if it was her, she was here for a reason.

Despite my belief of it being Alex, a nagging tug in my gut warned me to wait before showing myself.

The bay door slid down, revealing only darkness beyond it. I stepped closer but stayed beneath the canopy of the tree branches. I was near Malcolm's ship, and I noticed they were still tucked away inside, as their doors remained closed.

A vice closed around my chest as I took another step closer, making it difficult to draw in a full breath. My pulse beat frantically in my ears, and it drowned out Covyn's noisy footsteps behind me. I hid against the last tree before it opened up to the center of the village and the only area free of vegetation, where both ships were now settled against the dirt.

My eyes narrowed as a figure came into view. They drew nearer but stopped just inside the shadows of the bay door. Whoever it was stood silent for several breaths.

The whispers of others turned my attention away from the stranger. A small crowd was gathering on the other side of the building from me.

From the corner of my eyes, I caught sight of the figure stepping into the moonlight. Her long, auburn locks bounced around her face like waves of fire. She examined the area and her gaze finally settled on the growing crowd. I swear I knew her. She looked familiar, but her features were dulled from the lack of light.

Moving out of the shadows of the trees, I squinted at the woman, still unable to fully see her face with my exhausted eyes. Where had I met her before? She turned her attention toward me and her lips twitched with amusement. She was enjoying our unease.

The bay door to Malcolm's ship jolted. I jumped back, startled by the sudden movement and twisted to watch as the door opening widened. Then my focus slid back to the woman's face. Her gaze met mine, before drifting to the other ship. She was not one of Alex's people, which meant there were new anamans in the area.

My mouth ran dry as I tried to build the courage to advance closer, but my feet would not budge. The villagers' whispers grew in volume, although none of them moved any closer either. We were all waiting for someone else to make the first move.

Aly and Malcolm walked out of their ship, their focus already turned toward the ship next to them. Aly's eyes widened. The woman's hands settled on her hips, and one brow lifted when she saw Aly. They knew each other.

Expanded Chaos

I rubbed my eyes to clear away my blurred vision. The woman's unclear silhouette greeted me again, and I groaned in frustration. "Who are you?" I yelled, croaking my words as if I were a frog. I gulped back the ball of terror rising in my throat.

The woman glanced my way, but she remained quiet. Then her gaze drifted behind me. I threw a look over my shoulder. Covyn was leaving the safety of the shadows and tiptoeing toward me. I turned back toward the woman and took a few steps closer. Her brows lifted as if to challenge my advancements.

"Why are you here?" I said, my voice clearer this time.

The woman chuckled and shook her head. She was not going to answer my questions, and her amused expression sent shivers down my spine. I met Aly's gaze. The fear etched in her features spoke volumes, but her mouth remained closed. If she knew the woman, why was she staying silent?

I whirled around to look at the growing crowd. Rafael stood near the front, staring hard at the woman.

"My cousin asked you a question!" he yelled, his voice thundering like lightning. But I could see his hand shaking. Even he was afraid.

The woman only smiled, then lifted her hand and

wagged her finger at him as if he were a small child. A similar memory exploded in my mind. Kia Lynn and Rafael had been in a fist fight near Mum's home. We were young, maybe seven full seasons. Kia Lynn's mama had been scolding the two with her finger pointing at each of them as she spoke, just like this woman was doing now.

It couldn't be her. She has been gone for over nine full seasons. We thought she was dead. My hands curled into fists when I turned back to face the woman. I squinted in an attempt to pierce through the shadows. She lifted her arm and tossed something toward me, then pivoted on her heel and disappeared into the darkness. The object rolled and stopped only a few steps from me.

I heard someone scream. As I whirled back around, Kia Lynn burst into the clearing. My chest tightened with fear as I glanced back at where the woman had stood. She did not return, and the bay door lifted even with Kia Lynn tearing madly toward it.

"*Mama*," she cried, her feet pounding against the dirt, creating a wind of dust in her wake. She held out her hand as she neared the ship.

Rafael sprinted after Kia Lynn and I followed. The ship jolted slightly and rose above the crowd as Kia Lynn jumped at it. Rafael's arms wrapped around her and hauled her back just as I reached them. I stepped in front of her and helped Rafael guide her to safety.

She screamed, her eyes glued to the silver vessel as it shot upward and disappeared over the mountain peaks. Kia Lynn reached at the space that was now empty, sobbing uncontrollably. She kicked back at Rafael.

"Let me go," she shrieked, elbowing him in the stomach.

He loosened his grip and she collapsed to the ground, smacking it with the palm of her hand in anger.

I rushed back to where I had been and scooped up the object. It was a piece of paper, crumbled around a rock. I tucked it into my pocket to look at later. Whatever it was, I did not want Kia Lynn to be more upset until I knew it would not hurt her.

"Kia Lynn," I whispered, setting my hand on her shoulder.

She shoved my hand away. "She was right there, Zoe Dawn. Why did you not stop her? Why did you not tell her I was here?" Her eyes narrowed into a deadly look of disdain.

I held up my hands in a defensive stance. "Do not blame me, sister. I did not recognize her as your mama until it was too late."

"Of course you didn't," she spat at me. "You have

your mum, you ungrateful keefie."

I stepped back in shock. Covyn grabbed my arm and slid in between me and my best friend.

"That's enough," Covyn snapped. She smacked her palms together in front of Kia Lynn's face.

Kia Lynn jumped, but she did not speak. She stared wide-eyed at Covyn, with only her chin quivering in response.

"Your mother showed up in the earliest moments before dawn and did not say one word to us." Covyn wiped at her forehead and pressed her pitch-black hair behind her ears. "She did not ask to see you. She did not tell us who she was. Instead, she stood there with a smirk on her face and challenged your villagers with her silent defiance."

Kia Lynn opened her mouth to speak, but when Covyn growled, my sister snapped her mouth shut.

"The only one you should be blaming is your mother," Covyn said, falling to her knees in front of Kia Lynn. She reached forward and grasped her hand, squeezing them. "And while you digest that information, we will be here for you. Always."

In this moment, my heart burst. Covyn was not only protecting me, she was caring for my sister in a way I had not expected. And she did it without thinking twice about it.

"But why would she leave me again?" Kia Lynn asked. Tears welled in her eyes, before tumbling down her cheeks like tiny rivers.

I circled around Covyn. The crowd was dispersing, but Rafael remained a short distance away. I noticed Alarix near the infirmary, watching with a guarded look from the shadows. It seemed odd he would not want to be comforting Kia Lynn.

As I knelt on the other side of Kia Lynn, I met Malcolm's gaze. His expression was hardened and he seemed lost in thought. There must be more to this situation than meets the eye. Did he have the answers or was he as suspicious as I was?

"We will find out why your mama did not wait for you," I said, rubbing Kia Lynn's back. "Covyn is right. The moonlight was setting, giving us little light to see her face. She looked familiar, but I did not know for sure. I even asked. She chose not to answer and I do not understand why."

Aly finished speaking to one of the villagers, then turned toward us. "I recognized Tallisa." Sadness clouded her features. She sat cross-legged in front of Kia Lynn. "Your mama would have taken you away from here. Is that what you want?"

I wanted to ask her why she remained quiet, but Aly did not need Kia Lynn's fury directed at her.

Kia Lynn gulped and glanced at Alarix who still stood near the infirmary. "I do not know what I want right now." She pressed her palms into her eyes. "Why did she have to run? Why would she not make certain I was not here before leaving?"

"Because you chose to activate your elemental connection, even after she went through all the trouble to keep you separated from Alex and Zoe Dawn," Malcolm said from behind me. "Tallisa does not want to stay in this dimension. Remember Jax explaining the bridge between other Earths? Your mother is here for one reason, which was to remove you from our planet."

"And now that she cannot?" Kia Lynn asked, her grief-stricken eyes melting into a look of agonizing pain.

"You misunderstand." Malcolm brushed his palms together as he paced. "She has the freedom to take you away, but not without consequences to Mother Gaia. Regardless, your mother will regroup. I am sure of this. And when she does, we better be prepared."

I glanced over my shoulder at him. His jaw was set tight, and the urgency in his eyes caused my pulse to quicken. He needed to regroup as well, in order to match whatever Tallisa would fire at us. No one really knew what her plan was, which in itself was terrifying.

Kia Lynn shifted to her knees and rose to her feet, brushing the dirt from her clothes. "And what do you suspect she will do then?"

Malcolm stopped pacing and turned to face Kia Lynn. He pressed the palm of his left hand against his forehead and shut his eyes. "It is possible she will return for you, and if she has discovered a way to escape this world and remove you from Mother Gaia, she will do so, no matter the cost."

CHAPTER SIX
Searching for Uncle Henry

ALEX

"*Dax*," I cried, leaping at him and catching him just before his head hit the ground. "What happened? Why are you here?"

He groaned as he rolled to his back and his head settled on my legs. I cradled his head in my lap, searching for wounds. There was a deep gash across his forehead and another that spread from his right ear down to his chin. I twisted his head to find a bleeder on the back of it as well. My gaze drifted down to his chest, then to his torso and hips. A section of his trousers was unusually black. Leaning forward, I screwed up my nose from the scent of charred skin. The wound was most likely from one of the anamans' laser weapons.

Pounding feet reverberated against the floor, heading straight for me. I didn't have the energy to fight an intruder and prayed it was Mom and Dad.

"Alex!" Dad hollered, just as he tore around the

corner and through the doorway. He skidded to a halt and Mom ran into his back.

"Jax, what are you doing?" she asked, rubbing her nose as she popped into view. Her eyes widened. "Is that Dax? What happened to him?"

"I don't know. He came in after me." I laid his head on the floor and scooted away from him before climbing to my feet. "We need to get him into the medical station."

Dad leaned down and heaved Dax over his shoulder. "I hope they did not destroy that as well."

The thought had not crossed my mind, and I had not checked that room. I followed after Dad, panic assaulting my nerves. My skin prickled from the thought of losing Dax and Uncle Henry.

Mom opened the door to the medical bay, and Dad rushed inside. The station was unharmed. I let out a nervous breath and squeezed my eyes shut to stop the tears threatening to well in my eyes. Dax would be okay. I had to believe that.

Dad closed the hatch to the medical station and turned to look at me. "Now tell us what happened."

"I wanted to find out if Uncle Henry had found out anything about Tallisa's whereabouts. When I arrived, the bay door was open and the ship was ransacked." My fingers had warmed, and the frost had disappeared once Dax came into the room. Despite what we thought earlier, my elemental ability was still coursing through my veins. "I was unable to access Henry's room."

I whirled around and looked down the corridor at his bedroom door.

Dad nudged me to the side, and Mom followed him. The bedroom door slid open after Dad scanned his hand and then he stepped inside. I gulped before moving in behind them.

Light flooded the room, revealing an unmade bed and clothes piled on Uncle Henry's chair, but he was nowhere to be seen. Nothing seemed out of the ordinary, aside from his missing presence, but whoever had invaded the ship knew exactly what they were taking and where they would find it.

"I will search the rest of the ship. Adina, take Alex outside and scour the area around the ship. Maybe Henry is out there." Dad did not wait for us to answer before he was racing for the lower floor, where we stored the riding machines, extra tools and supplies, and the additional poles that would soon be surrounding the landing platform.

Mom grabbed my hand. "We will find Uncle Henry. And Dax will be fine."

"I hope so," I muttered, following her outdoors.

We circled the ship. Nothing on the outside looked out of place, and Uncle Henry was still missing. I watched Mom follow the trail of wires up the hill leading toward the small lake. I picked up my speed to catch her.

"Did you find something?" I asked, matching her stride.

"Maybe Henry is the one who left the mess out here." Mom stopped and separated a thick vegetation patch. She shook her head. "If he was running for his life, maybe he took the time machine with him."

"But why would he run out here and not come into the village?" I asked, checking the brush around me, just in case.

"If he was cornered or they were blocking his way," Mom replied, storming farther up the trail. "There could be many reasons why he was unable to make it to the village. I should have never left him alone in there."

The regret and grief in Mom's voice stopped me in my tracks. She was blaming herself.

"Mom, this is not your fault," I said, tucking my hair behind my ears.

Mom did not answer but continued searching. I quietly followed.

"This place was a mistake," Mom muttered softly.

"Henry promised this dimension and time would be safe, but we have had nothing but trouble. How could he have gotten this so wrong?"

I wrapped my fingers around Mom's arm and pulled her to a stop. "Mom, please. This isn't helping."

She turned toward me, and a flood of tears burst from her eyes. Leaning closer, I pulled her into an embrace and held her tight against me. Her sobs rocked her body as she clung onto me and wept into the crook of my shoulder.

"Adina. Alex. Dax is awake," Dad called.

Mom pressed away from me and wiped her face with her hands. "I'm okay, Alex. I am just exhausted and would really love to stop worrying that you or someone else I love will be abducted, hurt, or killed. It weighs on my mind daily."

I twirled a lock of her hair. "I understand, Mom. Your emotions are normal."

She smiled through her tears, then picked up my hand and held it to her heart. "You are my love, Alex. I would move the stars to protect you." She tugged me forward.

Our shoes pounded against the dirt as we jogged back to the ship, and I flew through the door of the medical bay. Dax was sitting on the station with his legs dangling over the edge and his head in his hands.

"Dax." I wrapped my fingers over his shoulders. "Who hurt you?"

His head rose, meeting my gaze. "Tatum." He inhaled a deep breath and leaned against my chest. "And Beatle."

I inhaled a sharp breath and looked at Dad.

"It seems they are not dead after all," Dad replied, sagging against the wall behind him. "It explains why the cloaking device is gone and the time machine, but why did they take Henry as well?"

Dax sat up straight. "The woman. The redheaded woman. She wanted Henry."

My heart dropped in my stomach. It couldn't be her. "Red hair? Are you sure?"

"Positive. She went on and on about a machine that would connect her to another world. Henry was the only one who knew how to make it work." Dax's gaze lifted to meet my terror-filled eyes. He sat back. "What did I say? Is she someone you know?"

"Did Henry act like he knew her?" Mom asked. She grabbed my hand and threw me a reassuring glance.

Dax squeezed his eyes shut but nodded after a few seconds. "It is possible." His eyes fluttered open. "He seemed repulsed by her, as if there was some kind of history. An old flame maybe?" He looked at me, then Mom and finally turned toward Dad. We all remained silent. "What am I missing?"

"It is possible she was my sister." Dad's shoulders slumped forward, and he tilted his head back to look at the ceiling. "And there is most definitely history with her and all of us."

I pursed my lips together when Dax turned back to face me. "Why are you so scared of her, Alex? Did she hurt you?"

My heart fluttered as a wave of anxiety smashed over me. I could only nod in response.

"I will strangle her with my bare hands," Dax hissed, sliding off the medical station and landing on the balls of his feet.

Dad stepped forward and steadied Dax. "Not the best time to be a hero," Dad said, patting Dax on the shoulder. "But our disdain for my sister is a mutual feeling."

A blinking light from my arm caught my attention. Someone had left me a message. I pressed the button for it to play.

"Alex, it is Malcolm. We have a situation in the girls' village. It is imperative you connect with me soon." The message played through my com.

"What is it?" Mom asked.

I switched to speaker and started the message again.

"Sounds like their night might have been as eventful

as ours," Dad said, sliding onto a nearby chair. His strained expression spoke volumes. "Let's call him back."

I opened the channel and activated my screen. Uncle Henry had wired Malcolm's ship to communicate with us if he needed and sure enough, it was less than a day away from them and we were both dealing with a crisis. A few seconds later Malcolm and Aly's faces popped up on the screen.

"Malcolm, we received your message. What is the situation?" Dad asked as I sat next to him. I snaked my free arm through the crook of his arm.

Malcolm's fingers ran over his whiskered chin. "We had a visitor early this morning and I have a feeling this will not be the last time we see her."

"Tallisa?" I asked.

"Yes," Aly replied with a sigh. "Kia Lynn is devastated. The rest of us are wondering what her reasoning was for not taking her daughter when she had the chance. Does she know if she takes her it could undo the balance that has been restored to Mother Gaia?"

"That would not stop my sister." Dad kneaded his palms against his temples. "Was she with anyone? Henry perhaps?"

"No, she came out alone. We never saw anyone else."

Malcolm leaned closer. "Is Henry missing?"

"Our ship was torn to pieces during the night," Mom replied. She pressed her hip against Dad's shoulder as she stood beside him. "And my brother was taken, along with our time machine."

"Was that not the machine that brought you to our planet?" Aly was now the one kneading her temples.

"Yes, Aly. That is the machine." I turned to look at Dad. "We don't have a choice. We have to go after her right now. If she returns for Kia Lynn, I don't think she will resist."

"What won't I resist?" Kia Lynn asked as she stepped into view.

A renewed sense of energy slid through me at the sight of her. It was good to see my sister's face again.

"Your mother if she asks you to leave with her," Malcolm replied, leaning back in his chair and intertwining his fingers on top of his head.

Kia Lynn nodded. "I don't want to leave, but I still am dying to see her. I have so many questions for her."

It felt like a knife cut through my heart, but I could not fault Kia Lynn. If this were my mom, I would not stop until I saw her again. And Kia Lynn did not know all her mother was capable of doing, starting with torturing me for her own freedom.

"Our ship is nonfunctioning. Again." Dad changed the subject as his weary eyes met mine. "We could use some help to get it up and running."

"We will come to you," Malcolm replied with a nod of his head.

Dad sat up straight, forcing me to do so as well as he had a hold of my arm. "We will need parts from my ship in orbit. Will you take me up there?"

"Not a problem. We will be there shortly."

Their faces faded, and I closed my screen.

"Mom, were you able to lock onto Uncle Henry's tracker?" I asked as I rose to my feet and took Dax's hand in mine.

"No." Her lips pressed into a thin line. "He doesn't usually leave it on, but I will check." She disappeared into the corridor with Dad following behind her.

I reached up and brushed Dax's curly locks from his eyes, then ran my finger across his already fading scar. He hadn't been in the medical station long enough to make it disappear completely.

"How do you feel?" I asked, licking my lips as my finger trailed down his cheek.

"Sore. Tired." He wrapped his arm around my waist and pulled me into an embrace. "I'm just grateful I made it to you in time."

"In time for what?" I asked, twisting my neck to look up at him.

"Did I not tell you?" He took a sudden step back, dropping his hands to his sides. "Was I really that out of it? I swear I told you when I was lying on the floor with my head in your lap."

I shook my head. "No, you mumbled a few incoherent words, but that is it."

"Beck and Jako. I found them." He smacked his forehead. "I can't believe I did not tell you."

Dad popped his head through the doorway. "Did I hear something about Beck and Jako?"

"Yes, sir," Dax replied, shuffling his feet nervously as I pulled away from him. "On my way home, I cut through a meadow not too far from my town, and I saw them: Beck, Jako, and all three guards, plus a few others I did not recognize. They are planning something."

"Of course they are." Dad shook his head and ducked back out of the room. "They will be our first stop once we have repaired the ship!" he shouted as he walked down the corridor.

I leaned in toward Dax. "How did my life become so complicated?"

He laughed as if I were joking. "Is not life always complicated?"

"Not when I was on my own."

He did not know about my past, especially the part where I grew up in the early twenty-first century, then, at the age of eighteen, was abducted by my Aunt Tallisa.

"When were you on your own?" he asked, drawing me back into another hug. He inhaled a long breath against my hair. "You smell good."

I could not help but smile. His innocence and chivalry were a breath of fresh air in this unruly world.

"It's a long story," I said, squeezing him tightly. "And a confusing one at that rate. You would definitely have to be sitting, and we don't have time for it right now."

"Give me a little bit of your story," he said, leaning back to see my face. Then he planted a kiss on my forehead. "Where did you grow up?"

I chuckled against his chest. "Right here. I grew up right here."

"But you just arrived, I thought." His fingers wrapped around my arms, and he pulled away, searching my eyes. "You are joking with me, right?"

I shrugged. "No. I told you it would be confusing. Do you know what a time machine is?"

His eyes shifted toward the ceiling as he drummed his fingers on his chin. After a few long seconds, he glanced at me. "No idea. If I remember correctly, time was a concept the ancients used to keep track of their days, but I have never heard of a time machine."

"That is how we arrived to this place." I pointed at the ground, which, by the way his eyes crinkled, I figured I confused him further. "The machine moves us from one time period to the next, but even more so, it creates a wormhole that can take us to other realities of Earth life."

His brows lifted. "I do not understand. Realities? Wormhole? What does—"

"I found him!" Mom cried as she raced past the door.

"Where is he?" I yelled, chasing after her.

She slid to a halt in front of Dad. "They have taken him to the west coast, near Mexico."

"Southern California?" I asked, craning my neck to see the location on her screen.

"One of the asteroids struck just south of the Mexico border and nothing is left of that area, except pockets of ocean water and heaps of dirt and sand. So, he is not too far south." Mom's hologram screen flickered as her fingers flew over the small keys. "He won't answer my call, but his beacon is on. That could mean many things and most of them are—"

"Don't think that way," Dad muttered, interrupting her grave words. He turned toward the bay door at the sound of Malcolm's ship landing as it echoed through the corridor.

Mom's com crackled. She opened the connection for all of us to hear.

"Adina, they know everything. Take Alex and leave." Henry's faint voice shook over the connection. "She found another way to bring the ships from our time through the wormhole, and she will stop at nothing until you are all dead. They will be here soon. Run. Hide. Do whatever it takes to keep Alex safe."

"Henry!" Mom cried, pushing on the connection button as its light flickered. "Are you there?"

"Still here." Henry groaned. "She will rip this universe to shreds if it means she can destroy our family. Please leave now."

Tears sprang in my eyes, and I wiped at them furiously. "We will come for you, Uncle Henry!" I hollered, afraid he would not hear me.

"Damn it, Alex, listen to me. Do not save me," he replied, then coughed loudly. He wheezed and coughed again. His voice quieted to a shaky whisper. "She is counting on it. The time machine is all you—"

"Who are you talking to?" a man yelled from Henry's side.

"No one." Henry screamed and the sound made my blood run cold. "Please, no, no—"

His voice cut off as the connection broke. We stood in silence, staring at Mom's arm and unable to breathe. Uncle Henry's screams rattled endlessly inside my skull, spiraling me back in time to the future where Tallisa had tortured me for her own freedom.

CHAPTER SEVEN
Papa's Revelation

KIA LYNN

"How is your mum?" I asked as Zoe Dawn exited her home.

Zoe Dawn shrugged as she pulled the wood door closed. "She is weary but much better. There is no more weakness or upset stomach, and Malcolm reassured me that the poison has been expelled from her body."

"Does he know what Nikita gave her?"

From the corner of my eye, I caught Rafael watching me from across the pathway, where he was working on their garden. I avoided his eyes, but Zoe Dawn did not miss the blush that rose on my cheeks when I glanced his way. She grabbed my arm and yanked me around her home and out of Rafael's sight.

She threw her arms up in the air and blew out a sharp breath. "What is going on with you two?" she questioned with a hint of irritation in her tone.

I sighed. I knew I would not be able to hide this from

her. "Do not be angry with me, sister. I know how much you despise your cousin, but we had a moment back when I escaped, and it has changed how I feel about him." I reached for her hand, but she pushed me away. My heart dropped into my stomach from her cold reaction, but I continued. "He is kind and gentle. If it were not for him, I would have been taken days ago by my mama's people."

"But what does that mean? He showed you his soft side?" She growled as if the thought of him being nice was a bad thing. "It does not change the fact he is a traitor."

I opened my mouth to respond, but she clicked her tongue to stop me.

"Is that not what you want? To be with your mother again?" Zoe Dawn puffed out her chest as her hands settled onto her hips. She did not wait for me to answer. "And what about Alarix?" She shook her head and stepped farther away from me. "I do not like where this is going. You are my sister and I will do whatever is necessary to protect you from the snakes in my family."

My fingers shook as my annoyance built in my chest. I threw out my arms in a dramatic show of exasperation. "Stop! This is my life, not yours. He has asked me to be his mate, and if I do choose him, you will respect my wishes." The words tasted like poison on my tongue, knowing I was betraying Alarix by speaking those words out loud, but I spit them out regardless.

Zoe Dawn's jaw dropped open. I spun on my heel and jogged away from her. With Malcolm and Aly gone to help Alex and her parents, I needed to find another way to ease Papa's pain. After hearing Zoe Dawn's mum was healing, it was hard to not insist he use the anaman healing station.

On top of that, I needed to speak with Alarix. I had not known there would be another man, but it did not excuse my behavior yesterday. It was important to make this right with him. Zoe Dawn on the other hand, would learn to live with my decisions.

Papa was out tending the garden when I arrived home. The color had returned to his face, and his legs and arms seemed to be steady and strong once more.

"Let me make you some peppermint tea, Papa. It will help with any pain." I scratched his back while he knelt in front of our cucumber plants.

"Thank you, love," he answered, tilting his head to see me better. "That would be very helpful. Will you please run up to the well and fill the buckets with more water too?"

A chill raced down my spine. I had not returned to the

well since the stranger had cut the rune in my calf. I had noticed the burnt magic rune had been tingling since yesterday, but I refused to look at it. My nightmares were filled with that moment, and I was not in any hurry to return there.

"Kia Lynn?" Papa asked, interrupting my thoughts.

I blinked and focused on his face. "Yes, of course. I will fill the buckets with water."

I slipped into the house and found my bag. After rummaging to the bottom, I pulled out the laser weapon Malcolm had given me after he had retrieved my bag from Beck's ship. I tucked it in my boot, then scooped up the two buckets. I could not be too careful.

"Be back soon, Papa," I said as I strolled away, doing my best to hide any fear I was feeling.

The trail was quiet. I moved slowly, glancing every which way. This time I would be prepared if someone tried to grab me.

After a long, slow walk, I could finally see the well. There was a man pulling water up, but his back was turned toward me. His clothes looked strange, like what Alex or Malcolm's people wore. I slipped behind a tree and waited several breaths before talking myself into peeking around the trunk.

He was lifting two buckets but still had his back

toward me. Then he turned around. I relaxed my tense shoulders and pressed away from the tree. It was only Alarix. He took a few quick steps back when he saw me and juggled to hold on to his buckets.

"Kia Lynn, I was not expecting to see you up here at this well," he said, trying to rebalance the buckets as the water sloshed from side to side.

"This one is closer than the other," I replied. Seeing him there, in those odd clothes and fetching water in a village that was not his, made me smile. "Did Malcolm give you new clothes? And who are you helping with the water?" I continued toward him and the well, drawing in deep breaths one after another to calm my racing heart.

He glanced behind him, then he blew out a long breath as he turned back to face me. Leaning over, he set the buckets on the ground. "We need to talk about what I saw yesterday."

Here we go. No time like the present to face my actions. I owed Alarix an explanation.

After placing my buckets on the dirt near the well, I turned the wheel to send the pail down to the bottom. I kept my eye on the stones lining the top of the water well.

"I will need to make a decision," I said, my voice nearly a whisper.

I could not meet his eyes. We did not have a long history, but when we met in the woods, several seasons before now, our connection had been immediate. It was rare to run into anyone from the other tribes, as our villages were stretched out across the lands. The coincidence of meeting was slim. When I saw him that day, the distance had not seemed to matter. My heart already knew him.

Now, I was in the middle of breaking *his* heart. I had not officially declared my mate before the Doyen, which meant it was still open for either of us to change our minds.

"I thought you already made your decision. Was I not your choice?" he asked, stepping close enough that I could feel the warmth of his skin.

"I thought I did as well, but it has not been sanctioned, and I did not realize my strong feelings for Rafael." The words tumbled out of my mouth like a boulder crashing down a cliff. "It was unexpected, and I will need a few days to sort out my thoughts on both of you."

His hand touched mine, and the wheel stopped. "Stay with me, Kia Lynn. I went against my parents' wishes, even when it threatened their lives, because you are the only one I could ever love."

I whirled around to face him. "What? Your parents were in danger because of us?" This was news to me.

He nodded. "A woman met with them on a day I was away from the village and insisted that they force me to mate with a woman she had chosen. She showered them with gifts and held the bribery over their heads. If they spoke of the arrangement, she would execute one of them, then leave the other to die of starvation or dehydration, whichever came first."

His explanation sounded rehearsed. My eyes narrowed for a moment, but his gray eyes stared innocently back at me. I turned my anger to the woman I had once trusted with my life.

"Nikita," I hissed, shaking my head.

New information on that woman kept surfacing. Even though Nikita had already confessed to Alarix's arranged mating, I was growing more disgusted by her every day. What was worse… she had called my mother her friend. That alone was difficult enough to wrap my head around.

"We can make a good life together," he whispered, brushing his fingers down my cheek. "Come home with me. Be with me."

I loved his touch. His smell. The way he looked at me. And I would never forget the moment we met, deep within the black mountains. Zoe Dawn and I had been searching for an ancient's town we had found on one of their maps. When we arrived, Alarix and his two friends were already there, digging into the side of the mountain.

"Do you remember the day we met?" I asked, turning back to the well and drawing the bucket of water over the edge. I dumped the contents into one of mine.

Alarix backed up and did not answer.

My attention shifted to his face as I straightened. "You were digging for something and stopped as soon as we arrived. Did you ever return for whatever you were searching for?" A nagging feeling swirled in my gut. "Zoe Dawn and I were planning on going back to find out what it was but never had the chance. What was it?"

"I don't remember," he replied quickly. He rubbed his hands down his opposite arms as if he were suddenly chilly.

The wind had stirred slightly, but the sun was still warming the land. It did not seem likely he was cold. His eyes shifted around the area, avoiding my gaze. I had struck a nerve that I was not even searching for.

I lowered the pail back into the well, turning my focus back to my work. "Must have not been too important." I threw him a tight smile over my shoulder.

"I will take you there after you agree to be my mate. We can dig for buried treasure together." His voice cracked with uncertainty.

"Is that what it was? Buried treasure?" I asked as I turned the wheel to bring the pail up again.

He sighed heavily. "I do not remember, Kia Lynn, and I am not wanting to discuss it right now. I am only concerned with your decision to be my mate."

After dumping the water into my bucket, I turned toward Alarix, then leaned over and hooked my arms under the handles.

"I will have my answer in three days. That is my right as a Black Mountain People. If you are not interested in waiting for me, it is *your* right to return home without me." I stormed past him and he did not try to stop me.

As I continued on the pathway toward home, I realized I did not trust Alarix. In fact, I was not sure I trusted anyone, with the exception of Zoe Dawn and Alex. Even Papa was keeping secrets from me, and Alarix had his own darkness I was not sure I wanted to know about.

Papa waved enthusiastically at me as I approached. His eagerness was different from his normal slow movements. My nagging feeling returned, and I slowed my pace instead of speeding up as my focus swept across the trees and brush all around me.

It was quiet out here on the edge of the village, but in

that moment I felt completely alone, aside from Papa. Even the usual noise that came from the village center at this time of day was gone.

"Kia Lynn, please hurry!" Papa shouted, pulling my attention back to him. He paced the edge of the garden, bouncing on his toes every few steps. This was not the father I had known for the past nine full seasons.

I nodded and picked up my speed without making the water slosh against the buckets' sides.

"What is it, Papa?" I asked when I drew nearer.

"You are right, my love," he said, taking one of the buckets and setting it on the ground.

I did the same with the second, then wiped the sweat from my brow with the back of my hand. "What am I right about?"

"No more secrets. I will tell you everything I know, but under one condition." He grabbed both of my arms and looked me square in the face. "You must find Mama. She is near. I know it."

My heart leapt into my throat. "How do you know she is near? Tell me, Papa. I will promise to go find her."

His gaze traveled up and down the pathway, then he pulled me in closer to him, his voice barely a whisper. "After our talk yesterday, I dug out an old anaman gadget your mother left behind."

My eyes widened and I opened my mouth to respond, but he held up a finger to quiet me.

"Hold on, Kia Lynn. I will tell you all I know." He released my other arm and scooped up both buckets as if they were light as a feather. He swung around and rushed toward our home. He was awfully light on his feet for someone who was ill. "Please be patient with me," he said over his shoulder.

I followed him inside and helped him set the buckets on their shelves. Then I led him toward his chair, but he yanked his arm free.

"I do not want to sit. My mind has been reeling since yesterday. I made myself sick after Mama disappeared. It drove me insane to know I could not save her, but when I found her communication device, I knew she would return someday." He held out a silver contraption similar to the one Zoe Dawn had stolen from Alex's ship. "I believe the day has arrived."

"How do you know this?" I asked, taking the device and turning it over in my hands. This technology had been a part of Mama's life. It seemed surreal. Just like everything else, she had kept this from me. I lifted my gaze to Papa. "Where is Mama?"

"Open it," he said, pointing at the middle of one edge. "Before your mother vanished, she told me if something ever happened to her, she would return to you if it was the last thing she did."

I pressed the spot he had pointed at, and the device flipped open. "What about you?"

He shook his head. "That's not how it worked with her. Yes, we loved one another and had several amazing seasons with each other, but she made it very clear that our union was temporary."

"That is not fair," I snapped. This was not right. Mama and Papa belonged with one another, just like Alex's parents. "You two were mated. Why would she leave you behind?"

"I knew what I was getting myself into," he replied, reaching forward and sweeping his hand over the top section of the device.

It lit up with what looked like an ancient's map. There was a blue dot blinking toward the bottom of the map. Papa pointed at it.

"Your mother told me that if she ever went missing, I was to check this device to find her. For many seasons I did exactly that, but after one let down after another, I gave up and tucked it away at the bottom of my clothing bench." His chest rose and fell with rapid breaths as he hurried through his explanation. "I had forgotten about it, until yesterday."

"All these years." My voice caught in my throat. "You kept this from me, all these years."

His fingers brushed a strand of my hair away from my eyes. "Only to protect you. Your questions reminded me that it was still there. When I pulled it out, the energy was drained, but I remembered Mama would leave it in the sun to recharge. It has been there all day. While you were at the well, I was finally able to access the information."

"But what does all of this mean?" I asked, waving my hand over the device. "Can I contact Mama like Zoe Dawn contacted Alex?"

He pointed at the red dot near the top of the screen. "We are here." His finger slid down to the blue dot. "And this is Mama. I have tried to contact her like she showed me, but she has not replied."

My face fell. "How will I ever make it to her? I have no idea how far away she is."

"She seemed to have resolved that problem as well." Papa's finger slid back at the red dot but veered off to a small blinking white light. "Mama told me these white lights were the anamans' small carriers. Only room for eight people. The anamans from our time do not have these, so they all had to come from her people."

I counted eight white blinking lights on the screen,

but the one he was pointing at was nearly halfway to the temple. One of them was by or in Alex's village, and another seemed to be near the ancient's town I had met Alarix in. My brows drew together. I did not think its location was a coincidence.

"I do not know how to use any of the anaman flying machines," I said, handing the device back to Papa.

"You do not need to know how to make them fly." He pressed the device back into my hands. "Before you leave, I will show you how to access it with this. Then, I will go over how to command the machine to take you to this spot on the map." He tapped on the blue dot.

I closed the device and set it to the side. "I won't leave you again, Papa. Come with me."

He shook his head. "I will not be able to walk that far, and besides, if your mother really wants me to join you, she will come back for me when the time is right. I trust her decisions."

Worry gnawed at my mind, and I desperately needed my herbs. Forget the fear of attempting to fly an anaman machine on my own. What about when I did see Mama again? Then what?

The memory of her smile pushed away all my unsure thoughts. Shaking my head to clear the cobwebs of my doubts, I threw my arms around Papa's neck. "I will find her," I whispered against his chest. "Then we will return for you. I promise, Papa."

CHAPTER EIGHT
Revelations

ZOE DAWN

"What do you mean she is gone?" I asked Kia Lynn's father, jamming my hands into my pockets. My fingers brushed over the piece of paper Kia Lynn's mama had thrown at me.

I came to apologize to Kia Lynn for trying to control her life, although I still did not understand her attraction to Rafael. Especially since Alarix was here with her. Now, her father claimed she had left to find her mother.

"Tallisa put into place a way for Kia Lynn to be with her if the circumstances called for it. A land ship will safely deliver my daughter," he replied, pruning one of his plants and never looking my way. His hands were steady for the first time in many seasons. "You have to understand her position. She misses her mother."

"How do you know this land ship is safe?" My teeth gnashed together to stop myself from spewing obscenities.

His arms fell to his sides. He was quiet for several breaths, then he threw me a glance over his shoulder. "Your anaman friend has a land ship as well. I saw it on the communication device. Why would she have a machine in her village that is dangerous?"

Alex's parents would not allow anything dangerous near their daughter. I nodded, satisfied that this land ship was safe for my sister, but her mother was another subject. "If Tallisa wanted to see Kia Lynn, why did she not wait for her when she stopped by this morning?" I asked. I yanked my hands out of my pockets and set them firmly on my hips. I held back my fury. He did not deserve my wrath, even if he was being compliant to help a woman who had abandoned her daughter.

He sighed and rose to his feet, stretched his neck to each side, and rolled his shoulders. I heard them crack from the movement. "I do not know all the reasons my mate has chosen to play her games, but I believe she wanted Kia Lynn to know she has returned and then allow her daughter to decide for herself. You should do the same, Zoe Dawn."

He turned his back on me and walked into his home without another word. My shoulders slumped forward. The shadows of the vegetation danced around me, and my gaze shot over to the longer shadows of the trees, realizing how late it was. If I did not start after her now, I would not make it before sundown.

As I walked away from Kia Lynn's home, I pulled out the paper and unfolded it. There was a picture on it. Tallisa stood in front of what looked like a castle, based on my understanding of the ancient years. On either side of her were two creatures with large, round ears adorning the tops of their heads. She had her arms wrapped around each of them with a warm smile stretched across her face. What if this was a message that only Kia Lynn would understand? I had to find her. Now.

I sprinted home, threw open the door, and came face-to-face with Mum and Rafael.

"You are better?" I asked, touching Mum's rosy cheeks with my fingers.

She shoved my arm away. "I am well and fine, Zoe Dawn, no thanks to you."

My breath caught in my throat from her harsh words. No thanks to me? Had everyone gone mad while I was off healing the world?

She poked me with her finger, pressing it against my kenaz marking. "I hear you have turned down our friends to the north on our mating agreement. Do you realize what you have done?"

Shock exploded through me like wildfire. "What *I*

have done?" I pointed at myself as I backed against the door. "You traded me for objects you will never see. Do you not see how wrong that is?"

"I did not trade you," Mum snapped, pushing Rafael's hand away when he tried to console her.

I glared at him. "Stay out of this, Rafael."

"Do not take your misdeeds out on your cousin," Mum said, shuffling to a chair and sinking onto it.

"My misdeeds?" I groaned and sagged against the door as I pressed my palms against my eyes. "Have you lost your mind?"

"*Zoe Dawn*," Rafael hissed. "Enough."

"Bite off, Rafael," I hissed back as I threw my arms into the air and waved my fingers at him. Turning toward Mum, I settled into a chair across from her. "Why did you do it?"

Mum blinked at me, but the tension in her jaw relaxed. "The village needed the seeds. Our crops have been dying more and more each year, but because of the north people's seeds, we have the best crop we have seen in many seasons."

Numbness infused my body, and a sudden chill prickled down my spine. The crops were doing well because of the elemental magic coursing through Mother Gaia. "You traded me for seeds? And you knew about this two seasons ago?"

"Once again, I never traded you," Mum hissed, white-knuckling the armrests.

"Then tell me, Mum. What do you believe you did?"

"Sister Nikita negotiated seeds for our village. They wanted a mate for their son as they are not Black Mountain People and do not participate in a mating ceremony." Mum's gaze flitted to Rafael, and she released her hold on the armrests. "When Sister Nikita described the women of age from our village, their son picked you. He did not want anyone else."

"And why was I not given the choice?" I asked, clenching my jaw. I did not have time to argue with her. The day was fading away.

Mum crossed one leg over the other and leaned back in her chair, regarding me with a sober expression. "You break the rules, my daughter. With these people, I knew you would be safe."

I growled and rose from my chair. "That is your reason? You *are* insane, Mum. Has Rafael told you what I have done to heal Mother Gaia? Have you seen the flourish of abundance that has overtaken our lands?" I pointed at my chest. "That was me." I choked back a rising sob. "And Kia Lynn. I do not need safety from a stranger or you for that matter. I am a queen, and I do just fine protecting myself."

I pivoted on my heel, stormed through the modest structure, and grabbed Covyn's and my bags.

"Where are you going?" Mum asked.

"Kia Lynn needs me." I glanced at her, then at Rafael. "We will not be returning."

Rafael straightened his stance at the mention of Kia Lynn. "What is wrong with Kia Lynn?" he asked, holding out his hand to stop me from packing my belongings.

I glared at his hand, shoved it away, and turned back to what I was doing. "Tallisa found a way to convince Kia Lynn to join her. She had a ship placed on the trail to the temple that will take Kia Lynn to her." I glanced over my shoulder at my cousin. "I am going to stop her."

"Her mother is alive?" Mum rose from her chair, shaking slightly.

"Yes," I muttered, squishing the rest of my items into my bag. "And Nikita, the woman who poisoned you and traded me for seeds, is Tallisa's friend. Kia Lynn might not realize how much danger she has put herself in."

"I will go with you," Rafael said, hurrying toward the door. "I only need a few of my belongings."

"I do *not* need your help," I snapped as I threw my pack over my shoulder. "Besides, Mum will need someone here to help her while she recovers."

Mum snorted as she shuffled past me. "I will be just fine without either one of you. Stop treating me like a helpless, old woman." She leaned over and rummaged through one of her bins, then pulled out a long dagger. "Take this for extra protection."

I shook my head and waved my hand in front of the weapon. "I do not need your weapons." Malcolm had given me an anaman weapon, and it would be far handier than a knife.

"I insist," she said, holding it out for Rafael. "I may have been a fool to trust Nikita, but I will not see you two leave without any protection."

Rafael took the dagger and followed me from the home. My gaze fell on Covyn, who stood on the other side of the pathway next to our garden.

"We are leaving," I said, tossing her pack to her.

She looked from me to Rafael, then back at me. "Where are we going?"

"To retrieve my sister. The crazy keefie," I hissed between clenched teeth as I stormed toward the village center.

Covyn jogged to catch up to me. "And where did Kia Lynn run off to?"

"She found where her mother is staying." I could see

Alarix staring at me underneath the umbrella of trees. Halting mid-step, I turned to face Covyn. "We should go to Alex's village first. She will know a faster way to catch Kia Lynn."

Rafael and Covyn didn't argue as I made my way to the northern opening to our village. The last time I walked through there was the day I had stolen the anaman device from Alex. Now, if I had to, I would steal again.

The trek up the pathway was extra grueling as the late afternoon sun beat down on us. Kia Lynn and I were usually returning home at this time, not leaving. I glanced at Rafael when we drew near the tree where I had hidden the contraption. It seemed eons ago when he had saved me from a trip over the edge. Maybe, if the stars aligned correctly, we would eventually learn to get along.

Covyn pulled out a black piece of fabric and tied it around her forehead, covering her hair. "It helps keep the sun off the top of my head," she explained when she caught me watching.

"Rafael will need one for his bald head," I replied as I picked my way around a few of the larger boulders in the path.

We stepped into the shadows from the cliffs on either

side of the path, and I swept my arm across my chin and then my forehead, wiping away perspiration. The chill felt good after all the heat. When we reached the blanket of branches covering the opening to the pathway, I signaled at Rafael to check one side while I investigated the other.

I shifted a branch to the side and peeked through. Silence and a darkened forest greeted me. When I glanced at Rafael, his thumb rose, signaling his side was clear. We crept to the other side of the barrier and secured the branches and brush back into place afterward. It felt silly, as it seemed like everyone knew where our village was these days.

"Now where?" Rafael asked, leaning in close to me so I could hear him.

I shoved him away. "Too close. Boundaries, cousin."

I slipped through the trees to my right and followed the trail Kia Lynn and I had used to cut through the vegetation. Circling around the broken pieces of smaller structures embedded in the dirt from hundreds of years of corrosion, I glanced back at Covyn and pointed at a pile of rectangular rocks.

"Watch for those," I whispered, giving her a thumbs-down. "They stick up in random places in this area, and I have stubbed my toes too many times to count."

She nodded in response and kept her eyes on the ground.

Soon we entered onto the main trail, and single file, we walked toward Alex's town. Rafael held Mum's dagger in one hand and a rock in the other. He obviously did not leave the village enough, but then, the anaman weapon was tucked away in my front pocket. One could never be too careful.

As we neared the building where I found the device, the sun finished setting completely, encasing us in darkness. The moon would rise soon, but we would probably make it to Alex before then.

Passing by the building, I wished I could go back to my earlier days of exploring. It was only the top level of the structure that stuck out from the dirt, and I knew if we could make it down to the sublevels, there would be loads of treasures.

I put a pin in that thought and led Covyn and Rafael around the building. We were close, but I remembered Malcolm saying something about the ship being on the opposite side of the village now, which meant we needed to circle all the way around.

"When will we be there?" Rafael asked, jogging up beside me.

Covyn came up on my other side and threw Rafael an

irritated look. "He does not believe I have been here before. I told you, Rafael, the village is just over this next hill."

"She is correct," I replied, linking my arm with Covyn's. "But we have to make our way to the other end. That is where the ship landed."

Rafael groaned and smacked his forehead. "Kia Lynn will be long gone before we arrive. Why did we come this way instead of going after her?"

"Even if Kia Lynn is gone, Alex's ships can track almost anything. This way, we can follow Kia Lynn." I punched Rafael in the arm and he threw me a dirty look. "Besides, we would have never caught up to her. She had half the day for a head start."

"When do you think she left?" Rafael asked, skidding to a halt.

"Late morning. Before mid-meal." I turned back to look at him. "Why?"

He was shaking his head before I finished speaking. "No. She had to have left after mid-meal. I saw her pick up bread, after she ate, and talk to several of the villagers about her papa's declining health." He clapped his hands together. "Which means we might still catch her if we hurry."

"Were you following her?" Covyn asked with a

smirk.

Rafael's gaze snapped over to Covyn. "No. It's a small town, if you had not noticed."

"No, I definitely *did* notice." Covyn chuckled and shook her head in amusement.

I grabbed Covyn's hand and tugged her forward. "Let's hurry. Rafael is right. Even if she has already made it to her mother's ship, who knows how long it will take for her to learn how to use it. We have a chance at stopping her with Alex's help."

We picked up our speed. When I saw the giant poles reaching high in the sky, I remembered Alex telling me they had a power to them that would keep out any threat. Steering clear of them, we circled around until we saw the outline of Alex's ship in the distance.

"There." I pointed at it.

Rafael burst into a run. I leapt forward and sprinted after him, with Covyn hot on my heels. He was going to get himself killed. I tackled him and we rolled in the dirt, hitting a tree trunk with a thud.

I groaned from the impact and stared up at the stars. A wave of darkness flickered against the night sky and I squinted at it.

"What was that for?" he shouted, jumping to his feet.

My eyes flashed to his face. I crawled to my feet and

brushed my dirty palms across my shirt. "They do not know we are coming, and they were just attacked. Do you want one of their weapons pointed at your head?"

"Zoe Dawn, is that you?" Alex called from the other side of a nearby pole.

I stepped closer, seeing her bright-blue eyes sparkling against the moonlight. "Yes, Alex. It is me, Covyn, and my cousin. We need your help."

Alex burst into tears. "And I need your help as well."

CHAPTER NINE
The Cruiser

ALEX

I turned off the electrical current to the fence, and Zoe Dawn, Covyn, and Rafael slipped into the village boundaries. Once they were through, I made sure the barrier reactivated, then turned around to greet them.

"You must have read my mind." I threw my arms around Zoe Dawn's neck. "My dad is up in orbit with Malcolm, and my mom has problems with our people that she could not avoid. Dax is finishing his healing inside the medical station. I am all alone right now, and all I can think about is my Uncle Henry being tortured by my aunt."

"Slow down," Zoe Dawn said, peeling my arms from her neck. Her gaze drifted down my body. "You are a mess, sister. What can we do to help?"

"I need to save my uncle." I glanced at Covyn, then Rafael. "Where is Kia Lynn?"

"That is why we are here." Covyn encircled me in a

hug and wiped away a lone tear from my cheek. "We need to help each other."

"Kia Lynn has gone to meet her mother," Zoe Dawn said matter-of-factly.

Her words cut through me like a hot knife. I tried to inhale, but the air seemed to suffocate me as it entered my lungs. "She did what?" I managed to gasp out.

Zoe Dawn's brows lifted from my frazzled reaction and then she shrugged. "Her father provided a way, and Kia Lynn took it. Now we need your help to stop her."

I sank to the dirt and cradled my head in my hands. I was living a nightmare.

"What is wrong with her?" Rafael asked.

They had a right to know. I tilted my chin to look at them. "Kia Lynn's mother is my aunt, and she's a tyrant." Bitterness swelled in my stomach and I swallowed hard to stop the bile from rising.

The three of them looked at me with confusion written all over their expressions. Then Zoe Dawn's eyes widened. Her hand flew out and grasped Covyn's arm to steady her as she ferociously shook her head.

"You mean the aunt who is torturing your uncle is Kia Lynn's mother?" Zoe Dawn asked, taking a surprised step back.

I nodded. "She really is a horrible person."

"When I knew her as a child, she was a woman everyone feared, but only because she spoke her mind. Loudly." Zoe Dawn heavily sighed and shot me a sympathetic look. "How is it possible for you and Kia Lynn to be cousins? You are not from our world." She shook her head again and held out her hand. "Never mind. You can fill me in later. We have a much bigger problem on her hands. I don't know who Tallisa is now, but if she takes Kia Lynn away from Mother Gaia, it could send Her into a tailspin."

After all we had done to heal these lands, we couldn't allow that monster to destroy my new home. We had to stop her.

Covyn held out her hand toward me. "Why does Dax need healing?"

I grasped her hand, and she hauled me to my feet. "Beatle and Tatum were with Tallisa when they abducted my uncle. Dax tried to stop them. The rest is history."

"Sounds like we all need one another," Rafael said with clear irritation clouding his features. He closed in on the three of us. "Zoe Dawn, can we get to the point? Kia Lynn will be long gone if we do not hurry."

Zoe Dawn glowered at her cousin, then turned to look at me, her eyes softening when she met my gaze. "Kia Lynn's papa had one of your communication devices. He gave it to Kia Lynn. On it were locations of what he called land ships, and one of them is here in your village."

"Land ships? What do they look like?" I asked, raking my hand through my hair and thinking back to all the vehicles we used in the community. "We have several small riders and cruisers but nothing I've ever heard called a land ship."

"They have to be large enough to fit eight people," Zoe Dawn explained. She waved her hand toward the center of town. "Kia Lynn's Papa said they are shaped like a rectangle with a door on the side. To activate the route, you add the instructions of where you—"

Recognition dawned on my face when I realized the machine she was describing. I clapped my hands together. "Oh, those!" I exclaimed, bouncing on my toes. "I know the machine you are talking about. We call them cruisers. We have one charging in the center of the town at our law enforcement building."

The corners of Zoe Dawn's lips quirked up. "And, can we use it?"

I shook my head slowly. "I doubt it. They keep that vehicle tucked away in case it is needed for local excursions." The town's people would be furious if I took the vehicle.

"You have a ship that can take you anywhere already," Rafael argued, throwing his arm back toward the ship.

"We can't just jump into the ship and take off in a moment's notice. It takes time to prepare it and using the cruiser for day excursions is much easier." I held out my fist toward Rafael. "We haven't officially met. I'm Alex."

He glared at my fist, then his eyes darted back to my face. "Are you going to help us or not?"

I dropped my arm. No wonder Zoe Dawn did not get along with her cousin. "If I ask, they will say no. If I try to take it, we will be caught." I turned to face Covyn and Zoe Dawn. "I want to go as much as you do. My uncle needs to be rescued and Kia Lynn cannot leave with my aunt. But even if we were able to use the cruiser, it will take a couple of days to take it from here to Southern California."

"What is Southern California?" A muscle in Zoe Dawn's jaw twitched and she waved her arm around erratically above her head. "Forget it. I do not care. We have wasted enough time talking about it. We need to stop Kia Lynn first!" she exclaimed, pressing her fingers against her chest and tracing the kenaz symbol etched in her flesh. "I will steal the cruiser. Just tell me where it is."

"Hold up." I held out my hand to stop her. "Dad said the cargo ship brought down new riders, including another cruiser. I bet it is still in storage on the ship."

"That's my sister," Zoe Dawn said as a smile broke out across her face and her arm fell to her side. "Let's go find out."

She pushed us all forward. I shut off the fence current again and led them onto the ship. The poles that were going to circle our landing area were going up first thing in the morning. I was supposed to be watching the ship until my replacement came in the next couple of hours. We had better be gone by then.

Instead of taking the stairs to the sublevel, I opened the cargo doors from the bay door entry. The sloped exit and the darkened room greeted me. Slipping to the floor, I looked back at the others with a smile.

"Follow me," I said, then pushed off and glided down the slanted metal flooring until my feet hit the bottom. "Lights on."

The lights turned on gradually, illuminating the dozens of riders stored in the belly of the ship. And off to one side was the cruiser.

I pointed at it once the others emerged behind me. "Is this what you're talking about?"

"Will it take us to Kia Lynn? And will we all fit?" Zoe Dawn asked, walking around the machine and giving it a once-over.

"Most definitely." I opened the door to the cruiser and peeked inside as the overhead light clicked on. "Just remember, this does not necessarily fly. It hovers above the ground a few feet. We will have to take roadways and wide enough trails, which means it will not zip us over mountains in just a few minutes like the ship does."

I moved aside as Rafael approached with a look of disdain plastered across his features. I did not understand his dislike for me, but I was too emotionally exhausted to ask. He climbed in first, followed by Covyn. Zoe Dawn patted me on the shoulder before she stepped inside.

"Good job, sister," she said, throwing me a smile over her shoulder. "This will be an epic adventure."

I had no doubt it would be.

"Were you leaving without me?" A voice echoed into the chamber from up above.

I jumped and whirled around to a grinning Dax. He sank to the ground and slid toward me.

My fingers dug into my bony knees as I leaned over to calm my racing heart. "You scared me, Dax." I straightened as he sauntered over to me.

He planted a kiss on my cheek and bounded into the

cruiser. "Good thing I woke when I did. You were all about to abandon me with strangers."

I drew in a long, shaky breath, silently apologizing to Mom for running off again and then climbed in after everyone. A clap of thunder nearly sent me flying into Rafael. Steadying myself with one of the handles near the door, I twisted back around and popped my head through the doorway. The rain pounded against the metal roof.

"Fantastic," I muttered, ducking back inside and closing the door behind me. "I hope you are all prepared because I did not bring anything with me, and it is pouring outside." The thin fabric of my tank top was not enough to keep me warm, even if the cruiser heater was able to turn on full blast. I might as well have been naked. I shivered and wrapped my arms around my chest.

"I have a few covers," Zoe Dawn replied, opening her pack and tossing me a course piece of fabric. "Now how do we find Kia Lynn."

The wool covering scratched my skin as I tossed it around my shoulders, but I welcomed the warmth.

Zoe Dawn and Covyn were sitting in the back row, with the tinted windows to their backs and to one side and the small restroom to the other. Rafael was lounging in one of the captain's chairs in the front, with his feet perched on the other chair, and Dax was lying down on the first bench, with his eyes closed and one ankle crossed over the other.

I glanced at the name of the cruiser stamped just above the doorway. Air Cruiser Six Dash Fourteen. Tapping my fingers on the name, I twisted to see Zoe Dawn.

"I will have to do a search for all cruisers in the area, then you can show me where Kia Lynn is." They didn't need to know I was winging this. I shoved Zoe Dawn's cover off my wrist and ran my left thumb over my right forearm. A few seconds later, I was connected to the cruiser. "Six Dash Fourteen, power on."

The lights in the cruiser flashed on, and all four of my passengers jolted upright. I heaved Rafael's feet off the other captain's chair and collapsed on to it. Facing the controls, I swiped my finger across the monitor until I reached the map. I chose the key for the cruisers' locations, and the computer began searching. Seconds later, the white lights of their positions popped up across the screen. There were eight of them scattered across the northwestern hemisphere, including the one we were in.

"Where is our temple?" Zoe Dawn asked, leaning over my shoulder.

"Your temple?" I inclined back on the chair and waved at the monitor. "I don't know your temple, Zoe

Dawn. Which direction did Kia Lynn travel?"

"South," Zoe Dawn responded, pointing. "The four Mountain Gods are near our temple."

"What four Mountain Gods?" I asked, sifting through my memories of any statues of gods in the area.

"The ones on the mountain," she replied, a hint of irritation in her tone. She stood up straight and her hands settled on her hips as she stared down at me. "Alex, they are large faces etched into the mountainside. You cannot miss them."

"Do you mean Mount Rushmore?" I glanced around at the four of them. They all looked at me with wide-eyes and raised brows as if I was the crazy one. "Are you serious? You worship the four presidents as your gods?"

"Presidents?" Rafael leaned forward, suddenly interested in the conversation.

"Never mind the presidents," Zoe Dawn snapped, tapping hard on the monitor. "Where are the Mountain Gods?"

I leaned closer and did a search for Mount Rushmore. When it pulled up, I pointed and turned to look at Zoe Dawn. "Is this where Kia Lynn was going?"

"No." Her finger pressed on the monitor where one of the white lights was shining. It was the only one between us and Mount Rushmore. "Right here. Her papa told me her mother's cruiser is on the path to the temple. This has to be it."

I moved the location of the cruiser over to the AI's monitor that drove the vehicle, then set the mode to automatic. The cruiser shifted up off its platform, jolting us slightly. Zoe Dawn scurried back to her seat, and I latched together my chest and waist seatbelts. The other four followed my lead as the cruiser slid up the ramp and out through the bay door. The rain pounded like rocks against the top of the vehicle, and they all looked up at the noise in surprise.

I activated my hologram screen and switched on my earpiece. "Bay door, close." I turned to face the back windows behind Zoe Dawn and Covyn and watched as the door shut.

A shadow shot out from the bay door at the last moment, and I worried too much water got inside, causing the suction to not hold properly. I squinted, but it appeared completely closed and there wasn't an alert notification to close it again. I swung back around and faced the front.

As I connected to Mom, I swiped the call away and instead settled on leaving her a written message.

Me: *Mom, I have borrowed the cruiser from the ship.*

Zoe Dawn, Covyn, and Dax are with me. Kia Lynn needs our help and this was the fastest way to reach her. Please don't be mad at me. I will stay safe. Promise. Once we reach Kia Lynn, I will send you an update. Much love, Alex.

I sent the message, then undid my restraints and leaned back in my chair so I could watch the rain from the sunroof.

Dax scooted off his chair and knelt next to me. He tilted his head to stare outside. "Is this something you enjoy doing? Staring at the rain."

"Actually, yes," I replied with a soft smile. I wrapped my fingers around his upper arm. "Dax?"

"Yes, my phantom sorceress," he replied, his dimples deepening with his teasing smile.

I sighed at his attempt at an endearing nickname. "Haven't you figured it out yet? I am no sorceress."

"Yes, you are." He lifted the armrest and laid his head on my lap. "Did you not personally witness the spectacular show with Mother Gaia?"

"That does not make me a sorceress," I whispered, but I smiled at the fading memory.

"You don't even know how powerful you are." His lips brushed across the skin of my exposed belly, and my breath hitched as warmth spread through me.

"Thank you for trying to save my uncle." My fingers combed through his thick curls. "Thank you for wanting to keep my family safe."

"For you, anything," he said, closing his eyes as my gaze drifted back to the sunroof.

The AI had calculated just over one hour until we reached Kia Lynn. Since it was saying the cruiser was still there, there was hope she would still be there when we reached it.

"When will we arrive?" Zoe Dawn shouted over the rain.

I twisted my head to see her, and Dax straightened. "It will take some time." They did not really understand time as it was not used in these villages, but I had explained seconds and minutes to Zoe Dawn. "Remember how I said in every minute there is sixty seconds?"

She nodded.

"We need to count to sixty, sixty times." It was worth a try to help them stay occupied. "Then we will be there or at least close." I pointed at the AI screen. "And Kia Lynn's white dot cruiser will be right next to our white dot. Just keep an eye on that."

Dax crawled back to his bench and climbed onto it,

then slid to a lying position with his eyes closed. "Wake me when we arrive."

I closed my eyes as well, drawing the wool fabric in tighter around me and letting the rain soothe away the fear drumming against my skull.

"Alex!" Zoe Dawn screamed.

I shot up and whirled around, nearly tumbling from my chair. "What? What?" My startled gaze bounced around the room as I tried to focus.

"Kia Lynn's white light," Zoe Dawn cried, leaping from the bench and pointing. "It disappeared."

I rubbed my eyes. Had I fallen asleep? As I blinked at the AI monitor, my jaw dropped. We were nearly there, but the other cruiser was no longer showing anywhere on the screen.

CHAPTER TEN
Brody

KIA LYNN

Chunks of bile gathered at my feet and the stench rose to my nostrils. I scrunched up my nose, but did not move. My forehead was pressed against a tree trunk, taking the pressure off my throbbing ankle. My stomach heaved again. I could not bring myself to look back at the decapitated heads of Brother Caprio and Sister Olir. Their rotting flesh was oozing with maggots and other insects.

The words etched on the warning sign hanging from each of their necks flickered in my mind.

THE DOYEN ARE NO LONGER
WELCOME. DO NOT RETURN.

The rain beat harder against the dirt, creating tiny rivers within the shallow crevices that led to the main trail. The two heads of the Doyen were adorned on top of spikes just inside the tree canopy. I would have missed them if I had stayed on the pathway.

I slowly straightened and slinked around the tree, circling wide around their dead eyes, then sprinted across the trail once I reached it. The land ship had to be close, based off the communication device I had checked just before the horrific view of the severed heads interrupted me.

A wet branch slapped me in the neck. I flinched and pushed the branch over my shoulder. My fingers grazed over the welt already forming. Doubt and fear of what was ahead of me, bubbled in my gut. I wanted to turn back toward the safety of Papa and my village, but I was so close.

I squinted at the dark void shadowed against the mountainside. It was a cave opening. That must be where Mama stored the land ship.

I dashed through the downpour of rain and skidded to a halt just inside the cavern. I turned back to take in the thunderous view from a drier perspective. It had not rained this much for many seasons. A soft smile twitched on my lips. We really had transformed Mother Gaia. So, why did it not feel that way? I shook away the thought before the sadness overtook my mind.

My covering was soaked. I pulled it off my head and wrung it out, then I returned my attention to the belly of the cave. This had to be the place, but I could not see far enough inside to see any land ship. And my ankle ached from twisting it when I had cut through the forest. At the moment, it had not started raining yet, and I had believed I would arrive much earlier if I left the pathway. Bad idea all around. I would never forget those dead, wide eyes staring at me.

Sinking to the dirt, I rolled up my trousers to my knees. I turned my left foot to inspect my ankle, but my birthmark caught my eye instead. It was glowing a bright blue. I leaned in closer. The lines were swirling as if it had come to life, and I realized it appeared similar to Alex's anaman markings. Was this my only physical mark to indicate my anaman heritage?

My gaze drifted to the scar. It stung as if it had recently been cut again.

Mama had asked her people to protect me by hurting me. It did not make sense. Why was she intent on leaving our world? Where did she want to take me? How would their protective rune really keep me safe? And now, I knew I had anaman blood running through my veins. Why had she kept that from me? I had dozens of questions, and only Mama would be able to answer them. Despite my deep desire to hug her and hide in her protection once again, I really needed her to look me in the eyes and explain the reasons for her actions.

I focused on my ankle that had swollen to three times its size. I had no choice but to figure out how to use the land ship and find Mama and her people. Walking any longer was out of the question.

Pressing off the ground, I rose to my feet and crept farther into the cave, waiting every few steps for my eyesight to adjust. The edges of a larger object materialized to my right. There was definitely something there.

When I closed in on the land ship, I ran my fingers along the surface. It was smooth and cold. I set my pack on the dirt and pulled out the anaman device. My teeth grazed my bottom lip as I smiled. The location of the device and the location of the land ship were right on top of each other. The rest of the voyage should be easy, if I could manage to power and maneuver the machine in front of me.

I held my finger against the white dot on the screen like Papa had instructed, and the screen flashed, then a row of colored rectangles spread down it. The one I needed was green. I pressed on it.

"Connecting," the anaman device stated loudly. The noise sliced through the roar of the rain beyond the cave opening.

Expanded Chaos

I nearly dropped the device and jumped to the side when the land ship's light flooded the cave.

"Connected to Air Cruiser Four Dash Eleven." The anaman device dinged, and the door to the land ship rose.

Excitement rippled through me as I scooped up my belongings and peeked inside the machine. Zoe Dawn and I had once come across an exposed ancient's machine that had washed out from a river. This was a clean and fully intact version of that. Plus it was a little bigger all around.

My foot teetered on the edge of the step, and I hesitated. After everything I had been through lately, was I really ready to start out on my own, in a machine I knew nothing about?

I glanced behind me, suddenly wishing Zoe Dawn was there. The rain was now coming down in quiet sprinkles, and a sliver of the moonlight shone through the clouds. Other than that, it was dark. I had come this far but was not looking forward to traveling such a great distance from my loved ones.

"It will be worth it to see her again," I muttered, stepping all the way onto the first step.

"It bloody well be worth it," a man said from the other side of the cave.

I shrieked and jumped, then bumped the top of my

head on the doorframe. Falling to my knees, I skinned them against the land ship steps before tumbling to the side. My right ear slammed against the dirt, and I winced from the sharp pain radiating down the nape of my neck.

"Come on, lass." His laughing tone made me want to vomit again.

I knew his voice. It sent chilling shivers down my spine, and my stomach lurched. I swallowed the rising bile. It was the man who had cut the rune into my leg.

"Get up and wipe yourself off. We have some traveling to do."

I squeezed my eyes shut, praying his voice was only a figment of my imagination. After several breaths, I rolled onto my backside and pried my eyes opened. My gaze landed on the legs of a man. He was tapping his foot impatiently. My shoulders sagged in defeat against the dirt as my gaze drifted to his face. He was staring with an amused smirk rising on his lips that slowly spread to his mossy-green eyes that were illuminated from the land ship light.

"You?" My voice trembled. I dug my elbows into the dirt and scooted away from him.

He reached forward and grabbed my foot. "Really? Have we not been down this road before? This does not have to be a difficult night for either one of us. You have already been enough trouble for me. Let's not continue down that path."

"Why did she send you?" I asked, shaking my leg to break loose of his grip.

"Because I get things done," he replied, yanking me toward him with one swift movement. "And she did not want you chickening out. There is too much at stake."

I fell back again, but he hauled me to my feet before my head hit the ground. Then he pushed me through the entryway of the land ship.

I held on to the doorframe. "No, please. I do not want to go with you. I changed my mind. If she has to send her goons to escort me, then she does not really want me in her life." Tears welled in my eyes, and I threw him a pleading look over my shoulder.

"Your tears have no power over me." His body pressed up against me and he pried my fingers from the doorframe.

I tumbled forward as he shoved me all the way inside. My eyes narrowed when I turned to face him, nearly choking on my rage as I wiped furiously at my tears. "Do not touch me again," I hissed between clenched teeth.

He chuckled as he ducked and stepped inside, then turned to close the door. I lunged at him and punched him in the back of the head. His forehead slammed into the section just above the door, and he cursed under his breath. He pushed back against me. As I leapt away from him, his elbow grazed my thigh when he threw it back at me. He whirled around and charged.

I scrambled to the farthest back row, jumped onto the cushioned seat, and held out my fists at him. "You touch me again, I will make you wish you had never met my mother." My chest rose and fell with each ragged breath.

He stopped midstride. His eyes narrowed slightly, but then he burst out with laughter. "You are definitely feisty like that mother of yours. It would serve you well if you ever had a chance to use it alongside your wind-walker abilities." The man pivoted on his heel and strode back to the front. "Your mother has a task for you to complete first, then we can follow her off this planet."

I quivered with indignation, but my shoulders relaxed, and I slid off the seat and landed on the floor. Sinking to the cushion, I wrapped my arms around my chest and searched the machine for a weapon.

I reached up to my neck and patted my chest, feeling around for the horse necklace I had given Alarix on the day we met. It was gone. My gaze swept over the floor, then I jumped up and ran my fingers across the entire cushion. I looked underneath the chairs, then crawled around on the floor until I reached the door. The ache in my ankle was intensifying.

"Not a wise choice," the man said.

I looked at him, but his face was still turned toward the front. "I left something outside. Let me grab it, please."

"Not a chance," he replied, wagging his finger at me without turning around. "Find a seat. We are leaving."

I slowly climbed to my feet and stood right behind him, looking at the anaman technology I did not understand. Their abilities to fly across land were more interesting as I learned about them. He was programming the machine to take us to Mama. I wanted to go, but not like this.

"Would you like to sit in that seat?" he asked, pointing at the other chair in front.

I huffed at him, before circling around him and collapsing in the chair. It swiveled to one side, so I kicked my feet on the ground, making it swing around. A smile burst across my lips but melted away almost as fast, as I remembered who was keeping me company. I straightened the chair and stared at the man. "If we must be traveling companions, could I at least know your name?"

He briefly glanced my way. His fingers flew along the screen in front of him, then he slid his hand to the end, and the next screen lit up with words. The land ship shifted. I gripped the armrests as I watched the cave fall away and the darkened forest grow above us.

"You can relax." He patted the side of the land ship. "This cruiser is top-notch technology. We just sit back and enjoy the ride."

"How does it know what trails to use?" I leaned back in my chair. The clouds were parting, and the moon and stars burst through, reminding me of home.

"The ships in orbit mapped out this entire planet. The cruisers are automated to find the best route that works for its size." He leaned back as well and propped his feet up on a ledge just underneath the three screens. "My name is Brody."

"Brody, it is most definitely not a pleasure to make your acquaintance." I pursed my lips together. "I am sure you understand why it is not."

He chuckled and nodded. "You might be surprised how pleasant I am to be around."

"I doubt that." I lifted my leg with the swollen ankle and pointed at it. "I was hoping to wrap this with something cold before I started out. Now that you have me as your prisoner, would you mind helping me out? It is throbbing."

He sat up straight, then leaned toward me and pulled

my leg closer to him. "It won't require cutting this time, but I can heal your ankle."

I yanked my foot away. "Over my dead body," I snapped, pulling both of my thighs against my chest and hugging them close.

"I will not cut you," he said, rising from his seat and opening one of the panels. It was filled with supplies. "You broke my last spell, and I hate cutting flesh to invoke my runes, but the circumstances called for it. Now, I have everything I need." He threw me a sideways look. "And the healing incantation is a simple one."

As he was talking, a deep energy flowing inside my core began to swirl like a tornado. I drew in a surprised breath and sat up straight. Closing my eyes, I focused on the air around me and instantaneously connected with Mother Gaia's magic and my two elemental sisters. I felt the power of three coursing through my veins and I knew I could heal myself. My left hand pressed against my chest and I wrapped my other hand around my swollen ankle.

A wind whipped against my body, and I grinned as my strength and the elemental energy built around me. Mother Gaia's divine spark still radiated within me, and Her presence embraced me as the pain in my ankle subsided.

"Stop that!" Brody shouted, shaking my shoulders.

My eyes fluttered open, and I shoved his arms away. "I do not need your runes or spells. Mother Gaia will heal my ankle."

His gaze swept across the land ship, then he focused on me. "Your elemental connection will be broken when we leave. Do you understand me?" He was shaking. The man feared my power.

I glanced at my ankle. The swelling was dissipating, and the throb was nearly nonexistent. "Then I will stay here. Drop me off." I jumped to my feet and thrust him against the wall.

His eyes widened for a split second, but he sprang forward before I could think of what to do next and he gripped both my arms. I kicked his knee, and it buckled underneath him, but he held on tightly as he dragged me down with him. I hit the ground with a thud. As I shook my arms, his fingers slipped away from one. He released my right arm, but yanked me close to him with the other.

"My patience is growing thin," he snarled in my ear, his breath hot on my cheek. "In this moment, you are seeing my kind side. Do not force my hand."

I tugged at my left arm, then swung my right and hooked him under the chin. He grunted and fell backward. I scrambled to my feet and kicked him in the ribs before turning to the exit. I searched for a way to open it, but there was nothing but the outlines of the door.

Brody's right arm wrapped around my neck, and the other encircled my waist. He yanked me back and pressed against my throat. I coughed, choking on what little air remained in my lungs. I thrashed my arms back and struck him in the side, pleading in my mind for Mother Gaia to free me. His grip tightened, and I sputtered as a dark film swam in my eyesight. He did not loosen his hold on me. The blackness bubbled up in my eyes, then they all popped, and I felt my arms collapse to my sides before darkness swept me away.

CHAPTER ELEVEN
The Empty Cavern

ZOE DAWN

"Was anyone watching the screen when the light disappeared?" Alex asked, wiping her eyes with the back of her hands.

My fingers were turning white from gripping the cushion in front of me. "I must have fallen asleep." Everyone looked my way. I released the cushion and stretched my fingers. "But just for a moment. Really."

I don't know why I was trying to convince them of anything. They had all fallen asleep long before me. I had never been the best sleeper and it was easy to keep my eyes open. Behind my eyelids were bizarre visions of people and places I did not recognize but at the same time I felt a yearning for them as if they were familiar, and that caused anxiety in my heart. It was easier to avoid them by not sleeping.

"Maybe it was a malfunction." Alex gripped the bar in front of her and hauled herself to her feet. She tapped on the screen. "Or maybe Kia Lynn disconnected something when she turned the cruiser on. There could be several reasons why it is not online right now."

"But it could be because she is hurt or someone has turned off the location," Rafael snapped. A crimson flush was speckling across his cheeks and he slowly rose from his seat.

Alex stood up straight and turned toward him. He came eye to eye in height with Alex, but the fury in his expression was enough to make her take a step back.

"Why are you lashing out at me?" Alex hissed, balling up her fists.

He took a step toward her, but did not reply. I knew this Rafael well.

"Back off, cousin!" I hollered, stomping toward him. My pulse quickened. His anger was misdirected. "You fell asleep when she did. I would know because I watched you *all* drift off into a slumber." I squared my shoulders at him and tilted my head to see him better as there was only a few fists' width between us.

"How will we be able to pinpoint her location if the cruiser is not showing it?" Dax asked, sliding up beside Alex and easing her out of the line of fire.

She pulled against his grip and glanced at the screen again. My attention shifted to her as Rafael's face fell.

He was out of line and he knew it, although admitting it would never drift across his stubborn tongue. He retreated and sank back into his seat.

Alex swiped her finger along her arm screen. "Six Dash Fourteen, locate Four Dash Eleven."

The monitor on the front of the cruiser flashed, and the map shifted several times before it beeped. "Four Dash Eleven is not accessible," the machine stated.

"Six Dash Fourteen, where was the last location of Four Dash Eleven?" Alex asked as her face scrunched with irritation.

Again the monitor flashed, then beeped. A red light blinked in a spot not too far from us.

"That is where it went offline," Alex said, pointing at the screen.

I knew this path well, and I was fairly certain of our location based off my view through the window. "Stop the land ship," I demanded. My hand pressed against the sealed door, and I noticed my other hand was shaking. I squeezed it into a fist. Ever since I connected to Alex back when I saw her for the first time, my steadiness had been wavering. "We do not want to be seen if someone else has joined her. Let's walk the rest of the way."

"Six Dash Fourteen, slow to stop." Alex gripped her chair.

When the cruiser jolted slightly, I wrapped my fingers around the metal bar protruding from the wall next to the entryway.

"I could get use to these lazy anaman rides," Dax said, with a grin from ear to ear, attempting to lighten the mood. His timing was horrible. "Much better than walking." He wrapped both arms around Alex and squeezed her.

Rafael blew out an exasperated breath and pushed past me. "How do we open this door?" He banged his fist against it.

"Slow your roll," Alex muttered, shaking her head at him as she wiggled from Dax's embrace. "Door open."

The door rose, revealing the darkened forest and the outline of the mountainside just beyond it. Rafael jumped from the cruiser, with Dax right behind him. I looked back at Covyn, who was still sitting in her seat, and held out my hand toward her. Her gaze remained focused on the floor.

"Are you ready for this?" I snapped my fingers to get her attention.

Covyn glanced at Alex, then back at me. "Someone should stay here. Don't you think?"

"Good idea," Alex replied. She held a cylindrical object in her hand and tapped it against her chair.

I whirled around, not in the mood to convince her to join me. "Suit yourself." I jumped and landed softly on the mossy ground.

Alex stepped up beside me. "Door close," she said, throwing me a tight smile.

She was on edge but doing her best to hide it from me. We would chat about it later. I did not like her secrets, and although I was not the first to reveal my skeletons, I suspected her hidden life had been far more impactful on the rest of us than we had been told. I had seen it in my dreams tonight, but I did not fully understand the darkness that followed her—yet.

I took one last look at the cruiser as its light disappeared behind the door, then jogged after Rafael and Dax. They had stopped just inside the tree line.

"What's the plan, Zoe Dawn?" Dax asked, twirling his dagger around his fingers. His black, curly hair flopped in his eyes, and he reached up to shove it to the side.

"First, don't stab yourself." I smirked at him and pointed past him, into the shadows. "Follow me." I swept by them and took the lead. The spot on the map was etched in my mind.

I crept forward, with Rafael nearly breathing down my back. He had a bad habit of invading my bubble. I could smell the mint leaves he was chewing and my irritation with him was clawing at my chest. Throwing my arm back, I pressed him away so I did not throttle him instead.

Thankfully, the rain had stopped and the moonlight was helping, but it was still difficult to make out what was what beneath the canopy of tree branches. I may have known the trail that led to the temple, but I had never explored this side of the forest.

I squinted and tiptoed over the scattered leaves and twigs, attempting to see the next best step, when Alex bounded up next to me. My heart leapt into my throat and I gritted my teeth to hold back the choice words that tickled my lips.

She pointed toward the right as she grabbed my shoulder. "I can see a cave through those trees. There's another wide path leading away from it," she whispered in my ear.

"I do not see anything, sister. How can you see it?" I asked, clicking my tongue with irritation. I tilted my head backward to focus on her better.

She shrugged. "I have always had amazing eyesight, even in the dark."

"You must be part cat," Dax whispered, planting a kiss on her cheek.

He was teetering on ridiculous. A man truly in love. It almost made me laugh at them both, but I was too focused on finding Kia Lynn, and we were running out of time.

"No, just part anaman," she replied with a proud smile.

Rafael groaned, clearly growing tired of their playful nature. "Let's go already."

He exasperated me more than anyone else, but I silently agreed with him.

I waved Alex forward, then followed right after, pushing Dax back behind me. Those two lovebirds needed space between them to stay focused. My boots were wet, and the chill was starting to seep through. I hated cold, wet feet. And I really wanted nothing more than to find Kia Lynn.

Sure enough, a shaded cavity formed as we drew near the mountainside. I blinked my eyes to double-check my vision, but it was still there, dark and obscure. Alex was already at the mouth. I jogged after her as she disappeared inside, but when I rushed into the cool darkness a light switched on and shone in my face. I skidded to a halt and threw up my arms to shield my eyes.

"She's gone," Alex said, moving the light away from

me.

The three of us followed her inside and, using Alex's light, swept over the entire area. It was empty. I pressed my lips against my teeth and snarled without thinking. My fingers folded against my palms, feeling this overwhelming desire to punch something or someone. Whirling around, I found Rafael standing there with narrowed eyes. I could see the blame in his eyes directed at me. He would do.

I pounced, and we both rolled. I landed on my knees, and Rafael grunted when his back slammed into the ground. For some disappointing reason, seeing him hurt did not make me feel better. My temples throbbed with rage, and red flashes shot across my view.

My fingers warmed, and a heat rose from my belly up to my chest, then flowed like lava down my arms. I leapt up from the ground and examined my hands. A crimson flush was brightening against my flesh. I flashed Alex a desperate look just as the flames on my arms and hands ignited. The energy consumed me. It was a fury I had never experienced before, and I had to find a way to dispel it before I really hurt someone. I squeezed my eyes shut, mentally pleading for the rage to not explode like a fireball.

I gasped as freezing water poured like a waterfall

from above, drenching me from head to toe. My eyes flashed open, and I did not miss Alex's outstretched hand. I stood as still as a statue, watching the liquid drip from my clothes.

My body shook uncontrollably and a deep sorrow shredded my insides. We were too late to stop Kia Lynn. I screamed, collapsing to the ground and beating my fist against the wet dirt.

As my anger and frustration dissipated, I pressed my hands into the dirt and allowed what remained of my anger and sadness to seep from me and into the earth. After several silent moments, I lifted my chin and blinked away the dust and tears. Something shiny caught my eye. I stretched out my hand and dragged a necklace from the mud. There was a small horse hanging from it.

Kia Lynn had most definitely been here.

I held it up for everyone to see. "She was here." The necklace swung like a pendulum as bits of dirt and mud fell from it. "There is no way she would leave this behind."

"What if it fell off and she didn't notice?" Alex asked, grabbing my elbow and hauling me to my feet.

I shook my head. "She is in trouble. I know it. If it was an oversight, she would have returned for it."

"Maybe she still will." Rafael stood near the mouth of

the cave, his clothes covered in dirt. His anger had melted from his expression, leaving grief in its place.

I was not sorry for attacking him. He needed to keep his trap shut. "How about you stay here, Rafael, and wait for her? The rest of us will continue on."

His fury returned with a vengeance as his face turned scarlet. "You would like that, wouldn't you?" he hissed, before storming from the cave. "I am returning to the cruiser."

"Excellent," Dax replied, smiling at Alex as if he was going to burst into laughter. "Family drama is my absolute favorite pastime. So delighted we have front-row seats to this one."

Alex shoved him. "I can't protect you from her fire if you choose to be a pest."

This time he did burst into laughter as he hopped around both of us. I smirked at him and kicked him in the backside when he wiggled his butt at us. He flew forward and rolled across the dirt, then leapt to his feet and threw out his arms as if he were the show all along.

"Thank you. Thank you," he said, bowing to Alex and then doing the same to me.

I glanced at Alex, who was biting back a laugh.

"I will throttle you, Daxie boy," I teased, flicking his ear when I walked by him. I dug into my pocket, and my fingers skimmed over something I had forgotten about. I stopped and whirled around. "I might have an idea where Kia Lynn is going."

Alex was kneeling and adjusting her boots. Her brows lifted as she looked up at me. "Where?"

I pulled the piece of wadded paper out of my pocket. "Tallisa threw this at me when she came to the village. I figured it was for Kia Lynn, but I forgot to give it to her with all the commotion."

Alex shot to her feet and held out her hand. "Let's see it. Do you know what it's a picture of?"

"I have an idea, but only because Kia Lynn told me about this place." I handed her the paper. "A happy adventure is what I remember."

She unrolled it and smoothed it out against her chest. When her eyes focused on the photo, they widened, and the color drained from her cheeks.

"What is it?" Dax asked, coming up behind her and resting his chin on her shoulder. "Wow! Those are funny looking animals standing next to that woman." He jabbed his finger against the photo.

"That woman is Kia Lynn's mother," Zoe Dawn told him, scooting in close to me and grabbing my elbow. "Are you okay, Alex?"

She tore her gaze from the photo and turned to face

me. "Yes, that's Tallisa. I know where they have gone. It will take us a couple of days to get there in the cruiser. We would be better off waiting for Malcolm to return with his ship."

"They can catch up," I said, tugging the photo from Alex's firm grip and nearly tearing it. "If you know where this is, then let's—"

A scream tore through the trees and echoed inside the cave. We all froze.

"*Zoe Dawn!*" Covyn screamed again. "*Help!*"

CHAPTER TWELVE
The Happiest Place on Earth

ALEX

Covyn's scream shot through me like an arrow. I bounded into action and sprinted toward her cries. My legs were long and my anaman traits were evolving. I could outrun Zoe Dawn and Dax any day.

I rounded the corner of trees and first noticed Rafael lying on the ground with Covyn leaning over him. Her hand was smeared with blood and she was pressing a piece of fabric against his head.

My gaze darted down the pathway. The cruiser was about to disappear around a bend up ahead. My body swayed as I rose a few inches from the ground. Levitating was not easy for me to do, but instinctively, my body knew how to react. My soul's energy connected with Mother Gaia like lightning digging through the dirt. With only a thought, I flew forward as if a tractor beam were dragging me after the cruiser.

"It is Alarix!" Covyn screamed after me.

Sure enough, as I drew nearer to the cruiser, I noticed one of our riders tucked off to the side of the road. He had followed us. I clenched my fists. He was the shadow I had seen shooting through the bay door of the ship and I had ignored it, too drained to trust my gut instincts. I really needed to stop making that mistake.

I held out my arms, enjoying the wind against my face, and focused on the cruiser ahead of me. He was picking up speed. How did he know how to drive one of those? Wasn't he one of the Black Mountain People? None of them so far knew anything about the anaman technology.

The more I integrated into this world, the more obvious it became that the illusions others portrayed were far more prevalent than reality.

Reaching the cruiser, I grasped on to the back end and pulled myself in close. My forearms shook and I gritted my teeth in stubborn exhaustion. I ducked my head and flipped over, landing on my feet on top of the cruiser. My knees kissed the cold exterior of the rooftop and I crawled to the front, clutching to the bar on the side with all my strength in my left arm. I closed my eyes for a second as the fear of dying knotted in my stomach. Peeking through my squinted eyes, I scooted forward and eased my hand over the edge of the cruiser, then pressed it against the identification screen next to the door. It scanned and beeped.

"Not authorized," the machine stated, but I could barely hear it against the wind whipping by me.

Alarix had locked me out. He swerved the cruiser to one side and picked up speed. I tumbled headfirst and slipped over the edge, nearly yanking my arm out of its socket as I slammed into the side of the cruiser. I groaned from the impact, but managed to keep my hold. My elbow was screaming in pain and I was losing traction from the slippery metal.

He was driving it manually, which meant he had been trained to know these machines. Even I wasn't an experienced manual driver, and I'd had plenty of time on board the ship in orbit to learn.

Luckily, Mom had insisted we have an extra safety measure put in place for a select few people. There was one other option to access the cruiser. I muttered a thank you under my breath and refocused on the scanner.

I hoisted myself up and readjusted my elbow hook around the bar. Alarix swerved again and I bit back a scream when my arm wrenched against the metal bar. I pressed my lips together and with my free hand, pressed the tip of my thumb, middle, and ring fingers onto the screen at the top right-hand corner. It scanned and my access blinked on my arm. I was once again in control of the cruiser.

"Six Dash Fourteen, slow to stop, then open door!" I shouted into the small speaker next to scanner, barely able to hear my own voice above the wind's noise.

The cruiser jerked as the AI regained control. I swung forward and then back again as it crawled to a stop. I leapt to the ground and skidded backward a few feet on the muddy pathway as the door lifted.

Alarix attacked and knocked me to the side. I balanced myself on one foot as I hopped away, then I swung my fist wide and it connected with Alarix's shoulder. I danced away from him. He took a few steps back, holding his shoulder and glancing behind me. The others must be coming.

"Who are you really, Alarix?" I asked. My chest rose and fell heavily with each breath.

An egotistical smile twitched on the edges of his lips, and he relaxed both arms to his sides. I bit back the urge to spit in his face. His arrogance was nauseating.

"I'm exactly who I say I am, Alex." He shook his head as his smile widened and a sinister expression slid over his features. "The real question is, who are you?"

My four companions circled up beside me.

"Just spit it out, keefie!" Zoe Dawn shrieked at

Alarix, flexing her hands and then balling them into fists. "We do not have time for your games."

Alarix pointed at me while keeping an eye on Zoe Dawn. "Where did she come from? Do you really know? They say from the skies, but is that all?"

"They all know I am not from this planet," I hissed as my chest tightened, terrified my secrets would pour out onto this road before I had a chance to explain.

"No, you are most definitely not from this planet." He laughed and circled around to the far side of the cruiser. He was going to make a run for the rider. "Better yet, you are not from our universe, are you?"

"What is he talking about?" Covyn asked, helping Rafael into the cruiser and popping her head back out. "There is only one universe." She was looking at me for the answer.

"Yes, in theory." I stayed focused on Alarix. "The bridge my dad told you about. There is more to that story."

"Why don't you tell them how you have broken our universe because of your selfish needs?" he snapped, slamming both of the palms of his hands against the cruiser. It did not budge from the impact. "Tell them how your ships broke through to our universe, and in doing so, ripped a hole in our darkened night." His finger lifted toward the sky and he jabbed it upward several times.

I tilted my head to look at the sky, mostly to avoid everyone else's stares but also because I had to see what he was talking about. The clouds had cleared, and billions of stars twinkled down on us, but I could not see anything unusual.

My gaze dropped to meet his and I shook my head. "Alarix, why are you—"

"*No!*" He shouted, interrupting me. Both of his hands flew above his head and he sharply waved them at the darkness. "Look again. You do not get to be forgiven for this. My only task was to stop you from following Kia Lynn so we can escape in peace. Just stay away from her. We are leaving for a new Earth."

He twisted one of his hands and wiggled his fingers at me, a sign of disrespect in this time, similar to flipping the bird in 2025. Throwing Zoe Dawn one last look of disdain, he pivoted on his heel and dashed out of sight. I heard him tearing down the pathway, back toward the rider.

"Wow. A bit of a drama queen, wouldn't you say? Should we go after him?" Covyn asked, still standing on the step to the cruiser.

Zoe Dawn was staring at me, but she shook her head in response to Covyn's question. "He is of no use to us.

We already know where Kia Lynn is going. Right, Alex?"

"Yes," I said. A sense of despair was crushing me. What had we done? My gaze drifted back to the sky and swept across my limited view. My heart dropped into my stomach. A small fraction glimmered even darker than the rest. I grabbed my chest, unable to take a full breath or tear my eyes away from the wavy blackness.

Dax's fingers trailed down my cheek, and his other hand settled over mine, which was against my chest. "Take a breath." He tilted my chin toward him, forcing me to look at him. "You have a gash right here. Let's clean you up."

I followed, unable to look Zoe Dawn in the eyes. My feet dragged up the three stairs and into the cruiser, and when I turned around to close the door, I felt her fury searing into the back of my head.

After about twenty minutes of resetting everything Alarix had disengaged, I had the machine up and running again. I set the coordinates and passed them on to the AI. We were heading to The Happiest Place on Earth, so why did I feel like my entire world was about to detonate? Tallisa was going to win, and there was nothing I could do to stop her.

I collapsed on my chair and swiveled around to look

at everyone. Rafael was lying on the front bench, with his head wrapped after Covyn had cleaned and bandaged his wound. Zoe Dawn and Covyn were in the back again, whispering to one another, and Dax was occupying the other captain's chair.

"Why don't you lie down on the empty bench and get some rest?" I suggested with a heavy heart.

"I want to clean your cut and keep you company," he replied, spinning around in his chair like a child. "And besides, this chair is way better than those benches."

I forced a smile. "Let's do that right now. I will get the antiseptic."

Dax cleaned my wound with a little water, dabbing the wet cloth against it several times, then blowing on it. "How does that feel?" he asked. He leaned over to grab the antiseptic.

I closed my eyes, grateful I had this time to avoid Zoe Dawn and the possible catastrophe I had caused when we entered this dimension.

"It stings, but I'll live," I whispered so only he could hear. "Add the antiseptic, then use this bandage" —I raised my hand that held a sticky gauze without opening my eyes— "to cover the wound."

He chuckled and took the bandage. I found it amusing how much he laughed. How nice would it be to not take anything serious?

I felt the cool antiseptic touch my skin, then the sound of the bandage wrapper when he tore through it. My eyes flashed open. The bandage had ripped with the wrapping. I sighed and held up another bandage from the package in my lap.

His smile widened. "Maybe you should open it this time."

With all the technological advances, I would think a bandage would have some upgrades, but the one in my hand was similar to the 2025 version. I guessed the old saying, "don't fix what isn't broken" held true for centuries long.

His delight from the sticky bandages shone across his expression as I pulled the dressing and showed him the sticky side.

"You people have skills." He pressed the bandage so it stuck to my skin, then sank onto his chair and examined the results of his doctoring skills. "Maybe someday you can take me to one of your ships, up there." His pointed at the sky.

I shrugged, biting back the terror rumbling up my throat. "Maybe. You have to receive approval from my dad first."

"That's already a done deal. Promise." He leaned

back in his chair and swung around in a circle.

I laughed at his confidence, but my joy was empty. I needed to speak with Dad.

"Move it, buster," Zoe Dawn demanded as she strolled toward us. She waved her hand at Dax. "It is my turn to speak with our fearless leader."

Here we go. I shot Dax a tight smile and turned to face Zoe Dawn when she took his seat. My heart hammered against my ribs.

"I have questions," she said, leaning forward and holding out the photo of Tallisa at Disneyland. "Starting with this. Tallisa is your aunt, correct?"

I nodded.

"What is the name of this place?" Zoe Dawn asked, smoothing the photo and pointing at the castle.

Drawing in a long breath, I took the photo from Zoe Dawn and turned it for her to see. "It is called Disneyland, The Happiest Place on Earth. It was once an amusement park where thousands of people a day would gather and pay to be entertained by thrill rides, food, and shows from morning until late in the night."

Zoe Dawn's eyes brightened as I spoke. "That sounds amazing. How do you know so much about it?"

"I don't know how I can even explain this to you," I said, then pressed my lips together to halt the quivering.

"Tell me about the castle and the two creatures next to Tallisa," she replied, helping me organize my thoughts.

"The castle is smaller than it appears here." I pointed at the pavers leading through the middle of the structure. "There is a bridge that connects through and leads you to another area of this amusement park. The creatures are really just people dressed in costumes. This is Mickey Mouse and Minnie Mouse."

"And why do they dress up like this?" Zoe Dawn took the picture back and folded it before tucking it in her pocket.

"For fun." I smiled, remembering the one time I went to Disneyland right after high school graduation with my friends. We played all day and all night. It was one of the best memories of my life before Tallisa ripped it away from me. I refocused on Zoe Dawn. "This amusement park began with a man named Walt Disney. He drew a mouse who sang and danced. From there, movies, television shows, toys, and parks were created after this mouse." My gaze swept over the unbelieving smirks on everyone's faces. "No really. It is all true. People adored him."

Zoe Dawn chuckled and leaned back in her chair. "Seems silly."

"It was," I replied, missing how easy it had been back

in 2025. "Those were the simple days."

"So we will see this Disneyland then?" Zoe Dawn asked.

"I have no idea if it is still there." I drew my knees up and hugged them to my chest.

She stared at me for a long minute as if studying me. "How do you know so much about this Disney place?" she finally asked again, shifting in her seat to stretch her sides.

Here it is. The moment I had been avoiding.

I sighed. "Because I did not grow up in your time, Zoe Dawn. I am from the ancient years."

Dax must have heard me as he bolted upright and looked at me.

"How is that possible?" The lines around Zoe Dawn's eyes crinkled. The mental cartwheels she was probably doing in her head right now almost made me crack a smile.

"The machine Tallisa stole from my parent's ship, it is a time machine," I whispered and bit at my fingernails to avoid Zoe Dawn's gaze. "It is how my Uncle Henry formed the bridge that brought us to your planet. It is also how I was sent back in time as a young child and then retrieved not too long ago and forced back to my parents' time in the distant future."

"When did you live in the ancient's time?" She was still calm, but I could see her mind reeling through her eyes.

"When I left, it was twenty twenty-five," I answered. Dax rolled off his seat and joined us by lying on the floor next to our chairs. I rose slowly, holding out my finger to Zoe Dawn before she could reply. "Hold that thought."

I held out my hand to Dax and pulled him to his feet, then opened the switch box next to the supplies container. I pressed for the two beds on the other side behind Zoe Dawn to unfold from the wall. As they did, I settled back on my chair.

"I forgot about those," I said, beckoning for Dax to take one of them. "The benches fold down as well, creating three more beds. We have some hydrated food and water inside the cupboards. You just have to request them like you did in Malcolm's cafeteria. And blankets and pillows are stored in the lower supply container, if anyone would like one."

Zoe Dawn's eyes stayed on me the entire time. "How do you live like this?"

"Quite honestly, I am still getting used to it," I replied, shrinking back from the fury rising in her expression. "Really, Zoe Dawn, this has only been my life for a short time. Before I was abducted by Tallisa from my life in twenty twenty-five, I had never known this way of living."

She leapt from her chair and leaned close to me. "I do not understand why Mother Gaia needed an intruder to be our elemental connection, but your arrival to our world has brought nothing but grief to me and my people. Tallisa would not even be here if it were not for you."

Dax popped up behind Zoe Dawn. "This is not how we fix our problem," he said, easing his hand on her shoulder and tugging her away from me. "Trust in Mother Gaia. She knows what She's doing."

Zoe Dawn thankfully did not resist him. She collapsed onto her chair and glared at me. "Mark my words, Alex. If any harm comes upon Kia Lynn, whatever Tallisa did to you will be the least of your problems."

CHAPTER THIRTEEN
A Toxic Alliance

KIA LYNN

A big yawn overtook my face as I sat up in bed. I blinked away the sleep from my eyes and scanned over the room. A ball of panic swirled inside my stomach as memories of being choked came billowing back into my mind. I was still in the land ship, and I had no idea where the brute had taken me.

I scooted off the bed and searched high and low for my boots, but they were gone. I was sure he had taken them on purpose, but I was not afraid to go barefoot. The door to the land ship was open. I tiptoed toward it and drew in a long, calming breath when the sun warmed my cheeks.

"Good morning, sleeping beauty," Brody greeted from beside a small fire. He was cooking something on a rock that smelled divine.

I still hated him, but I was starving. Picking my way through the sticks and mossy vegetation, I settled on top of a nearby boulder and drew my knees against my chest.

"That really was uncalled for," I muttered, referring to the night before.

"Breakfast is uncalled for?" he asked, not looking up from his work. "I would have to disagree."

I had forgotten about that word. Breakfast. It seemed a strange word for morning meal, but at least this time I knew what it meant.

"No, keefie," I hissed between clenched teeth. "Maybe next time just restrain me. Better yet, do not ever put your hands on me again. I do not like to have my eyes forced closed."

"There's a lot of things I don't like either. One of them includes not being hit in the face." He chuckled as he removed the meat from the rock and tossed it onto a piece of cloth. "But we don't always have choices. It's not like this life is free."

I noticed the bruise on his chin and my lips twitched with a quiet joy. At least I had a tiny fraction of a triumph. "Why is it not free? I have always been free to do as I please, until I met you." My gaze drifted from his chin to his eyes.

He rose to his feet and held out the cloth with the meat on it. "Your Mountain Gods are a ridiculous notion, and you follow the laws of a self-made leadership.

Freedom is not what I see in your lifestyle. Would you like to eat or argue with me?"

I glared at him, but took the food. "Both." I bit into the meat and chewed with a look of defiance on my face.

His eyes sparkled with amusement, and it took all my self-control to stop myself from stabbing him with a piece of wood lying next to my feet. I did, however, allow my imagination to mull over the image of him lying at my feet with a stick embedded in his eye, and the thought nearly brought another smile to my face.

He strolled back toward the fire and continued working on more food. After I ate my fill, I jumped to my feet and ducked back inside the cruiser. I did one more sweep for my boots, but they were nowhere to be seen. I tossed my pack strap over my shoulder and peered around the edge of the doorway. His back was toward me as he bent over the fire. I crept out and slid alongside the cruiser until I had rounded to the other side. Then I took off at a sprint.

When I neared the tree line, a figure stepped out of the shadows. It was Brody with my boots dangling from his grasp. I gasped and slid to a halt, the rocks and sticks scratching the bottoms of my feet.

"Would these make your escape easier?" he asked as one corner of his lips rose.

Expanded Chaos

I despised his amused expressions. "Give those to me!" My hands clenched into fists, but I did not move toward him.

"You forget I am on strict orders from your mother," he said as his amused smile grew, and he tossed my boots over my head. "We can dance if you would like, but when I drag you in front of your mother bruised and beaten, she will have no one to blame but you."

I glanced over my shoulder to see where my boots had landed. They were not too far back, but I could not calculate if they were worth the risk. If I ran to the left, away from my boots, I would have the best chance to escape, especially since my speed had increased when I connected with Mother Gaia and the other elemental girls.

His gaze shifted to my left, and he shrugged. "Go for it. Did you ever question why I was able to make it from the fire all the way over here without you knowing?"

My shoulders slumped. How *had* he done that?

"Look, lass," he said, stepping over a small boulder nearly hidden in the vegetation. "I am not your enemy. I have orders, and that is all this relationship is to me. If you run, I will catch you." He swept past me and scooped up my boots as he walked toward the land ship.

I watched him go, then trudged after him. I was

exhausted from fighting last night and I really did not want a repeat of it. Most of all, this was my chance to see Mama again. If I ran, I might never find her on my own. Not to mention, we were in the middle of nowhere, with no clear idea of which direction to run. I reluctantly climbed into the land ship and set my pack on one of the benches. My boots banged against the ground next to me.

"You will need those," he said from the doorway, then he disappeared again.

I sank onto the bench, tugged on each boot, and was securing the first one when I heard shouting outside. I bounded up, stepped forward, and tripped from my lose boot. My left knee twisted as it smashed into the ground, and I screamed as I fell to my side. The sound of my skull smacking the floor echoed through my head.

I rolled to my back and melted against the ground, drawing in a deep breath. No need for Brody to beat on me. I was excellent at doing it myself. My fingers rubbed the spot on my head. A fat bump was already forming.

Terrific.

Just as I lifted my knee to see the damage, a shadow blocked the sunlight streaming through the doorway. I glanced that way. Scrambling to my feet, I limped backward as I searched for a weapon. Beck's confident smile greeted me as if we were old friends.

"Fancy finding you here," he said as he climbed into the land ship. "Not who I was searching for, but you will do nicely."

"What are you doing here, Beck?" I asked, holding my pack in between us. I had to have something inside that could stop him.

Magic, genius, I scolded myself. Duh.

I could just start a small whirlwind and send him flying away from me. I focused on the air, gathering the colorful enchantment as it formed around me. It swirled slowly, but with a flick of my wrist it gushed ferociously between us. I shoved it all at the bald man. The current of air collided against him, and he teetered on his feet before grasping the chair next to him.

He laughed and waggled his finger at me. "Now, now, Kia Lynn. None of that. We need to save your strength for more important matters."

I built the wind around him, twirling it faster and faster. His lips melted into a frown as he swayed from the tempest force. He leapt at me. I jumped, but it was too late. His hands wrapped around my arm, and he yanked me to the back of the land ship and shoved me hard into the glass behind me.

I yelped, kicking him as hard as I could in the legs. He twisted his body enough to protect his groin, then squeezed my throat until I started seeing black clouds drifting over my eyesight. I gasped for air, but nothing came. As I clawed at his hand, his smile widened on his cheeks and a pleased expression sparkled in his eyes. He was enjoying this control over me.

Just before I lost consciousness, he dropped me to the ground. I gasped in a lungful of air. He gathered a fistful of my hair, hauled me toward the front of the land ship, and tossed me onto a chair. Jako appeared in the doorway with ropes and other items. He tossed them to his dad and chuckled at me before ducking outside again. Terror gripped my chest.

Beck pulled a hood over my eyes. I screamed as loud as I could and finally freed one of my arms from his grasp. I punched him in the gut, but he seemed to barely flinch. His arms circled around me to hold the ropes in place, but then he grunted and the restraints loosened as the rope fell to my lap.

I tossed the hood off my head. Brody was on top of Beck, decking him in the face. I threw the rope to the floor and scrambled to my feet before leaping from the land ship. Sprinting toward the tree line for cover, I did not have the courage to look around and check for Jako.

My loose boot slipped from my foot, and I slid to a halt, whirling around to go back for it. Just as I grabbed it, something sliced through my right thigh, sending agonizing shocks of pain ripping through my entire nervous system.

My cries echoed across the field and tears flooded down my face. I collapsed to one knee and reached down to touch my hip. I rubbed the spot that hurt, then looked at my hand. Blood. I swayed at the sight and bent over as my meal wormed its way up my throat and splattered all over the ground.

"Did you really think you would escape?" Jako asked as he approached me.

I hopped back to my feet and scrambled away from him, wiping the spit from my mouth as I whirled around and limped at a slow run toward the tree line. His footsteps quickened. I threw a look over my shoulder and when our eyes met I knew I was in trouble. A deep seeded hatred stared back at me. I pushed forward, doing my best to ignore the throbbing pain tearing up my thighs and spreading in every direction through my body.

Crossing into the shadows of the tree branches, I searched for a hiding spot, but he was too close behind me to lose him now. I kept running, weaving in and out of the vegetation.

My boot was still in my hand. I circled around a larger tree and flung the boot at Jako as he rounded the trunk after me. It smacked him in the head. He snorted and almost dropped his weapon, but I only infuriated him more. He tore after me.

"I will rip you apart, limb by limb, Kia Lynn!" he screamed at me as he closed in.

I swerved around another tree and turned back toward the land ship. Maybe Brody had subdued Beck—or better yet, immobilized him for good. Brody was still my best chance.

"*Brody!*" I screamed, weaving through tall brush. I wish I had his protection rune right now.

Gritting my teeth, I focused on putting one foot in front of another. With one boot missing, it was more difficult to keep my balance. Not to mention the bottom of my bootless foot was shredded. I felt pieces of my skin tearing off as sticks and stones ripped at my flesh, but I did not stop.

Sunlight greeted me when I sprinted back into the meadow. Jako was nearly breathing down my neck. I pushed harder. Up ahead, I could not see anyone outside the land ship. What if Brody was dead?

"Jako!" Beck yelled from the other end of the meadow. "Leave her be."

I glanced his way. Brody was standing next to Beck, both of them relaxed in their stances as if they were old comrades. I kept running, flying around the land ship, and only stopped when I knew Jako was no longer behind me. I pressed my back against the ship. My chest rose and fell deeply with each haggard breath, and I nearly lost the rest of my meal as the pain in my thigh pulsated with the beat of my rapid heartbeat.

After hobbling to the corner, I glanced around it. Beck and Jako stood near Brody, talking with smiles on their faces. Jako pointed back at the tree line, and they all burst into laughter. They were talking about me. No, they were mocking me. I limped into view and sagged against the frame as the world began to shift to one side. Or was it me who was swaying?

I heard someone call out my name, but everything was spinning. I opened my mouth, but instead of words coming out, I felt drool slide down my chin. The trees tilted and I crashed to the dirt, knocking the wind out of myself.

"Kia Lynn, I have you," Alarix whispered in my ear.

"You," I murmured. I blinked to clear the fog from my eyes and focus on the face in front of me. Sweat dripped into my eyes.

His fingers wiped away the perspiration. "Quiet, now," Alarix replied, planting a kiss on my forehead.

I was lifted off the ground. Was I dreaming? When

had Alarix arrived? It felt like I was floating as the blue sky disappeared and white clouds replaced it. Was I dying? The pain in my thigh, knee, and foot floated away with the wind, and I relaxed into the calming light surrounding me. Maybe this really was the end for me.

I snuggled in close to something soft behind my head and drifted off into the clouds.

CHAPTER FOURTEEN
Black Hole

ZOE DAWN

The morning sun would only rise higher, so I knew we needed to leave soon, but I had to connect with Goddess before the madness raging inside my skull consumed me.

I was angry, frustrated, and in a deep state of grief. Mother Gaia was in trouble, and I did not know how I would save her. The damage Alex's people had inflicted upon the skies petrified me, and Kia Lynn had just left me without a thought of how her absence would affect me or the rest of our people.

Fury was ignited in my heart and even I feared the thoughts of revenge ravaging the recesses of my mind.

I sat cross-legged against a tree trunk, with a sideways view of the cruiser. Tracing over the kenaz marking on my chest, I closed my eyes and focused on the sounds of nature. The tree bark and sap scent swept under my nose, and the soft breeze calmed my shaking mind. The cool earth below me reminded me of who I was connected to and how powerful I really was. I dug my fingers into the dirt, letting it all in, breathing fully and sending my energy into the depths of Mother Gaia.

Something rustled nearby, and I slowly opened my eyes. Alex was approaching. Did she not know how to listen? I thought I had made it clear I needed to be alone.

"Go back to the cruiser!" I shouted, trying to not let my rage ignite again.

She shook her head. Her black hair blew in her face so she pushed it back and tucked it behind her ears. "I know you are angry with me, but this is something we should do together. We are more powerful together."

"It will not make a difference if Kia Lynn is missing," I hissed, gritting my teeth.

"We can at least try," she replied, sinking to the dirt and sitting cross-legged directly in front of me. She held out her hands. "We both want the same thing, Zoe Dawn. Let me help."

I stared at her for a long moment, then wrapped my fingers around hers. "I am doing this for Kia Lynn."

"I know you are." Alex closed her eyes.

I examined her still face before shutting my eyes. It really was not her fault, but I needed someone to blame, and she was an easy target right now. And besides, if she had stayed in her dimension, as she had called it, we would not have been in this messy predicament.

The energy flow between our hands was unmistakable. Her touch was electrifying my nervous system, as if she were a missing piece to my soul. I almost yanked away, still angry and hurt by all that had happened, but the sensation spread so quickly, it felt like we were merging as one. She was the water and I the fire, dancing and playing through the wind together.

Between us a bright white energy flowed from the earth and Mother Gaia swam through us, filling our bodies with celestial love. I was hooked.

"Daughters," a voice in my head sang. "You are the elementals, the ebb and flow, and with my bond, the highest order of this planet. We, together, are the utmost importance in creating balance and harmony. Divided, I *will* collapse once more. Danger does approach from up above as well as on steady ground and we must heal all in order to complete our final transformation."

Her words sent a chill down my spine. Tiordan's instincts had been correct—we had not finished our elemental duty.

"The ocean is crying for you, Alex." Mother Gaia's voice swirled in and out of my mind, carried between me and Alex and tying us together. "Do you hear her? Do you sense her pain? She sees the evil unfolding before her. There is more work to do and the three of you must unite to bring forth transcendence."

Alex's grip tightened, bringing my awareness back to her. I scooted closer to her as Mother Gaia's energy intensified.

"Zoe Dawn, your fire breathes new life. When the Phoenix falls, it will rise once again. Use this gift to shower the divine spark upon the world's people and bring them all together in unity so our collective souls may shift as one. The threats must be eliminated from our world. Banish or destroy, either is acceptable."

Mother Gaia's essence stretched beyond space, and a vision of Kia Lynn swam in my head. She was lying flat on her back. There was so much blood. Was that Alarix kneeling beside her? My breath caught in my throat. Was this real?

"Where is she?" I cried, squeezing Alex's hands. I did not want to lose the sight.

"Stay on your path, daughters." Mother Gaia's voice was loud in my mind. "And do not allow the emotions of your physical bodies to separate you again."

Her energy dissipated slowly, twirling around us until it sank deep into the dirt once more. I was frozen. Exhaustion swept over my body, and my shoulders slumped forward. When I opened my eyes, I was greeted by Alex's stunned expression.

"Did you see Kia Lynn?" Tears gathered in her eyes. "She is hurt."

"I did see," I replied, gulping back the terror rising in my chest. "No more fighting, Alex. I may not know why Mother Gaia picked you, but I am trusting Her. Let's go find our sister."

I rose to my feet and hauled Alex up beside me. She leaned closer and wrapped her arms around me, then melted into my embrace as her body shook with emotion.

"I didn't ask for this, Zoe Dawn," she muttered and took a step away from me, her eyes searching my face for something I was not ready to give. "But I'm here now, and I will do everything I can to right the wrongs of my family. Tallisa will need to be removed from this dimension once and for all."

"That will only rip apart Kia Lynn's heart again." I knew Alex was right, but how would we ever convince Kia Lynn of this?

"I know it will," Alex said, raking her fingers through her hair. "But we have to stop her from ever risking our connection to Mother Gaia."

She led the way back to the cruiser where Dax was leaning against the machine and Covyn was lounging on the first step. Rafael stood just inside the cruiser. His head was wrapped with gauze and he wore a pained expression. He should be lying down, but I was not in the mood to mother him.

"Are you two love birds ready?" Dax teased as he climbed into the cruiser after us.

Rafael moved out of the way and shuffled back to the lower bed that Alex had revealed earlier.

Covyn lifted her brows at Dax. There was no amusement in her eyes. "Alex knows better than to move in on my partner," she said with a snarky tone. She patted Alex's shoulder.

I had not thought Covyn to be the jealous type. We would have to work on that.

"Never would even think of it," Alex replied, sinking onto her captain's chair and throwing Covyn a tight-lipped smile before focusing on the cruiser's controls.

Dax beat me to the other captain's chair, and his copper eyes sparkled when I pretended to deck him. Instead, I grabbed the sides of his head and planted a kiss on the top of his forehead.

"It is my turn to hear Alex's stories," Dax said, swatting me away. "You have dominated enough of her time."

"What I want to know is why you would come to a

place like this, when you lived in the ancient years," Covyn said from the back of the cruiser. "Weren't the options endless in those days?"

Alex laughed and shook her head. "Far from it. They were most definitely different from now, but the government was in full control of the people through smart phones, televisions, fear-mongering... You name it, they were probably using it to keep us under their thumb."

"What is a smart phone?" Dax asked, kicking his feet up on the dashboard and leaning back in his chair.

Alex finished instructing the cruiser. The door closed, and the machine shifted upward and we sped off, traveling faster than a horse, reminding me of the speckled creature in Zion. I missed Malcolm's horses, especially Chester and his soft nose that would nudge me if I did not keep scratching behind his ears. I could not wait to return to him. If only the chaos would stop interrupting the adventures I had planned.

Alex twisted around to look at all of us and returned my smile. "It is similar to the chip in my arm, except it was a rectangular device you held in your hands. You could communicate with people around the world with them."

"Really?" Rafael asked, rolling to his side and

engaging with Alex for the first time since the cave. "You actually could talk to someone who was on the other side of our huge planet?"

She nodded. "I can do so now with my chip, but I don't really know anyone that well who lives that far away."

"Tell us more." Covyn leaned her arms against the cushion in front of us and rested her chin on her hands. "The vehicles, you called them, right? What were they like? The roads we come across are littered with these machines. There were so many."

"Yes, they were everywhere," Alex replied, patting the armrest, "and similar to this cruiser, except they had wheels and we drove them ourselves. No automatic driver for most cars, and the few that did were still glitching when I left. I don't know if they ever worked out the kinks in those designs, as I skipped over all those years."

"What about the bad stuff?" Rafael asked, leaning against the side of the cruiser and shoving a pillow behind his back and head. "Based on some of the books I have read, there were wars and—what did you call them?" He snapped his fingers. "Gangs. Mafia. People who intentionally hurt others, even children. Is that all true?"

Alex's face fell and her teeth grazed over her bottom lip. "All of that. Yes. The year I left behind was one of our better years. Peaceful, in fact. Just five years before, a deadly virus emerged and swept across the world in a matter of months. Our economy collapsed, fights broke out, racism was exposed, and people were being held accountable for their actions on a much larger scale. That year changed the world on a wide scale."

"What is racism?" Covyn asked as her hand reached over and grasped mine.

Alex's gaze shifted around to each of us, then she looked down at her hands and picked at her fingernails. "It was an ugly stereotype that has since died out. If there is one thing I am grateful to have left behind, it is that." Her eyes lifted to mine and I saw tears shining in them. "Enough of my gloomy past. Maybe later we can talk about it more. How about a lesson on The Happiest Place on Earth?"

Dax nodded enthusiastically. The boy was a diehard kid, and I loved how easily he made me laugh.

Alex turned back toward the monitors. She messed around with the controls, and from the ceiling, right behind the sunroof, a section split and then rotated down. It looked like one of the monitors, except much larger. Alex and Dax were blocked from view, but then they came around the sides and took a seat on the bench in front of me.

"Six Dash Fourteen, play Disneyland archives from twenty twenty-five," Alex instructed the machine.

The screen flickered and a moving picture sprang into view. There were people everywhere, for as far as the eyes could see. They looked like a herd of animals as they walked through iron gates. Their clothes were strange colors, and many of them had circle objects covering their eyes. Their head coverings were in all shapes and sizes, but the one thing on everyone's faces was a smile. They were enjoying their lives.

"Are those the smart phones?" Rafael asked, pointing at an object several of the adults carried in their hands.

Alex nodded and a smile lifted her cheeks. "Most everyone had one. We could take photos on those phones and share them on social media. It was the thing to do back then. Share our entire happy lives with the world."

What a strange time. All my exploring into a past that did not belong to me and my new sister had been there. I felt a small tug of jealousy. It would be an adventure to witness the world from her time.

The moving picture showed people climbing in boxes and riding down rickety tracks, laughing, and taking these photos Alex was speaking about—just like the one

Tallisa had thrown at me. The strange-eared creatures were everywhere. They were not all the same, but I had to remember it was just a costume with people inside.

The cruiser beeped and the lights flashed. We all bolted upright as it slowed without Alex commanding it. She shot out of her seat and disappeared behind the screen, which lifted soon after.

"Mom. Dad. Is that you?" Alex asked. Her hologram was shining.

"Alex, finally." Adina's exasperated tone brought me to my feet. "We have tried everything to force our way through to your com. We will discuss the cruiser and you leaving at a later point. For now, Dad is on his way home in Malcolm's ship. They have discovered something in space, and finding Henry has now become our only focus."

"What is wrong, Mom?" Alex asked, throwing me a guarded glance over her shoulder.

I left Covyn and slowly walked toward Alex.

"The time machine did not close the wormhole completely." The emotion in Adina's voice shook me to the core. "I don't know how we missed it, but it has grown and is creating a small black hole." She quieted, and Alex blew out a sharp breath.

"Mom, what does that mean?" Alex asked, wringing

her hands together.

Adina cleared her throat. "It could mean many things, but the theory is that both universes will collide if it grows any bigger, and they will be destroyed."

Alex's bottom lip quivered, and she slowly lifted her chin to meet my gaze. Alarix's accusations had been precise after all.

CHAPTER FIFTEEN
Reckless

ALEX

"Alex, are you there?" Mom asked again.

My gaze remained locked with Zoe Dawn's. Mother Gaia had warned us. Alarix's words rang in my mind, accusing me of destroying their world. It was all true.

I could barely breathe as I turned back toward the hologram. "I'm here, Mom. What are we going to do?"

"I am going to patch you through to Dad," she replied. I heard her fidgeting with something and then Dad's face popped into view.

"Baby girl," he said as relief spread across his expression. "You can't just leave like that."

"I'm fine, Dad." I reached toward the cruiser's monitor. "Hold on. I'm going to transfer you to this other monitor." I linked my chip to the cruiser's and swiped them over to the screen. Both of their faces slid into view. "Much better. Say hello to everyone."

Zoe Dawn waved. "Hello, Jax and Adina. We are

keeping your daughter safe. Promise."

"We want to believe that is true," Dad replied, leaning back in his chair. I saw Malcolm in the background. "But you all tend to be a little reckless. Where are you going?"

"To save Uncle Henry and Kia Lynn," I said before anyone else could reply. I waved at Zoe Dawn. "Tallisa left this photo for Kia Lynn to find. We knew they were in Southern California, but now I believe they are all meeting in Disneyland or in that area at least. Show them, Zoe Dawn."

She slid the photo out of her pocket and unfolded it, then held it near the camera. "Tallisa threw this at me when she came to our village. I never showed it to Kia Lynn, but her father must have received some information because that afternoon she was gone."

"Alex, disengage the block on your location," Dad told me, working on something on his end that I could not see. "After we pick up supplies and Mom, we will meet you wherever you are. There is no reason for you to do this on your own."

I did as I was told, grateful they would be able to take charge. Being a leader was exhausting.

"How long do you think you will be?" I asked as I opened the channel for them to find us.

"Not too long," Mom replied. She was also

rummaging around, and it was hard to see her when she kept moving her arm.

"The time machine is our only hope to stop this wormhole from growing," Dad stated, jumping back to our other problem. "Since this is how we believe Tallisa snuck into this dimension, the question is now, why didn't she do anything to stop it from getting to this point?" He looked up from what he was working on and focused on me. "This was her home for over a decade. Why would she want it to implode?"

"What is implode?" Rafael asked, sneaking up behind me.

"It is the opposite of explode," I said, not wanting to explain how their world would literally be crushed. "Don't worry. Dad is an expert at fixing problems. He will find a way to stop this from happening."

Rafael nodded, but I could tell he was still digesting the information. When he finally realized what was happening, I imagined he would do more than yell at me.

Mom and Dad's images flickered, then blurred. I smacked the computer, but it only made it worse.

"Hey, can you still see us?" I asked, leaning in closer to the screen.

"Not really," Mom replied. "Jax, are you messing with the connection?"

"No, I'm still working on finding their location. The map is moving all over the place." He shook his head, and the screen blurred even more.

"I do not like what is happening," Zoe Dawn said as her fingers wrapped around my upper arm. She pulled on me slightly. "What is going on?"

"Mom?" I fidgeted with my ring and when Mom didn't reply, I reactivated my chip connection. The screen went black. "Dad. Mom. Are you there?"

Dax came in closer and examined the monitors. The map to Disneyland had blurred as well. "Can you access them from your arm?"

"I'm trying," I replied, hiding behind my hands and shaking my head. "Nothing is connecting."

"The other two screens have gone black," Covyn said, shaking me. "What are we to do?"

I dropped my hands and glared at her. "I don't know," I snapped, shoving them all away from me. "I need some breathing room. Please."

"She has no idea what she is doing," Rafael said from the bench. He tucked his hands behind his back and stared at all of us. "Just like the rest of us. We are a bunch of keefies, running around like chickens. Worst plan ever."

The cruiser jolted. I fell forward and landed on my

hands and knees, cringing when my kneecap shifted from the impact. Zoe Dawn managed to hold on to one of the bars near the doorway, but Covyn tumbled to the ground, smacking her head against one of the benches. Dax was white-knuckling my chair, but somehow held himself steady.

The cruiser was no longer moving.

I crawled toward Covyn, but Zoe Dawn beat me there. She helped her sit up and checked her head.

"You will have a bump," Zoe Dawn said and kissed her there.

Dax hauled me to my feet.

"I can't reach anyone," I said, trying to connect via my internal chip. My heart sank into my stomach. I really didn't know what I was doing.

"Take a breath," Dax said, rubbing my shoulders and kneading a knot at the base of my neck. "Let's go outside and find out what happened. Maybe the cruiser took a wrong turn."

I rolled my eyes. Mr. Optimistic. As cheesy as he was, I still needed his positive mindset right now. I drew in a long, deep breath, while Zoe Dawn helped Covyn onto the back bench and tucked a pillow under her head.

She turned back to face me. "Let's see if Dax is right. Are you coming, Rafael?"

"Nah. I am all adventured out." He scooted to the back and closed his eyes. "From the sound of it, we are all doomed to die anyway."

Mr. Pessimistic. I didn't even bother rolling my eyes at him.

Zoe Dawn was already walking outside. I followed her, with Dax in tow.

I held my hand above my eyes to shade them. We were just outside a meadow, which was surrounded by a thick forest. Where we were standing was a pathway that must have once been an old road. It was much wider than most of the trails and pathways.

"Everything looks fine!" Zoe Dawn yelled from the back of the cruiser. "Do either of you see anything out of place?" She peeked around the corner at us.

I jumped from the steps and circled around to the front. Nothing was out of place on this end either, aside from it no longer hovering and now sitting firmly against the ground. A white rectangle. Who would have thought these would be the future RV's?

Dax shouted something, but I could not make out what he was saying. I had made it to the other side of the cruiser. Zoe Dawn was on the back end. She glanced at me, then we both circled around on opposite ends.

Standing a few feet away was Jako, holding an

anaman weapon to Dax's head.

"Wonderful!"

I whirled around. Beck tapped his toes on the steps of the cruiser as his arms folded over his chest.

"Exactly who I have been searching for," he said, grinning from ear to ear. "How did we get so lucky?"

I backed up a few feet. Zoe Dawn's eyes narrowed and then she nodded her head. Her fingers reddened. Beck just smiled at her, then yanked Covyn through the doorway. A cloth had been shoved in her mouth, and her hands were tied behind her back. I strained my eyes to see past them. Rafael had to be in bad shape if he was not causing an uproar.

"Toss any of your fire or ice at me, and this will be the last time your friend takes a breath." He pulled out his weapon and pressed it to her back. "Now, why don't we all gather inside and make plans for our journey together?"

"Over my dead body!" Zoe Dawn screamed, balling her hands into fists.

Jako forced Dax toward the cruiser and aimed his weapon at Zoe Dawn. "That can be arranged," he hissed, cocking his head to the side. "I'm a great shot. Ask your friend Kia Lynn."

A crimson flush rushed across Zoe Dawn's cheeks,

spreading like wildfire down her arms. "What did you say?" Her tone had lowered a few octaves, and I swear the devil himself would tremble from the fury shooting from her eyes.

Beck only chuckled, clearly amused by his son's words. "Do not poke the bear, Jako. We don't want her to explode."

Rafael shouted. "What is going—" A shoe smacked Beck in the face.

Nice one, Rafael. He must have been in the restroom. Beck flinched and twisted to look inside the cruiser.

"You're new," Beck said as he dragged Covyn back inside the cruiser and pointed his weapon at Rafael. "I think you both should sit down and shut up."

Jako beckoned at me to follow Dax. Zoe Dawn remained glued to her spot on the ground.

"We only need one of you," Jako said with a smile. He sauntered closer to me. "You know I don't have a problem with hitting a girl. It wouldn't be our first moment." He licked his lips, and I noticed Dax staring at him with a crazed expression sliding down his face.

I held my hand out at Dax to stop him from doing something stupid. "I will go with you, but first, what happened to Kia Lynn?"

"Same as what will happen to you if you try to run,"

he said, grabbing my arm and wrenching me toward the cruiser. "She might live, but I hope not." He laughed and ducked into the cruiser after me.

Zoe Dawn climbed in behind us. I could feel her raging fire bristling just beneath her skin as she slipped by me. Jako tied each of our hands behind our backs, then Beck pointed at the bench behind Covyn and Rafael. We took our seats.

"Now," Beck said, once we were all secured. "Who knows how to drive this beautiful piece of machinery?"

"Me," I said, scooting to the edge of my seat. "Where are we going?"

"Don't you worry your pretty little head about that," Beck replied, waving me to come closer. He pulled out a small square computer and pressed a few buttons. "There. The scrambler is turned off for a moment. I need you to disconnect our location and turn off all access to the AI's network. Make it quick."

He untied my hands, grabbed me by the neck, and pressed me onto the front seat.

I turned toward the monitors, trying to quickly figure out in my head how I could disconnect everything but still leave a route open for Dad to intercept a message.

"Do you need me to program our destination into the AI?" I asked as my fingers flew across the keyboard.

Beck knew I was always connected unless I deactivated my chip as well, but he hadn't specified anything about that. Now that the scrambler was off, I could possibly use it.

"No, I will do it. Just take care of all access points." He leaned over my shoulder. "And, Alex, I am not stupid. I will know if you leave anything undone, so please do not test my patience."

I bit down on my bottom lip and disconnected any chance of Dad finding us. If he happened to be looking during the few minutes it was still accessible, then we might have a chance. If not, this was the end of the road for us.

Next, I deactivated all access points to the network and closed my work. Beck straightened. He looked over the information on the screen, then nodded as if satisfied.

"We would have made a great team, Alex," he said, towing me out of the seat and thrusting me back with the others. "Too bad you had to go crash my ship. Now I'm going to destroy your village and steal your parents' ship. What do you think of that?"

"Is that where we are going? Back to my home?"

"Wouldn't you like to know," Jako said, laughing as he leaned back in the other front chair, and making it clear it was not a question. He faced us.

Expanded Chaos

We were over halfway to Southern California. By nightfall, we would have been there. I exhaled loudly, defeat taking over my thoughts as I dropped my forehead to the cushion in front of me. Mom and Dad had to save Uncle Henry. They were the only hope he had now.

"Before we return to your village, I need to meet up with my new friends. You are going to love them," Beck said, bursting into laughter as if he had told the joke of the century. "Buckle up, ladies." He pointed his finger at each one of us. "We are about to embark on the adventure of a lifetime."

He manually switched on the cruiser, like Alarix had done. The wheel slid out from a panel in front, followed by the pedals at his feet. He found the button to close the door, then settled into his seat and wrapped his hands around the steering wheel. Slowly inching forward, we continued down the road leading us to Disneyland, except now our final destination was a promise of more torture and possibly a gruesome death I did not want to imagine.

CHAPTER SIXTEEN
Alarix's Secrets

KIA LYNN

I felt a cool compress press against my forehead as I swayed in and out of consciousness. Nothing seemed real or tangible, but the fabric lying on my skin tugged me back to an unfriendly and unforgiving world. I wanted to see who was beside me, but it hurt too much to open my eyes.

"She is still burning up," I heard Alarix say.

My pulse quickened from the familiar voice. "Where am I?" I asked, reaching out to find him.

His hand encircled mine, and he placed it back on my belly. "We are still in the cruiser. How are you feeling?"

I groaned from a pain in my thigh. "I hurt. Why am I in so much pain, Alarix?" I pried my eyes open and squinted at him. He was kneeling beside me.

"You were shot by that raving lunatic," Alarix explained, screwing up his face with clear loathing bubbling in his eyes. A frown melted down his expression when he glanced over his shoulder. "Jako needs to be held accountable for shooting her daughter. Are you going to make sure that happens?"

Brody shifted into view and shook his head as he peered down at me. His hands were busy fidgeting with something I could not see. "Have you met her mother? When Tallisa sees what happened to Kia Lynn, I don't think anyone will be able to stop the wrath that will follow." He patted Alarix's shoulder before walking away. "My advice would be to stay out of her way."

I pressed the palms of my hands against my eyes and rubbed them. "How are you here, Alarix?" My memories were jumbled, and their conversation made absolutely no sense.

"It's a long story," Alarix replied, wiping the compress across my forehead again. "It might take some time for your memories to return. But first, we really need to cool you down."

"Why do my thigh and foot hurt so badly?" I asked, groaning as I attempted to sit up.

"Don't move just yet." His hands pressed on my shoulders. "Let me take care of you. The wound in your thigh is still very tender."

"Why do I have a wound in my thigh?" I asked, growing impatient with his broken answers.

"Do you have any more of that medicine?" he asked Brody, still ignoring my question.

His fingers trailed down my face. I sighed. It felt so nice, my question was forgotten and my eyes fluttered shut.

"I have my herbs," I replied, trying to roll to my side.

"Brody has something stronger." Alarix held me on my back, but my leg was cramping. Or hurting. Maybe both. I could not tell anymore. "I am going to help you sit up, but just for a moment. This medicine tastes like goat waste, but it will take away the pain in your leg and foot."

I peeked out through my eyelashes and nodded. "How do you know what goat waste tastes like?" I asked in an attempt to lighten my mood. Alarix's lips twitched into a small smile, then he pulled me to a sitting position and crouched behind me, propping me up. Brody had a white cylindrical object in his hand.

"I will squirt this in your mouth. Just swallow it." He leaned in closer, but I held my mouth shut. "You will feel back to normal once this makes its way into your system." He took a seat next to me and his eyes softened slightly. "I promised I would not cut into you again to invoke my spells. These herbs have been brewed and blessed by the best of the world's mystics. It is a concoction from your Mother Gaia."

I stared at the object, pressing my lips together. Even using Her name was not convincing enough, coming from him.

Alarix leaned over my shoulder and patted my arm. "I'm right here, my love," he whispered in my ear. "When the pain is gone, we can talk over everything that has happened."

His voice was soothing. I leaned into him and finally relented, opening my mouth. The liquid was foul—goat's waste was an understatement. I scrunched up my face in disgust and nearly spit it in Brody's face, but somehow I swallowed it. Brody handed me a water container. I gulped down a mouthful, but it made my stomach churn. I thrusted it back to him, then Alarix slipped out from behind me and helped me lie back down.

A faint memory of Beck fluttered through my mind. He was standing in the doorway of the land ship. "Was Beck here?" My eyes opened wide at the thought, imagining the man walking into my view right now.

"He was," Brody replied. I couldn't see him, but he was near.

I groaned, and this time Alarix let me roll to my side. "Please tell me he isn't on the land ship."

"No, I needed him to help me with something else. He

was happy to assist," Brody said casually as if they were old friends.

I bolted upright and cringed when pain shot from my thigh down to my toes. Ignoring the ache, I pressed my palms against the cushion and leaned forward, trying to stand. It was too much. I collapsed against the back of the bench and glared at Brody.

"Beck tried to kill me," I snapped, raising my trembling hand to my forehead and wiping sweat from my brow. "Why would you let him go free?"

"Her temperature is going down," Alarix said, interrupting me and using the cool cloth to help me wipe away my perspiration.

"Good," Brody replied, glancing back at Alarix, then turning to me. "Beck will be punished for what he has done to you, but for now he will be of some use."

For the first time since I had awakened, I became extremely aware of my body. My gaze drifted to my thigh. My trousers had been torn in one spot, and a white cloth had been wrapped tightly around my leg. It was the same type of cloth Brody had used when he cut the rune into my calf.

"What did you do to me?" I asked between clenched teeth. Angry tears welled in my eyes, and a deep sense of rage boiled inside my stomach. He promised to not cut me again.

Alarix sank onto the cushion next to me. "He didn't do anything. It was Jako."

"Jako was here too?" I asked, my voice barely a whisper. I gulped back my rising dread. Rage and terror was a lethal combination, but they snaked relentlessly around every muscle in my body. I covered my face with my hands and shook my head, fighting away the explosion waiting to erupt. "Why can't I remember? Why did you let this happen to me?"

"You refused my protection spell," Brody replied nonchalantly.

I peeked at him between my fingers, my eyes shooting darts of fury at him, but he had not even bothered to look my way.

"And Jako was out of line. He never should have chased after you, let alone shot you. When we reach your mother, she will decide his fate."

I froze, then dropped my arms to my sides. Mama was really here. The rage and terror cooled within my chest and settled back into my stomach, where it slowly dissipated. My gaze fluttered to Alarix.

He was not supposed to be with us. "How are you even here?" I asked, running my fingers across his chin. "Do you know Brody?"

He avoided my eyes. I gripped his chin and forced him to look at me.

"I-I can explain." He stuttered, flinching when my fingernails dug into his skin.

"Was this all a game to you?" I released him and pushed him away from me. My emotional rollercoaster was roaring back to the top. I felt foolish for trusting a man I had met briefly on an adventure none of us should have been on. "When we met, was it all staged?"

He vigorously shook his head. "Far from it."

My eyes narrowed. His reluctance to talk about what he was digging for the ancient's village and now he was here with Brody. Either nothing was adding up or the truth was being exposed.

"I promise." His voice rose an octave. "We were there looking for one of these cruisers."

"What is a cruiser?" I asked, shoving him harder.

He scooted all the way to the end of the bench. "This." He waved his hand around the room. "What we are in right now is a cruiser."

"Not a land ship?" The words spilled out before I had the chance to digest his words. My confusion overwhelmed my mind, and I realized I did not really care what the name of this machine was.

He shook his head. "It is a cruiser. My father sent me

and my friends to dig out a cruiser that had been covered by a mudslide." Alarix rose to his feet and stepped all the way back to the wall as if he knew it was best to put some space between us before he spoke his next words. "Beck and your mother recruited my parents right before I met you. When they discovered you were Tallisa's daughter, Nikita demanded I break off our relationship, and my parents did not give me a choice."

A burst of wind slid across my back and over my shoulders. "You did not have another mate?" I asked. My rage had returned. I hated being manipulated.

He shook his head and his gaze drifted to the floor. "They threatened my parents. My family. I had to make up a story to keep everyone safe."

"You are no hero," I hissed as I tried to rise to my feet. I screamed in agony when the pain in my foot and thigh collided. Collapsing back onto the bench, I glowered at Alarix, then Brody. "You are both cowards, submitting to my mother like a bunch of dogs."

Brody laughed, which did not surprise me.

"Little lass, you do not even know what is about to befall this world. Your connection to the two other elementals and Mother Gaia means absolutely nothing. And your little show, the one that supposedly *healed* our world, will be destroyed within the next few days. You realize you failed, right? The healing is not complete and it never will be. What a waste of time." He finally glanced back at me, and if I wasn't in horrific pain, I would have ripped his smirking lips right off his face. "Hold on to your britches because we are ripping you from this dimension whether you like it or not."

I opened my mouth to reply, but instead screamed at him. Alarix cowered toward the back of the land ship, but Brody turned back to face the controls, unfazed by my rage.

It was silent in the land ship after that. The ache in my thigh lessened, and I unwrapped the cloth from my foot. The bottom of it was shredded. I closed my eyes and faintly remember throwing my boot at Jako. If only I'd had both boots on, I would have escaped.

As the sky darkened, a light off in the distance caught my eyes. I scooted to the edge of the bench and squinted at it.

"What is that?" I asked, pointing.

Brody smiled, and the side of his face I noticed lit up with excitement. "That is The Happiest Place on Earth," he said, stretching his neck from side to side before rising from his chair. "That's what your mother calls it. I imagine it means more to her than most others, but you can ask her about it when we arrive."

The Happiest Place on Earth. Mama had talked about it my whole young life. We were supposed to travel there together to see if it still existed. And now, I was about to step foot in this place that had only lived on in my head.

Brody handed me a pair of shoes. "They are not as fancy as your boots, but you really won't need those anymore."

I took the shoes. After wrapping my foot again to protect it, I slipped both shoes on and pulled myself to my feet. I limped to the front of the land ship and pressed my palms into the paneling below the front window.

"You know I hate you, right?" I asked Brody, never taking my eyes off the lights ahead.

"The feeling is mutual."

Alarix was quiet. My feelings for him were mixed, but at this point, I just wanted off this machine. If I never saw him again, I would probably be fine with it. No man was worth this turmoil.

If Mama's stories were correct, this place would have been destroyed by the hundreds of harsh seasons when most of our ancestors had been forced to dwell underground, while the vegetation took ownership once again. But as we neared it, I realized the broken buildings were still standing. Why was it free of dirt, vegetation, and buildup after so many seasons? Just like Covyn's town, it seemed as if someone had maintained it.

I pushed the thoughts away. The land ship was slowing and people were gathering. Large letters adorned the building. I squinted at them. DISN CA IF NIA ADVEN RE. I did not understand what they meant, but it seemed there were missing letters due to the spacing. Mama had described the entryway to her favorite spot on Earth, and those letters matched the vision of them in my head. Somehow, after years of her absence, Mama had kept her promise.

Alarix came out of his hiding place at the back of the land ship. I turned to look at him. His expression had sobered, but there was fear behind his eyes. He was frightened of me. I almost laughed out loud, but instead shook my head and pursed my lips to show my indifference. He really was a coward.

The door rose, revealing the growing crowd. How many people, anamans and humans combined, had Mama recruited? There had to be hundreds gathering.

I followed Brody outside and stood on the top step, taking in the scenery that stretched out before me.

"*Kia Lynn!*" a woman shouted.

I scanned over the crowd, but I could not see her. Then a flash of red hair caught my eye to the left. My eyes widened when I saw someone pushing through the masses. She waved and bounced on her toes when our gazes met.

I flew down the stairs and shoved my way toward her, but then the crowd parted and she stood in front of me. Her auburn hair was flowing like fire over her shoulders and down to her waist. The sparkle in her green eyes had not changed as her smile overtook her entire face. I did not wait for her to invite me. I threw myself into her arms and wept against her shoulder, clinging on to her with all my strength.

All the questions I had, all the fury I had felt for her leaving me, and all the pain and hurt and anger I had been holding onto for so long drifted away as I inhaled her scent. The memories of her undying love were all I needed right now. Nothing else mattered.

CHAPTER SEVENTEEN
Fighting For Our Lives

ZOE DAWN

My head was resting on Alex's shoulder when I woke with a start. I straightened my posture and examined my surroundings.

We were still inside the cruiser, but we were encased in darkness with only a sliver of the moon shining against the blacked out windows. Blinking away the sleep, I stared at the back of Beck's bald head. He continued to manually running the cruiser, despite Alex insistence that automatic was easier on the machine.

He did not care for any of our opinions. That was abundantly clear.

I wiggled against the cloth wrapped tightly around my wrists. They dug relentlessly into my skin, and now my arms and hands were numb from being held behind my back for so long. I rolled my shoulders, stretched my neck to each side, and sent my heat to my wrists. Maybe now they wouldn't be paying any attention. I hoped. The last time I tried to burn away my restraints, Jako had head-butted me.

My nose still throbbed. When I was free, he would be the first to go.

My warmth increased, and I concentrated it against the fabric. Alex stirred in her sleep. I froze when Jako glanced my way, but then he chuckled and said something quietly to his father.

Despite the numbness, I pulled against the cloth, pumping my fists to push my inner fire and awaken my nerves. My skin prickled with life, and the restraints stretched from the heat. I put more pressure on them, and the fabric strained more. I wiggled my fingers and tried to roll my wrists, but they needed more room.

I peered at Jako and Beck again. They had fallen quiet, and Jako's head was resting against the top of his chair, but his eyes were wide open. Any light from my fire would alert him to what I was doing.

I warmed my wrists, holding back the flame but easing the heat against the fabric. It crackled, and the warmth spread through my hands and against the cushion of the seat. I jerked forward, afraid the entire seat would light up with my fire. If that happened, the only person I would hurt was Alex.

My fingers shook as I clasped them together and I

pressed the heat once again into my wrists. Wiggling against the fabric, they snapped in one spot, then another. I sighed with relief as my arms fell to my sides.

Easing my arms in front of me, I rubbed them until the pin prickles eased. Alex stirred again, and her head fell to my shoulder. I guess it was my turn to hold her.

I reached behind her back and untied her restraints as she slept. She instinctively moved her arms onto her lap and wrapped one of them around my arm, snuggling in closer. My pulse quickened. I hoped Jako would not do a sweep before she woke.

I held her tightly, soothing away the nightmares that made her so restless. She had already screamed for her mom and dad two times since she had fallen asleep and once she had whimpered, before weeping against the hard cushion we were propped against. Tallisa's whispered name had followed. The woman had really done a number on the girl.

Dax bolted upright on the bench in front of me. Then he scooted to the edge of his seat. "I need to relieve myself, Beck. Will you please untie me?"

"No, no," I hissed quietly, trying to get Dax's attention. I kicked at his bench, but he did not turn around.

I reached toward Alex and shook her, all the while

keeping my eyes on Jako and Beck. They were both ignoring Dax, but I knew how persistent he could be. Unless I got his attention, there was no way he would let up on them.

Alex shifted and I turned toward her just as her eyes fluttered open. Her unfocused eyes blinked several times and reached up to scratch her nose. I pushed her hand back down to her lap, squeezing her hands to silently remind her they were supposed to be restrained.

"Hey, what was that for?" she blurted, looking at me with squinted eyes.

Now Dax glanced over his shoulder. I glared at him, then turned with softer eyes to look at Alex.

"Quiet, Alex." I patted her hands, showing her she was untied.

Jako rose from his chair, craning his neck to look at us. "What are you two ladies doing in the back? Do I need to come separate you? Don't you remember the last time I had to subdue you?"

Beck laughed, and Alex's eyes widened. She must have remembered our present circumstances. Her gaze fell to her hands, and I noticed her fingers tremble before she shoved them behind her back.

"I was just having a nightmare," she said, pushing me away with her hips. "When will we be stopping next? My legs and arms are hurting."

"Deal with it," Jako snapped, sinking back on his chair and throwing his feet up on the dashboard.

"Jako, seriously," Dax whined, wiggling against the cushion. "I really need to go. Do you want me to piss my pants?"

"Suits me just fine," Jako replied, holding up his fingers and wiggling them at Dax.

Dax growled and scooted to the end of the bench. "Come here and do that to my face, you coward."

Beck whispered something to Jako that I could not hear, then jabbed his thumb back at us. "Go untie him and guard the door."

Jako rolled his eyes but did as his father instructed. He yanked Dax up from his seat and shoved him past us. After tossing him up against the paneling, Jako undid Dax's restraints and forced him into the cramped restroom. While Dax was inside, Jako's gaze wandered over to me and Alex. A mischievous grin rose on his lips, and he leaned his full weight against the door, blocking Dax inside.

"I never really liked the guy," he said, laughing at our expressions. "Such a buzzkill."

Sweat dripped off Alex's chin. Or was it water?

"What about me?" Covyn asked, turning around to

look at Jako.

Jako's eyes narrowed. "You made your choice, Covyn. And you chose wrong. Not my fault."

"You used to be a cool guy," Covyn muttered, shaking her head as she looked away from him. "Now you're just your daddy's little submissive baby."

"What did you say?" Jako's cheeks burned red.

Dax pressed on the door and when it did not budge, he knocked on the paneling. Jako's attention turned back to Dax, but not before he threw a dirty look in Covyn's direction. Then a smile reappeared on his face and he turned his amused grin toward me and Alex. His silent laughs made my blood boil.

Dax shoved his full body weight against the door. "Knock it off, Jako."

Jako snickered. As Dax pushed harder, the dark-haired man stepped aside so Dax flew out and landed on his face right below Alex's feet.

Alex's entire body tensed, and she bit down on her lip to hide the quiver.

Dax rubbed his forehead and pulled his knees underneath him. Jako didn't give him a chance to recover. He reached down and grabbed a handful of his hair. Dax's hands shot up to his head just as he was yanked to his feet. He held back a cry, but I did not miss the glistening of tears in his eyes. He was shoved against the wall next to the restroom, and Jako smashed his face into the paneling.

I nudged Alex. This was our chance, and we had no choice but to improvise.

She nodded and held her hands on her lap, rubbing them together. I did the same focusing on my fire. As I watched Jako knock Dax in the back of the head several more times, my fury erupted and I pushed the flames from my hands. I launched them at Jako.

He shrieked and bounded toward the front of the cruiser as his arm burst into flames, leaving Dax to tumble to the floor. The sounds of Jako's desperate cries brought warmth to my heart. I do not think I have ever despised a person more than him.

Alex and I leapt to our feet at the same time, following Jako. Beck whirled around. His frantic gaze landed on me, and when he saw us approaching, he slammed on the brakes.

My whole body tensed before it snapped forward. I threw out my arms in front of me, but when I collided with Jako, my skull cracked against his. We rolled across the floor. I gasped for a full breath and watched as Alex recovered and jumped back on her feet, building her ice storm around the two men. I scooted away from them and gave her space as I worked on my flame again.

Covyn landed on the floor next to me, pulling me with her tied hands to help me to my feet. As I stumbled to an upright position, I rose quickly, then turned back to face them. I focused on my fire, but a hand reached through the ice pellets flying around the men and knocked me over the head with the back end of an anaman weapon. I tilted, stars glittering from every direction like the darkest of nights back home. I tumbled over and smashed into the floor.

I was growing frustrated with the strikes to my head. Mum had taught me to hold my own in a fight, but even with my fire abilities, I was struggling to gain the upper hand. My head throbbed as I rolled to my back. I pried my eyes open in time to watch Beck lunge for Alex. He dodged a dagger of ice and yanked her long hair. Her head snapped backward and her arms flailed out to stop him, but Beck flung her to the ground before she had the chance. She slid across the metal, and the top of her head slammed into the side of the cruiser. Her body went limp.

Red flashes of light sparked in my eyes. A deep sense of wrath grew inside my core, and my heart wrenched for my friends. With all the blessings we had received from Mother Gaia, we were still not powerful enough to fight against their brute strength.

"Get me the rope," Beck hollered at Jako, brushing Alex's frost from his arms.

Jako handed him a roll of rope and stood guard while Beck wrapped it tightly around her chest and all the way down to her stomach. Her arms were snuggly pressed tight against her sides, with the rope digging into her flesh and drawing blood just above her wrists. She squirmed and kicked out at him as she came to, but Beck kneeled on her legs, driving a scream of agony from her lips.

I lifted my head, but something hard pressed against my skull.

"I dare you," Jako said, hovering over me with rage bristling across his expression. "Do it, so I have a reason to smear your brains all over this cruiser."

I held my hands in front of my face, then collapsed to the floor again, watching from the corner of my eyes as Beck strung Alex up by her bent knees from the ceiling. She was completely immobilized with her ankles strapped to her upper legs. It looked like one of the most awkward and uncomfortable positions. The pain in her wide eyes was evidence enough to that.

We were royally screwed.

Alex cried out. "Let me go!" she screamed, biting at Beck when he leaned over and stuck his tongue at her.

He shoved a piece of cloth in her mouth.

"That will keep her quiet," Beck said as he turned to look at me. "Now what are we to do with you?"

Dax sprang into view, obviously recovered from being struck in the back of the head several times. He launched himself at Jako, knocking his weapon out of his hands. It skidded to the corner of the room. Rafael rolled to the ground next to me and placed his hands against my arm.

"Untie me, Zoe Dawn," he cried, wiggling his fingers to loosen the knots.

"Stop moving," I snapped at him, pushing away the black fog still swimming in my eyes. My stomach coiled as I tried to concentrate on untying him.

Covyn leaned over us, pushing my trembling hands away. Somehow hers were free. She finished loosening Rafael's restraints, hauled me to my feet, and helped me limp to the door. Rafael had joined the fight, already attacking Jako and Beck. His fist slammed into Beck's jaw, then he turned toward Dax and Jako and beat against the back of Jako's head, just like he had done to Dax.

From the corner of my eye, I saw Covyn reach over the controls and press one of the buttons on the wheel Beck had been using to maneuver the cruiser. The door slid open.

The night air rushed over my heated skin as Covyn pulled me to the first step. I struggled against her hold on me, trying to look back at Alex, but Covyn dragged me down the stairs. My toes bounced off the edges of each one until we dropped to the dirt.

"We. Need. To. Save. Alex," I said in between pained breaths. I pulled against Covyn and stretched my arm back toward the cruiser.

"First we save you, Zoe Dawn," she barked, tightening her grip. She might be a tiny one, but her inner lioness was taking control.

We stumbled along the rocky ground. My feet kicked up pebbles and dirt, unable to fully lift with each step. The noise from the fight grew quieter as we neared a grove of trees. I took a chance and looked over my shoulder, just as a bright explosion ripped through the atmosphere above our heads, lighting the entire sky. As I twisted my neck, my entire body locked up from the white clouds barreling toward us from the heavens. I reached out to grab Covyn's hand, but a wave of energy hit us like a boulder and tossed us like ragdolls into the air.

Everything went black.

CHAPTER EIGHTEEN
The Sky is Falling

ALEX

The explosion's echo bounced around endlessly inside my skull. The cruiser tilted, then crashed to its side. I cringed just when my head did the same, smacking hard into the paneling.

I know I cried out. I thought I heard myself screaming, but then someone landed on top of me, covering my face entirely. It was silent and dark. Whoever it was, they were not moving. I screamed again and thrashed my head around, but the dead weight pressed against me more.

I stopped fidgeting and drew in a shaky breath, blowing against the suffocating clothing of the person smothering me. My joints ached, and the flesh covering my wrists was tearing against the weight of the rope. The only noise I heard was the beat of my rapid heart pounding in my ears.

Time seemed to slow to a snail's pace. I was in

complete darkness, and the body was unyielding against my face. I swallowed hard, trying to keep my breathing soft and steady, but panic was rising in my chest, battering me like the ocean's waves.

With every second, my air supply dwindled, and a murky tug on my mind brought my world to a standstill. I sucked in hard for that next breath, but it did not come. My lungs cried out for air, deflated completely and burning as the much-needed relief did not arrive. The darkness edged me closer to my end. I knew I was teetering as a warm euphoria relaxed my aching muscles.

"*Alex!*" someone shouted.

I tensed again. They were so close, dragging me back from the oblivion I had nearly submitted to.

"There you go. Take another breath. I'm working on these knots, so keep breathing. Please."

The voice was familiar. I floated between the starry sky and a white light, then I gasped and my eyes snapped open. My chest rose and fell rapidly as I sucked in one frantic breath after another. The ropes were loosening, and I remembered the voice.

"Rafael," I said along a breath, barely able to speak his name.

"Just keep breathing, Alex. I am almost done." His fingers were tugging at something to my side.

My arms relaxed, and the rope was carefully unraveled from my body. I shifted my weight as life returned to my arms and hands. Rafael crawled to my legs and worked on the rope that held my knees in a bent position. My gaze fell on Dax.

"Oh my Goddess," I cried, pointing at him. "Please tell me he is alive."

"Yes, he is breathing but out cold," Rafael replied as the second rope fell away from my feet. "Let's go. We are using the back door."

My gaze shot to the back. The section between the restroom and the last bench was blown open. "How did I not know that was there?" I crawled to my hands and knees, pulled myself to my feet, and sagged against the ceiling to clear the blackness edging across my eyesight. Then I refocused.

Rafael lifted Dax by his arms and dragged him to the first bench. "We can slide him over the sides of the benches, one at a time, then I will pull him from the cruiser. It will take some strength on your part."

I nodded and followed after him, limping slightly from having my ankles and knees twisted so tightly together. Beck was dead next to where I had been lying. I glanced at my clothes. They were covered in his blood.

Something struck the side, now the ceiling, of the

cruiser. I jumped.

"Are you sure we should go outside? What was that explosion?"

"I don't know, but Zoe Dawn and Covyn are out there, and Jako followed after them," Rafael replied, lying Dax over the end of the first cushion, which was now pointing toward the heavens. "Come on."

He climbed over Dax, then held out his hand to help me up. I grasped it, and he hauled me up beside him. We teetered on the edge, before Rafael climbed back over Dax. We carefully shifted him across the three benches, and Rafael pulled him the rest of the way outside, just as another piece of shrapnel struck the earth only a few yards away. Dirt sprayed in every direction, causing a cloud of dust to blow our way.

I took a chance and looked at the stars. White clouds spiraled in every direction, like a massive octopus. Something had been destroyed in low orbit. I tumbled to the ground and tried to push the fear from my mind. All those people on the large ship. My chin quivered. My people. Dead.

"Help me, Alex," Rafael grumbled, propping Dax against his body with his arm around Dax's waist. "Hold him on the other side. We need to make it to the trees for cover."

He had to have realized that nothing would stop this shrapnel from hitting the ground, especially a tree. But I did what he said, taking one shaky step after another. As we drew closer to the tree line, I saw Covyn sitting on the ground with Zoe Dawn sprawled in front of her.

"I can't drag her any farther," she whispered. Her voice shook with exhaustion and grief. She held up her arms, which were trembling. "I just can't do it. I tried, Rafael. Please help."

He nodded as we passed by. "I will come back for her. Follow us."

I heard another piece of the ship hit the dirt, but it was farther away. We picked up our speed anyway. The trees were large, with wide and thick branches. We found one not too far in that tilted to the side, enough to create a covering. Rafael eased Dax on his back. Then he was off again. Covyn fell to the dirt next to Dax and rested her head on his chest.

I sprinted after Rafael. He was already lifting Zoe Dawn in his arms, but I noticed they were shaking.

"Let me help, Rafael," I said, touching his trembling bicep.

He shifted Zoe Dawn and set her on her feet. I wrapped her arm around my neck and circled my arm around her waist. We hurried for the trees. My ears perked up. I heard something zipping down toward us.

"Faster, Rafael," I managed to squeak out, as terror gripped my chest like a vice.

When we reached the first trees, the projectile object struck the ground with so much force, my body went limp, and I was ripped away from Zoe Dawn. I bounced once, then rolled sideways, smacking my upper back hard against a tree trunk.

I gasped for air, clutching my side as pain shot across my chest. Coughing, I forced myself to roll to my belly, then eased my knees underneath me. I drew in another breath and blinked away tears. Finally, I pressed up to my hands and knees and scanned over the growing wreckage.

Zoe Dawn and Rafael were sprawled out about ten feet away from me. Neither were moving.

I fell back onto the tops of my feet, then pressed against the tree trunk and guided myself to my feet. Everything hurt, and I was fairly certain I had a cracked rib. I hobbled toward Rafael and Zoe Dawn. There was no way I would be able to drag them both to cover, but I had to figure out something to protect them. I had no other choice.

I knelt down in front of Zoe Dawn, something dripped onto my arm. I wiped at it and lifted my fingers to see it better. The copper scent stopped me in my tracks. Reaching up to my forehead, I ran my hand across it and into my hairline.

"Ouch," I whispered, touching a gash on my scalp.

It felt deep, but I could not think about it right now. I brushed both hands down my sides, cringing as my cracked rib reminded me to go slowly. My fingers found Zoe Dawn's pulse on her neck, and I sighed with relief. I crawled to Rafael to check his pulse as well. He twitched, and his hand flew up to his face as he groaned. Smeared blood had been wiped across his forehead and chin, and I did not know where it was coming from.

"Easy, Rafael," I said, trying to find the source of the blood. "You are bleeding, and I can't find the wound. Do you feel any pain?"

He nodded but did not open his eyes. "My head and neck," he mumbled, slightly slurring his words.

I gulped. If his neck was hurt, I did not want to move him. "Hold as still as possible." I reached behind him, searching for any signs of trauma. My fingers touched something sharp protruding from Rafael's shoulder. It felt like metal, but it also could've been bone. I didn't know enough about human anatomy to even make a judgement call at this point.

"Does your shoulder hurt at all, right here where I'm

touching?" I asked, pressing softly around the object.

"I can't feel you touching me," he whispered as a drip of blood rolled from the corner of his mouth.

A weight settled on my heart. I did not know much, but blood in his mouth and an inability to feel my touch meant there was something horribly wrong with him. "Rafael, can you turn your head toward me?"

He did but started coughing. More blood dripped from his mouth.

I ran my hand to the top of his shoulder. "Can you feel your left shoulder at all?"

He didn't answer at first, then he slowly shook his head.

"Keep your head turned toward me." I reached across and touched his other shoulder. "Can you feel my touch now?"

"Yes, I can feel that," he replied, his voice a lot stronger.

I trailed my fingers down his chest. "And that?"

He nodded.

I crawled to his legs. "Can you move your legs?"

He bent his knees and planted his feet firmly.

"Good," I whispered, patting his knee. He wasn't paralyzed. I was not a doctor, but I was positive the pain in his neck was radiating from the protruding object. "I still don't want you to sit up, but we have to move you."

"Are those things still falling from the sky? Is it the stars again, like before?" he asked, his eyes following me as I pulled myself to my feet.

"No, it isn't the stars," I replied, straining to see anything that could help me pull Rafael to under the tree cover. "And I really hope that was the last of what hasn't burned up in the atmosphere."

He wiped away the blood from his lips and lifted his hand in front of his face. His eyes widened. "That's why I have an awful taste in my mouth. This cannot be good."

"No, it isn't good. Just stay still." I turned away from him and hobbled a few yards away. "Mother Gaia, I could really use your assistance right now," I whispered to the sky.

It was quiet. Too quiet. I exhaled in defeat, holding back a rising sob. We had come so far, for nothing. Not only would Zoe Dawn and Rafael probably die if we didn't find help soon, but this planet would be ripped to shreds if Uncle Henry was unable to prevent the collision of the other dimension. I dragged my feet back to Rafael as a sorrowful numbness infused my body.

My ears perked up. There were footsteps crunching along the sticks and rocks. I held my breath to listen. They were drawing closer, and Jako was still out there. I ducked, then crouched next to Rafael.

"Do you need my help?" Dax's voice was music to my ears.

I leapt to my feet, ignoring the ache pulsating from my side, and bounded into his arms.

"Careful, my phantom sorceress," he said, wincing from my tight embrace. "I'm not sure I have all my parts in the right places at the moment."

I laughed, which sent searing pain from my side to my toes. "Me too," I squeaked out, letting my arms fall to my sides.

Covyn crept around a tree and stepped under the crescent moonlight. Her gaze swept over the area and landed on Zoe Dawn. "What happened?" She rushed to Zoe Dawn's side and pressed her hand to her girlfriend's cheek.

"We were thrown," I replied flatly, limping back toward Rafael. "Rafael has something in his back and he's bleeding from his mouth and somewhere on his head. Zoe Dawn has not recovered from the blast."

Rafael reached his right hand toward me and clasped my hand. "I need you to help me stand."

I shook my head. "If you stand and then faint, you will have more injuries on top of the ones you already have. I'm not taking the chance."

"We are sitting ducks out here in the open. Jako is still around, and if he returns, I will be dead anyway. We need to find some shelter." His fingers intertwined with mine. "Help me sit. We can do this in steps."

I glanced at Dax for support.

"He's right," Dax replied, circling around to Rafael's other side. "We need to move out of the open and regroup. And we have to help Zoe Dawn." He sank to his knees and eased his hand underneath Rafael's shoulder. "On three."

I pressed my lips together and pushed one hand underneath Rafael's lower rib cage and the other against his shoulder. Then I nodded at Dax.

"One," Dax said.

I swallowed hard, scooting my knees closer to Rafael.

"Two. Three." Dax finished.

We lifted and Rafael yelped in pain, but we kept going until he was sitting. I shifted behind him and examined the protruding object. It was a piece of the ship and not a bone, but it was buried into his muscle and I knew better than to yank it out.

"Are you dizzy?" I asked, checking for any other wounds.

"A little. Give me a moment."

There was a gash on the back of his head and another

on the side near his ear, but the blood was drying, so I wasn't as worried about them as I was the shrapnel knifing him in the back.

"Dax, once I'm up, you will need to carry Zoe Dawn and let the women help me," Rafael instructed, pressing his right hand into the ground and shifting his knees underneath him.

"I should go back to the cruiser and disconnect Beck's scrambler," I said, holding Rafael steady without putting too much pressure on my ribs. "Then I can reach my parents from my internal chip."

"Not without me." Dax shook his head. "Not with that murderous tyrant running loose out there."

"Let's find shelter for the injured first, then you two can be heroes." Covyn was still kneeling next to Zoe Dawn, holding her hand against her chest.

"I am ready," Rafael said, patting my hand that was holding his shoulder.

Seconds later, Rafael was standing. Covyn left Zoe Dawn and wrapped her arm around Rafael's waist. I did the same and we slowly moved under the thick of the tree canopy. Dax stepped up next to me, with Zoe Dawn over his shoulder.

"Leaving so soon?" Jako's voice cut through my heart.

Expanded Chaos

We all froze, and Rafael glanced over his shoulder.

I heard his breath catch in his throat. "Jako, no. Please, don't."

CHAPTER NINETEEN
Family Lies

KIA LYNN

"*Brody*," Mama hollered after examining the wounds spread down my face and body.

I stared at her in awe, pinching myself to make sure I wasn't dreaming.

"Why was my daughter not protected like I asked *you* to do?" Her fingers combed through the hairs of mine that were loose, then rolled one of my dreads between her thumb and forefinger.

"She refused the protection rune," Brody replied, sauntering toward us with an over-confident smile blossoming across his face. "Then we ran into Beck and Jako. All those chats over the com, and he did not realize who I was at first."

"But why is Kia Lynn hurt?" she asked, clenching her jaw as a crimson flush speckled up her cheeks.

"The boys got out of hand." Brody shrugged but took a quick step back when Mama lunged at him.

She yanked him by the front of his shirt. "Boys do not get out of hand when it comes to my daughter. When those two arrive, I want them brought before me. Am I making myself crystal clear?"

Brody gave her a curt nod, and when she released his shirt, he trotted away without a backward glance. Seeing Brody afraid of Mama lifted my spirits, but only a fraction.

Mama turned back toward me. A smile lifted on her lips, and she ran the tips of her fingers down my cheek. "I have waited a long time for this moment. We have so much to talk about. Are you hungry?"

What a surreal moment. I could not stop staring. "I am famished." My stomach growled in agreement. "And exhausted."

"Food first, then off to the medical unit. You will need to be in tip-top shape for what's to come." Mama wrapped her arms around my shoulders and flashed me her unforgettable brilliant smile that I had missed so much. "These next few days will be exciting for all of us."

She led me through the slowly dwindling crowd and we weaved around several stacks of broken gray rocks with mounds of dirt mixed in. The large letters above our heads were worn, and chunks of them were scattered across the roof. I peeled my eyes away from them as Mama pulled me through the old iron fencing. On the other side, a magical land of structures rose in front of me.

My gaze drifted upward and over, and I came to a full stop before twirling in the middle of a line of stone buildings. "It is as if they never saw the calamity of the falling stars," I said, holding my arms out and stopping to stare at Mama.

"Many hands kept this sanctuary clean," Mama replied, taking one of my hands and patting it. "I wanted our reunion to be in a place that meant something to us both."

"Can we stay here forever?" I asked, linking my arm with Mama's like I had when I was young. "I cannot wait to explore all of it."

Mama smiled and tugged me forward. A few doors down, she led me into a room bustling with noise and filled with the sweet scent of bread and other delicacies. My stomach grumbled in reply.

After waving at someone I could not see, Mama patted the top of a nearby table and pointed at a chair. "Take a seat. They will bring you anything you want to eat. I have to tend to some business but will return soon." Her hands pressed against the sides of my head, and she loudly planted a kiss on my forehead. "I missed you, Kia Lynn. You and I will be creating a wonderful future together."

With that, she turned and left. I sank into the chair and leaned back, sweeping my gaze around the room. It had wood beams holding the structure up, probably from years of wear and tear, but I was not positive after speaking to Mama. Someone had maintained this Disneyland, and I had a suspicious thought it might have been all for me, to convince me to take this trek in the first place.

"You must be Kia Lynn," a woman, with a dainty nose and narrow lips, said as she set a plate full of vegetables, steamy meat, and bread in front of me. "You look just like your mother." Her skin had a bronze tint to it, similar to Zoe Dawn's, but the faint swirly gray lines etched into her flesh gave away her anaman lineage.

"Yes, I am Kia Lynn. How did you meet my mother?" I asked, tearing my gaze from her arm and looking at her mink-brown eyes.

"Here," she replied with a soft smile. "My parents found this place when I was young, and they joined the community that already resided here. Tallisa was well known in these parts, even back then."

"You are about the same age as me? Nineteen full

seasons?" I asked. It seemed strange Mama had been traveling here when I was young without bringing me.

"I am twenty-one years old. We do not use full seasons here." Her eyes twinkled with amusement, but I did not understand what was so funny.

"And you met my mama when you were young?" My fingers drummed against the table as irritation flooded my mind. No matter how I spun it, suspicion of my mother's intentions nagged at my mind.

She nodded and looked pointedly at my food. "Eat. I'm sure you have had a long journey, and I know your mom is anxious to spend time with you." She started to walk away but stopped and glanced back at me. "You know, you are lucky to have a mother who would move heaven and earth to bring you to a better life. That is what she is doing for all of us here."

The woman hurried off, leaving me to chew on her words. They treated Mama as if she were their savior.

I dug into the food. Delicious was an understatement. When I finished, I licked my fingers and sighed with contentment. Even with all the distrustful behavior of Mama, I was feeling better. Now, I needed to find her. Those questions I had forgotten about when I first arrived, were now encroaching on my every thought.

I slipped through the doors and followed the wide

path but stopped when it split. To the left were more buildings, but the right appeared more open. I stepped onto the much-darker path to the right to investigate what was around the bend. As I circled around the side of the buildings, I heard familiar voices up ahead.

Nikita. I was certain it was her. I crept closer.

"Completed the connection to the ship." Nikita's voice drifted toward me. "The final preparations are being made to leave. We still need him to instruct the maintenance crew on the functions and upkeep of the machine, which he will begin first thing in the morning. When they are comfortable managing it on their own, and the remainder of the repairs are completed on the ship, we will eliminate him."

"Henry has two days to make them comfortable," Mama replied with obvious disdain in her tone.

I gasped, covering my mouth to smother the noise.

"I don't know if that will be enough time." It was Tatum who answered.

It was quiet for several breaths.

"Fine, Tallisa. We will make it happen," Tatum stated. There was clear irritation laced in with his tone.

I ducked and slinked forward, peeking around a wood beam on the side of the path.

Mama stood facing me, her hands on her hips and a

look of contempt etched across her features. "We need to discuss Kia Lynn now that she is here. She is not to know about Henry, and I do not want her hearing about her two friends, especially after my past with Alexandria. Henry and Alex ruined my chances to return to you and my daughter unscathed, and now she is the only one who can keep us from being followed once we leave this dimension."

Nikita wiped her hands down the sides of her trousers. "Such a shame. After all these years, she only wanted to be with her mother again."

It sounded like she actually cared about my feelings, but I knew better. It was more deceit from both of them. Either they realized I would not comply with their plans or they knew if they stole me away from my world I would hate Mama forever.

"I will make sure I give her plenty of my time." Mama's lips pursed to one side. "Three days and this will be all over. I can finally leave it all behind, especially the elemental threat hanging over my head."

"You do realize Beck only wanted them for his own gain," Tatum said, rolling his shoulders back and stretching his neck as if to relieve strain. "He would have taken Kia Lynn as well, if Brody had not interfered."

"Yes, I am well aware of Beck's disloyalty," Mama

replied. A smile blossomed across her face. "He will reap what he has sewn. Let him burn with the planet."

Tatum chuckled. I was in complete shock. We really were leaving everyone behind to perish. This was not my mother, at least not the mother who had disappeared nine full seasons earlier.

"If my people discover our plans before we leave, we can kiss all of this goodbye," Nikita replied, not amused with the thought of the planet on fire. "I am taking a huge risk by not checking in with them."

"All of them will be too busy trying to mend the rip up above. It will all be over soon and you can leave behind their repressive rules as well. I need to return to my daughter," Mama said, squeezing Nikita's arm as she walked by. "When she is tucked away in the medical station, we will meet with Brody and the others and prepare for tomorrow." She paused next to Tatum and placed a hand on his forearm. "And under no circumstances is Brody to be told our plan to leave her behind. His soft feelings for her will only become a problem if he was to discover it."

Tatum and Nikita nodded.

Her words were like a knife to my heart. I gripped my chest as despair ripped my insides to shreds. My gaze was locked on her approaching figure. I backed away and tiptoed up the lane, then hurried toward their eating hall as much as my limp allowed. Once I reached the doorway, I turned around and leaned against the wall.

A few moments later, Mama sauntered around the corner, smiling as usual and acting like she was not about to abandon an entire planet full of lives. My scalp prickled with shame. This was the one person in my life I thought I could trust, and even she was a disappointment. I had believed I could save her, but she was already saving herself—and using me to accomplish it.

Somehow, I needed to find Henry and warn Zoe Dawn and Alex.

"How are you feeling?" Mama asked, holding out her hands toward me.

I took them and forced a smile. "Much better. Is it possible for me to wander around for a while before I go to the medical unit? I really would love to see this place."

Her smile faded slightly. "It is dark, Kia Lynn. You won't see anything at this time of night." She intertwined her fingers with mine and pulled me down the pathway and to the left. "In the morning, you can explore to your heart's content."

"Then will you stay with me for the night?" I asked, reaching over and grabbing her arm to pull myself in closer to her. The hurt from her deceit was ripping my heart to shreds.

"When you wake in the morning, I will be right beside you," she responded, patting my hand and leading me down another turn to the right.

At the end of the building, I saw one of the anamans' ships settled just beyond some shorter trees. The healing station would be on there. I exhaled with defeat. Henry would have to wait.

On the ship, Mama led me to a sublevel just like on Malcolm's vessel. The healing station stood in the center of a room, bulky and intimidating.

I tugged on Mama's arm. "What about the smaller devices that you just run up and down the injured area? Can I use one of those instead?"

She slowly turned toward me, her eyes narrowing slightly. "How do you know about those?"

"A-a-a friend showed me one," I stammered, not sure how to explain it was her brother's mate who had healed me before.

"That friend is not from around here," she replied, stepping close to me. "Those devices were not invented by the anamans until much farther in the future." She ran her finger along my hairline and tucked a strand of hair behind my ear. "Kia Lynn, we do not associate with traitors, and that is exactly who my brother and his dreadful daughter are. Do you understand me?"

I swallowed hard, pushing down the dread that was rising in my throat. "Yes, Mama." I did not know what else to say. She even terrified me.

"Good girl." She took my hand and led me to the healing station.

"Take your shoes off and climb in, my love," she instructed, pulling the monitor toward herself.

I did as I was told and rested my head on the firm cushion. My gaze met hers. "Promise you will be here when I wake?"

"I have moved heaven and earth to be with you, Kia Lynn."

That was what the girl in the eating hall had said.

"Of course I will be here when you wake." She shot me one of her wide, brilliant smiles, but it quickly melted when she refocused on the monitor.

The glass dome lowered, and I pressed my hand against it as panic swelled in my chest. But then my mind relaxed, followed by my muscles, one by one. A sense of euphoria spread like a whirlwind down my body, with only one thought tumbling inside my skull.

She is a liar.

CHAPTER TWENTY
The Void

ZOE DAWN

The ache in my body was the first thing I noticed when I awakened. Why did I hurt so badly?

My eyelids fluttered open. The stars twinkled through the branches of the trees. Rolling to my side, I groaned from the pain radiating like fire across my entire body. Covyn was not too far away, leaning against a tree trunk with her head between her legs.

"What happened?" I asked, my voice barely a whisper.

Her head snapped upward, then she leapt to her feet and collapsed by my side. "Don't you ever do that to me again," she cried, wrapping both of her hands around my face. "I was terrified you would never wake up."

I chuckled but stopped when the ache burned my insides. "You will not get rid of me that easily," I said through a labored breath, pushing against the discomfort.

She leaned over and pressed her lips to mine as tears

tumbled from her eyes onto my cheeks. When she broke away, I reached up and wiped them from her chin.

"Will you help me up, please?" I asked, giving her an amused smile. I still had no idea what had happened, and my mind was filled with a strange void. It swirled like a dark fog and pressed against the edges as if it wanted to rip itself from me.

"Are you sure you should be standing?" She did not move but instead pressed her hand on my shoulder to hold me down.

I raised my brows and grabbed her arm. "Slowly. My body hurts, but you are smothering me, and I need to know where I am hurt."

"Oh," she replied, scooting back. "I was not meaning to smother you." Her head hung as she sulked.

I sighed. After propping myself on my elbows, I pulled my knees to the side and sat up straight. "I am horrible in relationships, Covyn. Forgive me for being brash. I woke to the stars and no memory of why we are here. Can you please help fill in the gaps?"

She hiccuped in response and after several breaths, she nodded. "It has not been easy."

I stretched my hand out and waved her closer. She scooted until our knees touched.

"Tell me what happened," I said, resting my hands on

her legs.

"Beck and Jako happened," she whispered, hanging her head again. "That old man has been an absolute nightmare my entire life, but Jako was my friend." I heard the pain in her voice. He had betrayed her.

I pulled her chin back up. "I understand that must hurt, but I really need the details so I can piece my fragmented memories back together. Just spit it out. What happened?" The last few words came out between gritted teeth.

Her jaw clenched from my harsh tone. "Jako has taken Alex back to the cruiser to fix it, and Beck is dead. You were beat badly by Jako earlier, and when we escaped the cruiser, something exploded in the skies and we were nearly hit by the pieces that fell around us." Her voice grew louder with each word, a hint of hysteria laced in her tone. "One chunk of metal struck so close to us that it knocked you out, and Dax was unconscious as well because of the cruiser falling to its side. Then Rafael was struck by shrapnel, and Alex has a cracked rib."

She stopped and drew in a long breath, then burst into tears. I shifted to my knees and pulled her into my arms, ignoring my screaming muscles. Her sobs came in waves, ebbing and flowing like the ocean's current. I held her close and let it all drain out of her.

When she quieted, I patted her shoulders and leaned back on my knees. "Was that everything?" My memories of Beck were jumbled, but I did remember freeing myself and Alex from his restraints and starting a fire on the cruiser. From there, it was a giant blur in my head.

"You are awake," Rafael said, limping toward me with Dax holding him up.

I pursed my lips as I examined my cousin. He was covered in dirt and blood. "You look awful, Rafael."

"Same to you, Zoe Dawn," he replied, sagging his right shoulder against a fallen tree not too far from me. Dax released him and he slid to the ground. "How are you feeling?"

"Awful but strangely energized." I wrung my hands together. "It appears as if we need to save Alex and stop Jako from whatever he is planning. Have any of you been watching them?"

Covyn shook her head. "He warned us not to leave here. If he even caught a glimpse of us peeking out at them, he would shoot Alex in the leg. He needs her alive to help fix the cruiser, but once that is done, he promised to finish her off."

"Well, that is unacceptable. We cannot have that." I climbed to my feet and stepped closer to Dax, mentally pressing against the black fog in my mind. It whispered as if it were its own entity, but I could not understand the words. I shook my head to break its hold on my thoughts and shot Dax a sideways look. "Are you well enough to fight?"

"For Alex? Absolutely," he replied, bouncing on his toes, his attention remaining focused on the path leading to Alex.

I looked back at Covyn. "Stay here with Rafael. I am just going to see if we have options." I did not wait for an answer as I ducked under a branch and disappeared from her sight.

Her spunk had vanished, and I was struggling to watch her weakened spirit. I also needed to move before the darkness consumed me. Was I losing my mind? I felt separate from it and at the same time, tethered like an animal in a cage. That strike to my head must have done a number to my brain.

Dax and I tiptoed through the brush and trees, only stopping when he said we were close. I waved him forward and crept toward the tall grass separating us from the cruiser. Dax ducked and crawled forward on his hands and knees. I followed suit until we were peeking over a section of grass right before it thinned out.

He pointed. "Jako is outside guarding the door. How will we sneak up on him? There is not enough cover."

I rubbed my chin. Pushing my fire through the air was easier when Kia Lynn helped it along, but it was possible to still do it. I brought my fingers to my thumb and pressed them together. The flame flew over Dax's head and just ahead of us, a spark exploded like lightning striking stone. Dax stumbled back, surprised by my attack. He rolled away into the cover of the grass, but the moment he did, my fire reached out on its own and ignited the entire field.

Dax screamed, and I stared in amazement as the inferno overtook the vegetation and spread toward the trees on the opposite side. From the corner of my eye, I saw Dax tumble from the grass and fall against a tree trunk, wheezing from the smoke that followed him.

He slid against the bark until he was back on his feet. "Zoe Dawn!" Dax shouted, pointing past me toward the cruiser. "Stop what you are doing. Alex will be killed as well." He gasped in another breath and shielded himself from the smoke as it billowed around him.

I turned my head to view the cruiser. Alex was limping toward us, holding her hand over her left side. Her other hand waved erratically at me. Jako was nowhere to be seen. I blinked and vigorously shook my head to break up the blackness devouring my mind.

I lifted my quivering hands and turned them over,

examining them. My entire body seemed so fragile but extraordinary at the same time. Blinking to clear the fog away again, I pulled back on the fire as dark clouds rolled in, and a thunderous storm dumped its rain on us.

My skin prickled against the chill, but the black fog lifted from my mind, and I finally could see clearly. I raced toward Alex and threw my arms around her tall stature. She was almost a head taller than me.

"Zoe Dawn," Alex cried, weeping against my shoulder as she leaned into me. "I have been so worried about you. Why did you light up the field?" She stepped back as the rain dissipated, and the clouds continued on their way.

Like a snap of the finger, the blackness returned to my mind. "Where is Jako?" I asked, gritting my teeth to hold back its control on me.

"I stunned him, then tied him up." She jabbed her thumb over her shoulder, not noticing the change in my demeanor. "He forgot to search his father before leaving me alone inside the cruiser."

"Then let's leave," Dax said, throwing me a terrified look, then pulling Alex into an embrace. "What do we need to do to get a signal to your parents?"

"I have already done it," she replied, holding her arm up and running her thumb along her wrist. "Mom. Dad.

Are you there?"

It was her usual call to them. They would be furious and worried and then we would listen as she reassured them. All the while, Kia Lynn was walking into the throes of danger, and the fog inside my mind begged me to let go of my control. Instead, I bit down on my bottom lip and held my tongue. And my fire.

"Thank God! Alex!" her mom exclaimed over her hologram screen. "We have been trying to find your whereabouts for hours now. What happened?"

"Can you pinpoint our location?" Alex asked, getting right to the point. The exhaustion in her expression spoke volumes. She did not have the energy to do anything more for us.

Thank you, Alex.

"Yes, we have you," her dad said. "On our way now."

"The explosion knocked the cruiser over," Alex told them, limping back toward the machine. She continued to protect the left side of her body. "Beck and Jako were able to scramble our receiver and forced me to disconnect all communications."

Alex's mom gasped. "Where are they now?"

I trotted to catch up to her, with Dax right behind me.

"Beck is dead, and Jako is tied up next to the cruiser." Alex turned so they could see the wreckage. "Rafael has shrapnel in his back, and he might have more injuries I can't see. Zoe Dawn and Dax both were knocked out, but they are awake now. They will need a medical evaluation to make sure they don't have concussions, and I have a cracked rib. It has been an ugly fight, Mom. I don't remember signing up for all of this."

Her voice shook with emotion, and it almost made me smile. A deep desire to spread pain to everyone, including my friends, bubbled up inside my mind. I reached for the stun gun tucked into the back of Alex's trousers.

Dax slapped my hand away. I glared at him and he matched the look.

"We are closing in on your location," Dad replied. "Malcolm will then take us to California to retrieve Kia Lynn and Henry."

"You should know, I suspect Beck is connected to Tallisa somehow." Alex sagged against the cruiser. The fatigue and pain in her expression deepened as she finally let emotion consume her. Tears streamed down her cheeks, creating rivulets through the blood smeared down her face. "She wants us to all die, Dad. And our people on the ship, they are all gone now." Alex collapsed to the dirt and pressed her forehead into her knees as the sobs rolled through her.

"Alex," her dad said over her cries. "Our ship is fine."

She quieted and slowly lifted her head. "I saw it, Dad. It exploded."

"It wasn't our ship. I will explain soon. Be ready for us."

I stared in awe at my friend and for the first time really saw her. I admired her bravery and knew no matter how angry I was toward her, she would never leave my side. That thought made the darkness spread down my neck, infiltrating my muscles and bones as if becoming one with me. It wanted Alex to trust it—to want to help with whatever it was needing to survive. She could be useful for what it had planned.

I held out my hand toward her. "I have your back, sister. Let's retrieve the others and leave this place." The next step was to bring all three elementals together, once again. Every cell in my body screamed for me to fight against the void, but my mind relaxed into the fog as it spoke to me through my own thoughts.

Alex smiled through her tears and took my hand. I helped her up, turned toward the trees, and whistled for Covyn and Rafael.

"I will go help Rafael," Dax said, still wary of my intentions as he circled wide around me. He shot Alex one last look before sprinting away.

Jako stirred on the other side of the cruiser. I held out my arm to stop Alex from advancing upon him. "It is my turn, sister. He deserves a dose of my fire to keep him in line."

Alex did not argue.

Hovering over Jako, I had this faint memory of us being in the opposite positions. His weapon had been pressed against my skull. He had wanted me to be submissive—to tremble at his feet. It made him feel big and powerful. It was as if I could read his thoughts from that moment in time. I licked my lips as a knowing smile twitched at the edges. Now, he would be served a giant platter of his own karma.

I ground my feet into the dirt, just as his eyes popped open. He squirmed against the ropes, but they held fast. I rubbed my fingers together, igniting a flame instantly, and I closed my eyes and allowed the dark fog to spread through every inch of my body.

I swear it laughed as it did so.

Another entity shot out from the dirt and swirled around me. Mother Gaia. I felt Her pulsating light prickle against my flesh, but She was unable to fill me with Her essence as the darkness cackled within my mind.

Her light pressed against me, then Her face materialized in front of me.

"Forgiveness," she whispered. It was no longer said within my mind but a voice carried by the wind.

I shook my head. The power of vengeance was far more alluring in this moment. My flames built as my fury returned, wanting nothing more than to be vindicated for my suffering. For my sister's pain. Mother Gaia had to understand why I needed this, and the fog encouraged me to continue.

I sensed Her sadness as She melted back into the earth. It would be fine, I convinced myself as I let Her go.

My eyes fluttered open, and I zeroed in on Jako's terrified face. I held out my hand, the fire ready to do my bidding, when Alex's freezing palms touched my neck. A shiver ran down my spine, nearly extinguishing every flame.

"I want him to suffer too," she whispered into my ear. "He has caused me more pain than I ever want to face again, but this is not the way, Zoe Dawn. Listen to Her."

I gritted my teeth and pressed my inferno at Alex. As it melted her ice, she leapt away, and I heard her grunt when she fell to the ground. I glanced her way. The fear in her eyes sparked a sense of euphoria within my mind. I paused to absorb the mounting joy, then shrieked when a load of water dumped on top of my head.

CHAPTER TWENTY-ONE
Water Elementals

ALEX

"Alex!" Zoe Dawn screamed, whirling around to look at me. She was drenched from head to toe, but so was I.

I held up my dripping arms to show her, then pointed at the sky. She tilted her head and her arms went slack, but her eyes still sparked with a flame of rage that frightened even me. Malcolm and my parents had arrived, and she was not happy about it, even though it was crucial for us to refocus on Uncle Henry and Kia Lynn.

"You had to know burning Jako alive would not be met with welcomed applause," I said, heaving myself off the ground and grinding my teeth to stop myself from crying out in pain.

"He is better off dead," Zoe Dawn hissed, wringing the water out of her curls, then wiggling her fingers at Malcolm's ship. "We would all be better if he were eliminated from our planet."

Her words seared through me like a burning dagger. Zoe Dawn had a temper that usually extinguished quickly, but now the heat radiating from her body was burning my eyes. I backed away.

Malcolm had landed on the other side of the cruiser, and Mom and Dad were already tearing across the rocky ground, kicking up pebbles and dirt as they neared us. Mom pulled me into her arms and squeezed me, just as Dad wrapped us both in his embrace.

"No more, Alex," Dad said, stepping back and lifting my chin so I met him eye to eye. A crimson flush was rising up his neck, and I knew he was trying to hold back his anger. "You are all we have. Do not make us worry like this ever again."

"You really should listen to your parents," Zoe Dawn said from behind us. "Be grateful you have parents who love you this much."

Dad whipped around. "And you, young lady."

I shrank back into Mom's arms. I had never seen him this furious before, and seeing Zoe Dawn's rage matching Dad's fury was terrifying. It was as if a dark cloud hung over them both.

But then he tugged Zoe Dawn into his arms, only flinching slightly from her noticeable heat. The steam simmered from her skin. "You are family. Do not make us douse your fire to stop you from something you will later regret."

Zoe Dawn pressed her lips together and tried to put on her usual tough face, but I could see a tiny smile fighting through. She patted Dad's arm and pulled away from him. Her red flush lightened considerably, and I breathed a sigh of relief. Something was not right with Zoe Dawn.

"You are just a giant softy, aren't you?" she asked, shaking her head. "Tsk. Tsk. Tsk. You really shouldn't show all your secrets, Jax." She winked at him, and I swear her irises swirled like black clouds, but then as quickly as it was there, it was gone. She reached over and hugged Mom. "Your daughter is tough as the rocks beneath our feet. I believe I would not be standing here right now if it were not for her."

Aly strode toward us, and several others ran past to help Dax and Covyn bring Rafael through the tall grass.

"Never a dull moment with you two," Aly said, embracing Zoe Dawn and planting a kiss on her cheek. She wiped her hand over Zoe Dawn's flushed forehead. "Are you well?"

Zoe Dawn pressed Aly's hand away and smiled. "Better than ever. I am ready for our next adventure." A flash of excitement shot through her eyes, and she turned toward Dad.

"We need to load the cruiser and get the injured down to medical to be examined," Dad instructed, waving his hands at Eshah and several others who had joined them. Then he noticed me clutching my side. His fingers brushed away my tangled hair. "We crushed you in that hug. Did we hurt you more?"

I shrugged my one functional shoulder and shot him a tight smile. "I'm beginning to think this is my new normal. Pain."

"That is not funny," Mom snapped, frowning at me. Her gaze shifted over my shoulder as Jako was dragged away. "We will interrogate him. Maybe he knows more about where Tallisa and the others are hiding."

"They have to be in Disneyland," I said, following Mom and Dad to the ship.

"What a strange place to instigate a war." Dad's brows bumped together. "I wonder why she chose it."

"Tallisa told Kia Lynn stories of a magical place that she would someday take her to visit," Zoe Dawn said, as she rammed her hand into her pocket and pulled out the folded photo she'd shown them on the cruiser's monitor before we lost connection. She handed it to Dad. "She intentionally threw that at me. Possibly thinking I would give it to Kia Lynn as a message. Alex says it is

Disneyland."

Dad unfolded the photo and nodded after seeing it. "That is indeed my sister, and Alex is correct. That is Disneyland, The Happiest Place on Earth. So they say."

"Then that is our destination," Malcolm said, stepping out of the shadows of the bay door. His gaze fell on Zoe Dawn. "Starting fires again, I see."

"I was helping you find us," she replied, patting his arm as she walked by.

"Right," he replied, pursing his lips at her receding back. He followed her.

I stopped and looked back at the cruiser. "What about the explosion?" I asked, hunching my back to help ease my rib discomfort.

"Another ship from our future time attempted to squeeze through the rip in space," Dad explained as he tried to press me into the ship. "We need to put you in the medical station as soon as Rafael is well."

I ignored his last sentence. "They were bringing one of their large ships through?" A fresh terror washed over me like ice-cold water. "You mean, the anamans from our time who want us all dead?"

Dad's foot tapped against the bay door. "Stop it right now. Worrying about it will not help," he replied. The lines around his eyes were deepening. "We will find

Uncle Henry, and he will repair the tear. No one else is coming through."

"You do not know that," I said, plodding down the corridor and sulking to my seat. "How will we stop Tallisa and fix the damage we created? It seems impossible."

Aly sank into the chair next to me and reached over the armrest to pat my knee. "Have you seen what you three can do together?" Her smile brightened up her whole face. "I have faith in you three."

It was not long before the cruiser was loaded and everyone was seated. Malcolm lifted the ship and sped off. For the second time in my life, I would be visiting Disneyland, but this time it would not be for wild rides, character photos, and turkey legs.

I glanced at Zoe Dawn. Her eyes were closed, and her usual animated expressions were gone. Instead, her face looked peaceful. Whatever happy place she had flown off to, I wanted to join.

It was quiet in the room, aside from the buzz of the computers. Everyone was exhausted or concentrated on the fight ahead of us. Dax and Covyn both drifted off to sleep, but my eyes were wired open.

We closed in on Malcolm's red peaks. In 2025, these were mountains inside a national park in Southern Utah, the same area only days before where I had connected with Zoe Dawn, Kia Lynn, and Mother Gaia. Who knew that moment had only been the beginning of our adventures together?

Malcolm eased the ship down onto his landing platform between the Zion buildings.

"We need more reinforcements," he said, turning toward Dad, then looking at me. "Alex, the wound on your head is still oozing blood."

Mom undid her restraints and pulled her handheld medical unit out of her bag. "Rafael is still in the medical station, but I have this." She waved for me to follow her. "Let's find a private room."

I followed, still limping and protectively hugging my ribs. The pain was throbbing, but my senses were numb and my heart was shattered. All the time that passed was another nail in Uncle Henry's coffin and the possibility for Kia Lynn to choose her mother over us. I wanted to believe our connection was unbreakable, but a mother's love had a power that could blind a person.

But did Tallisa really love anyone besides herself?

"Here we go," Mom said, interrupting my thoughts. Her fingers found mine. "I have you, Alex. Just lie down and let me work my magic."

I smiled at her comment. Magic was our new way of

life, but the anaman technology still surpassed most of our abilities thus far. Scooting onto a chair, Mom switched on the mechanics that slid me down until I was lying on my back.

"Dim lights low," she commanded, and the glaring lights above us dimmed.

I closed my eyes and relaxed my arms to my sides, sensing the healing unit glide just above my head. With Mom, safety had never been a worry for me. From the moment I first met her, I had known she would protect me at all costs. My parents literally bent time and space to place me in a time they believed would be far safer than the time I was born. If they were willing to go that far, I had no doubts in their love for me.

Mom gently nudged my shoulder. I blinked and yawned as a blanket of euphoria settled over my body. Focusing on Mom, I reached up to my head and ran my fingers over the wound. It was gone.

"You fell asleep," she said with a soft smile teasing the edges of her lips. A single tear slid down her cheek, and she wiped it away quickly. "You promised you would be safe."

"I'm sorry, Mom," I replied, wrapping my arms over my chest, grateful there was no more pain. "I did not think it would come to this. Beck and Jako were last seen near their village. The thought of crossing paths with them did not even seem possible."

Mom ran her fingers over my forehead. "I know you are all grown up, and I need to allow you to spread your wings like most parents do, but I just got you back." Her chin quivered, and I reached over and squeezed her arm. "I can't lose you again, Alex."

"I love you, Mom, and I'm sorry you were worried." I scooted back and adjusted my chair so I was sitting upright. I wanted to tell her I would be safe, but after all that had happened, I was not positive I could make her such a promise. I rose to my feet and wrapped her in a hug. "I am so grateful you are my mother."

She leaned back and smiled. "Let's go see where we are. Malcolm said we would be landing near the ocean, where we can regroup and wait for the rest of our team."

I followed her out into the corridor. "Who else is coming?" I asked, linking my arm with hers.

"Dad contacted the other ships. We have a crew joining us to help retrieve the time machine and Uncle Henry, and hopefully stop Tallisa from leaving." Her muscles tightened at the mention of my aunt. "They are also preparing their people to move to another dimension if worse comes to worse."

I stopped midstride, pulling at her arm. "That's not an

option, Mom. These people trust us. We cannot allow this world to crumble."

"But what if we cannot stop it?" She already knew my answer, as her eyes widened in horror. "No. *That* is not an option."

"I won't leave, Mom." Sweat trickled down my spine from the thought of dying, but I pulled my shoulders back and stood my ground anyway. "This is my home, and I am not running, no matter how awful it becomes."

Dad stepped into the corridor. "Come see this." He jabbed his thumb over his shoulder. "It was not here when we scanned the planet before settling."

I hurried after him with Mom reluctantly following us. Once on the bridge, I slid to a halt. Three tall buildings stretched high into the sky, their black glass gleaming under the starlight. As Malcolm lowered the ship, I noticed an obscure pointed object nestled in the middle.

Taking a few steps closer to the window, my eyes bulged out of their sockets. It was a pyramid, and plastered across the side facing us was the all-seeing eye—the one etched on the United States one-dollar bill. It was a symbol many had questioned in the twenty-first century as belonging to a secret society that controlled our world.

"What does it mean?" Aly asked, coming to stand next to me and Mom.

I was speechless as I turned to look at her, then at Malcolm. His face spoke volumes. He knew history better than I did. It being here meant there were forces far more powerful than anyone else sitting right below us, and they had arrived like a thief in the night. I gulped back the dread.

"Where are we?" I finally choked out.

"Not far from Zion," Malcolm replied, his gaze never leaving the buildings. "It was once a city filled with many large buildings, but most have crumbled or have been destroyed over the many harsh seasons."

The ship zoomed backward, widening my view. Then I saw the giant Ferris wheel, half buried under dirt and vegetation. I rushed forward and pressed my hands against the glass, squinting through the darkness and scouring the land. The few buildings standing either were nearly covered as well or so broken they were unrecognizable.

"Slowly go that way," I said, pointing toward the left. "This looks like it was once a road."

Malcolm steered the ship alongside what appeared to be a pathway in between the buildings, and my focus zeroed in on the tip of the Eiffel Tower. The fake one. It was there, protruding above the ground, but like most everything else, it was covered with vegetation.

"We are in Las Vegas." I turned to look at everyone, but only Mom and Dad nodded in recognition. Everyone else looked confused by the name. "This was a major city in the ancient's world. And that" —I pointed at the barely noticeable Eiffel Tower as we drifted by— "was one of the buildings that attracted visitors from all over the world. Whoever made this their home, they picked this area for a reason and I suggest we don't wait around to find out. One problem at a time."

Malcolm glanced my way. "Agreed. A question for a later time."

The ship soared away from the broken city and its new inhabitants, and I settled into my seat between Dax and Aly.

Dax leaned over. "I want to know all your stories."

Zoe Dawn swiveled her chair and looked around Aly. A darkness edged across her eyes, and a smug smile twitched on her lips. "Me too, Alex. I want to know all about you."

I threw her a flat stare, but she burst out laughing and turned her focus back toward the front. Maybe Zoe Dawn had hit her head harder than we thought. I made a mental note to speak to Mom after Rafael was healed.

Expanded Chaos

The beach was at our feet before I knew it. Waves crashed against the sand just like they had the last time I was here. It was what I loved about the ocean. Consistent. Strong. Seeing its vastness pulled me to it like a moth to a light.

Malcolm set us down not too far from the sand. The buildings and structures were less covered in this region, and it almost looked like they were only abandoned recently. I wandered away from the rest of the group, absentmindedly examining each home as I neared the call of the ocean. A whisper blew with the breeze, and I hurried closer, anxious to feel the water flow against my skin.

A row of houses led straight into the ocean, several of them covered from the rising waters. The sandy beaches were pushed against the buildings that were not submerged, breaking through the windows from hundreds of years of pressure.

A light was blossoming against the horizon as I reached the piles of sand. I yanked off my boots and socks, followed with my jacket. Dropping them on the sand, I raced for the water and splashed it everywhere as I bounded through it. I kept going until I was chest deep, then I dove in. The view underneath was surreal. Like a Hollywood dystopian movie.

Water swelled around me like a million kisses across my body. I closed my eyes and sank into its energy. The whispering filled my ears. There was an urgency thrashing against my mind, and I strained to make sense of their words. Then the voices quieted, and as if I were cradled in many arms, I was lifted into the air and gently set back onto the beach.

They had a message. Their cries echoed in my skull. I twisted at my waist and peered toward the ship, which I could not see from this angle. Tallisa never intended on taking Kia Lynn with her. All of this, her entire scheme, was just a ploy, and her daughter was the key to ensure our deaths.

CHAPTER TWENTY-TWO
Broken Heart

KIA LYNN

The glass dome was still sheltering me when I pried my eyes open. I looked around, but Mama was not in the room. I released a disappointed breath and tried to ignore the ache knocking at my heart. I do not know why I had believed her.

Thank Goddess, Alex had shown me how to open these from the inside. I stretched my hand above my head and swiped on the glass. A green-hued light shown back at me, and I pressed it. The glass rose and tilted to the left, then slid down and out of the way.

I swung my legs over the edge and breathed in deeply. All my physical pain was gone. These machines were miracles. And Mama had known about them my entire young life. It made me wonder what other information she was choosing to hide from me and Papa. It was a shame these machines did not have the ability to heal a broken heart.

Henry was next on my agenda. I slipped on my shoes and opened the door. It was quiet on the other side. Hurrying down the corridor, I used my memory of Beck's and Malcolm's ships to lead me outside. Once I was there, I glanced quickly at the sky. The sun had not risen yet, but it would soon.

I crept back the way Mama had brought me the night before. I checked the doors of each building, but none of them opened. Then I remembered the structure behind Mama when she was speaking to Nikita and Tatum. There had been several guards stationed outside its doors, and the only reason for so many was to keep others out or hold someone in.

I turned and did not stop until I reached the road that led to the eating hall. A man was perched on a chair next to one of the buildings, with his head propped against the wall. He was snoring. Mama would not be happy he was sleeping on the job, but I did not have time to worry about him and was grateful he was not awake.

After sprinting across the open space, I slid to the other side and hid behind a large tree. When I did not hear anyone come after me, I tiptoed to the large beam I had hidden behind last night. As I peered around it, my shoulders sagged in defeat. There was a guard standing next to each door. I don't know why I expected anything less. Mama really did not want anyone to know what was inside.

I slid through the grove of trees and crept to the side of the building. I circled around to the back and noticed a door up ahead without a guard. After checking one last time in every direction, I crept forward, ignoring the panic rising in my chest. As I neared the door, a man stepped out of the trees, adjusting his trousers and not paying attention to his post. I ducked behind another tree and held my breath. When my heart calmed enough so I could listen better, I twisted enough to sneak a peek through the branches.

He wasn't by the door. My pulse quickened again and I squinted at the empty space. Someone moved near the ground. I rose on my toes and noticed the guard settled on a cushion a few feet from the entrance. He rolled away from me and after several breaths, his arms relaxed. It was not long before he was snoring.

I tiptoed past him, then slowly inched the door open. It creaked and I froze. The guard rolled to his other side, facing me and mumbled something incoherent. I held my breath and slid inside, closing the door quietly behind me.

The inside of the building was cool and dark, but there was enough light streaming through from the nearly risen sun. I opened the nearest door. The room was empty, aside from a chain lying in the middle of the floor. One by one, I looked in each room, searching for one that could possibly be hiding Henry. Soon, I entered a massively open section of the building. An anaman ship was parked in the middle. I tiptoed toward it, stopping when my toes slid over an embankment. I did not fall.

My heart was thrashing harder than ever before, but the air held me like an invisible step. If I wasn't scared out of my mind, I would have enjoyed this moment. I scooted my shaky feet backward to firm ground and pressed my hands against my chest.

My gaze traveled upward and then back down. The ship was not as small as the others but not as massive as the ones that had crash-landed after no longer having the ability to stay in high orbit. All my life, we had kept our distance from them, but Mama had pointed one out when I was young. A charred vessel had been pressed against the landscape north of the black mountains, and in an area the Doyen had forbidden us to explore. We had traveled that way once together and I would never forget the long adventure.

Mama and Zoe Dawn were more alike than I had realized, until this moment. No wonder I had clung to my best friend after Mama disappeared.

The vessel inside the building was smaller than that one, but its size seemed insignificant in this moment. Mama intended to take everyone off this planet, but even this ship would not hold all the people I had seen when I first arrived.

"Kia Lynn," someone whispered, ripping me from my thoughts.

I tensed my shoulders as I whipped around in a circle.

"Over here," he hissed.

Someone waved from around the bend of the ship. It was Henry.

"Hurry," he whispered again, his arm waving erratically at me.

Edging around the crater, I slinked toward Henry. My heart continued to ram against my chest as I watched for other guards. There was no way Henry was here by himself, not if Mama was in charge. As I neared him, I realized why no one was lingering around. He was chained to an iron fence, and half his face was swollen. I was surprised he could even see me.

"At least they haven't broken anything," Henry said as he noticed my gaze slid over him. "They have to keep my hands and only one eye in good working order, or I won't be able to repair their ship. How did you break in here, Kia Lynn?"

I nodded back the way I had come in. "A back door. The guard was sleeping. Seems not everyone is as afraid of my mother as she would like them to be."

"Is anyone else with you?" he asked, pulling on the chain to give him slack.

"I am alone." I looked around for a bed or a mat. "Is this where you sleep?"

He pointed at a bucket. "Don't go over that way. I'm only allowed off the chains when I have five pairs of eyes watching my every move." The skin on his wrist was raw. "Why are you here?"

"Mama is up to something atrocious," I replied, circling around him and investigating the area. "I wanted to see her so badly, but now that I am here, I do not think she intends on allowing anyone on this planet to live." I puffed out my cheeks and blew out the air. "Why does she hate you so much?"

"It is a horribly long story."

Something clattered on the other side of the ship.

I ducked behind a beam. "I need to contact Alex," I whispered, squinting to see through the dark room. "Can you help me?"

"Has she not left yet?" He sighed but nodded, already knowing the answer. "Do you know how to use the anaman ships at all?"

"Not really, but I am a fast learner." I scooted closer to him. "I watched Brody in the land ship or cruiser, whatever you call those machines. It seemed simple enough."

He winced when he rolled his wrists. "Perfect. Can you get back to the cruiser?"

I pursed my lips, thinking back to where we had left it. "I think so. If they have not moved it."

"Override sequence is—" He paused and looked behind me, then refocused on my face. "Can you remember these numbers? If not, behind you on that table is a notebook and a pencil."

I rose to my feet and crept around the beam. The table was not too far away, but it was out in the open, and I still could not tell if anyone else was around. Someone had made that noise earlier.

When I handed Henry the paper and pencil, his hand was shaking. The open sores on his wrists looked infected. He wrote down the number and handed it back to me.

"I will return for you, Henry," I whispered, stuffing the paper in my pocket. "I really believed my mother was a warrior. One of the good guys. It is breaking my heart to find out otherwise." I didn't expect him to be empathetic to my pain, but I had to say it anyway.

"When you speak with Alex, tell her—" He drew in a raspy breath and then coughed it back out, covering his mouth with his shaky hand. "Sorry." He swallowed hard. "Tell her Tallisa has been talking about a secret weapon, something about outer space and the ability to tear open the universe."

My mouth ran dry when I heard those final words, and I gulped back the rising dread. I could not answer, so I nodded in response.

It did not take me long to slip back out the door. The sleeping guard was gone, and the sun's rays were spreading across the eastern sky. I glanced both ways, checking for the man. There was no sign of life nearby, so I sprinted through the trees, rounded the corner and tiptoed toward the front of the building.

As I drew closer, I heard the guards in that area speaking with hushed tones. They were facing one another and the one turned toward me squinted at the vegetation when I brushed against a branch. I froze and stared at him between the leaves, holding my breath. I waited for him to make a move. After several long moments, he refocused on the other man and laughed.

My breath came out in shaky waves, but somehow I kept it quiet as I slipped around the corner and out of their sight. I did not have much time.

The cruiser was still in the same place we had left it last night. Relief washed over me as I sprinted to the machine. I used the numbers on the paper to open the door, then entered them again once the monitor buzzed to life.

"Connecting to Alexandria Martanium," the cruiser said.

I had never heard Alex's full name, and it made me smile. What a mouthful.

"Hello," Alex answered, then her face appeared on the screen.

"Alex, it is me. Kia Lynn." I bounced on my toes, excited I had actually made a machine work.

"Kia Lynn!" Alex exclaimed. "Are you okay? Are you with your mother?"

"Yes, I am fine." I squinted at what was behind Alex. "Where are you? Is that water?"

"It's the ocean," Alex replied, but I could see she was walking away from it. "I'm on my way back to my parents and Zoe Dawn. I need to fill you in with everything I have learned before you make the decision to leave with your mother."

"I am not leaving." I shook my head and sank onto the captain's chair.

"Good," she replied. I could hear relief in her tone. "Listen. When we arrived with our ships, the portal from our home did not close all the way. Over time, it has grown. It is how your mother slipped back to our dimension."

"Dimension?" I did not understand.

"I will explain later." Alex wiped at her eyes. "The portal is ripping open, and if it gets much bigger, it will force the two universes to collide. Your mother is planning on using your wind to force it open."

It felt like my heart stopped. "But that would mean—" I could not say it. Instead, I slouched in the chair, hiding from the monitor. Everything I had overheard last night finally made sense. Mama was leaving me here, not someone else like I had thought.

"I know this is painful to hear, Kia Lynn. Your mother has been planning this from the start." Her breath was coming in short as she picked up speed. "I believe all the games were a way to see what you would do to see her again. It is a way to train you for that moment, and she has three days to convince you to destroy your own world, while she whisks herself away to safety."

My pulse was deafening inside my head. I had played right into her hands, and now she was convinced I would really do whatever it took to please her—just like all these other keefies she had under her control.

"Alex." I bolted upright. "I found Henry. He is chained in a building, fixing their ship. And the ship, it is not that big. Is there another one hidden somewhere else?"

"Possibly in high orbit," Alex replied. "They could be preparing to take people up, but if I know anything about my aunt, she is not going to jeopardize her own life for anyone else's. If that is the only ship they have, she will leave the people behind."

I had to confront Mama. Stop her.

"Kia Lynn, I'm here. Do you know where the time machine is?"

"Henry did not say anything about the machine," I replied, rising to my feet. I wiped the sweat from my palms and turned away from the monitor. "But I will find it and somehow contact you again. If I do not see you, tell everyone I am doing what is best for Mother Gaia and the people of this world. Good-bye, Alex."

"Wait, Kia Lynn!" Her desperate cries shattered against the back of my head.

I leapt from the cruiser and sprinted back to the entrance. In the daylight, the Disneyland area looked like the perfect adventure for Zoe Dawn and I to explore. Instead, I was going to walk to my deathbed or into something equally painful.

The guard was now awake. He rubbed his eyes and blinked at me but did not say anything. The fear that rose in his expression made me think he was terrified Mama would find out he had been sleeping. I strode past him without another look, then raced back to the small ship. Mama would be looking for me there. When I rounded the corner, I saw her standing outside of it, speaking to Nikita.

I picked up speed and barreled toward that hateful woman. Her black, long hair fell in her eyes, and she smoothed it back as she turned toward me. Mama held out her hand as if it would stop me. Nikita's eyes bulged from their sockets at the sight of me.

My feet pressed off the ground, and I flew at Nikita. My arms wrapped around her, and I tumbled over her head and threw her toward the ship. The thud of her body crashing into it was not enough to stop me.

"*Kia Lynn, stop!*" Mama screamed at me. I could sense her racing after me as I picked up Nikita by her hair, then slammed her against the ship again.

"Everything started with you," I hissed in her face. Our noses nearly touched. "Mama was nothing like she is today. You are the reason she is willing to sacrifice her own daughter."

Mama's fingers wrapped around my shoulder. "That is nonsense, Kia Lynn. Let Nikita go."

Nikita smiled despite her swollen lip. "Listen to your mother."

"Quiet, Nikita," Mama snapped. She reached over my shoulder and pried my fingers from Nikita's chest. "Let's talk, my love. Just you and me."

I released Nikita and she slipped away from us, chuckling as she walked away. Watching her receding back, I made a vow to finish what I started when I saw that woman again.

Mama's hand cupped my chin. "What has gotten into you, Kia Lynn?"

I shoved her arm away and stepped back. "Do not pretend to care, Mama. What was your plan for this portal in the heavens? Me? You were going to convince me to rip it open and destroy my home, while I remained here. Is that your plan?"

Mama's eyes widened as I spoke, but then she relaxed and pursed her lips in amusement. "What rubbish. Where did you hear this? Henry? You do know he would do anything to turn you against me."

"Why did you not wait for me in our village?" I asked, folding my arms over my chest.

"There was too much hostility," she replied, her smile

returning to her face. "Did you really want your mother to be ripped to shreds by those people?"

"I was there, Mama!" I shouted, throwing my hands in the air. "No one was hostile. They just asked who you were. Why are you lying to me? Better yet, why did you abandon me?"

The smile melted from her face as if she were facing a painful memory. Then she shook her head and focused on me with narrowed eyes. "That day was out of my control. The anamans who attacked our village belonged to the same settlement as my brother, and they forced me to leave you."

"*Liar!*" I screamed. Spit flew from my mouth, but I did not care. I wiped it away from my lips and pressed my palms to my eyes to push back the tears. "Is there anything you have told me that is the truth?"

She shrugged. "I have loved you from the moment I laid eyes on you. *That* I have never lied to you about. But life is unfair, and I have had to make hard choices to survive. This is just one more of those choices." Her hand lifted in the air, and she beckoned at someone behind me. "Your sacrifice will not be forgotten."

I whirled around, but something dark was thrown over my face. Snapping my fingers, I called on the wind and pressed against those surrounding me. The air bent to my will and built up its pressure faster than it had ever done before. The covering over my face flew off with the raging wind, and I sneered at the three men falling over themselves as they tried to escape the tornado raging around them.

Glancing over at Mama, I cocked my head to the side. She was unfazed by my storm.

"The only sacrifice you will witness is me walking out of your life. I hope it was worth it." I pivoted on my heel and left without another glance.

CHAPTER TWENTY-THREE
Ball of Fire

ZOE DAWN

"Kia Lynn is confronting her mother," Alex said, pacing the ground in front of me. "I shouldn't have told her."

"Told her what?" I asked, picking at the dirt under my fingernails. The situation seemed over dramatized. Kia Lynn was capable of taking care of herself. Besides, I had better things to be doing, like returning to the buildings in Alex's Las Vegas. The dark structures held a secret that I yearned to uncover.

"Are you even listening to me?" Alex asked, interrupting my thoughts.

I stretched my arms out in front of me, then smiled as I yawned. "Sure, Alex. Tallisa is wanting to use Kia Lynn to rip open the portal that could possibly consume our world. Why are you blathering on about this to me and not your parents?"

The dark void snickered inside my mind. Its humor

annoyed me, but the surge of energy I was experiencing was worth the irritation.

Alex was staring at me and her eyes were shooting sparks in my direction. "This is Kia Lynn we are talking about. Are you really going to sit here while the rest of us stop her mother from destroying our world?"

My arms lifted above my head, then I mockingly bowed to Alex. "I will follow you, my queen. Lead the way."

Her eyes narrowed. "Whatever, Zoe Dawn. Do what you need to do." She pivoted on her heel and stormed away.

I watched her go and after a few breaths, I bounded to my feet. The other ship had landed right before Alex returned from the beach, and the group of people were circled around Jax and Malcolm. They had this covered. I had other plans.

The idea of this time machine nagged at my mind. The void wanted me to find it, and I had to admit, my curiosity of traveling to another point in history was overtaking all other rational thoughts. Kia Lynn would understand. She knew I was an explorer, and what better way to do it. The machine was my first priority, then I would find a way to return to Las Vegas.

I slipped the anaman weapon into the pocket of my

trousers. Once the ships landed closer to Tallisa's camp, I would sneak off on my own.

"They do not know we are coming," Jax said as I walked past the circle. "Most urgent is retrieving the time machine and Henry. Both will be required to seal the portal."

I slid to an abrupt halt and circled back around to face the group. "What about Kia Lynn? Is she not your concern anymore?"

Jax turned to look at me. "Of course she is, but one problem at a time. Tallisa will not be able to leave or force Kia Lynn's hand if we have the time machine and the portal is closed."

I rolled my eyes to the sky. He had a point, but I really wanted that machine for myself.

"We believe Henry is being held inside this building," Jax said, continuing as if I had not said anything. He pointed at a large screen with a map spread across it. "Tallisa has turned off his communication abilities, but his tracking is intact."

"How do you know it's not a trap?" someone shouted from the back of the group.

Jax peered out at the group. "We don't. And honestly, she is probably hoping I will come for him. As most of you know, she and I did not separate on good terms."

Expanded Chaos

The whispers grew louder in the group.

Malcolm held his hands in the air. "*Quiet!*" he hollered, jabbing his thumb back at Jax. "We have to be smarter than Tallisa. She might be expecting, even wanting us to attack. Let's give her what she wants. A distraction right in that very spot. One team is the distraction, and another sneaks in around the chaos and rescues Henry."

I liked Malcolm's plan. I wanted to be on the second team. Then once we had Henry he could tell me where the time machine was being held.

I raised my hand and waved it around until Malcolm turned my way.

"Yes, Zoe Dawn."

"I will lead the second team," I said with a curt nod.

Malcolm and Jax glanced at one another. "Fine," Malcolm replied, pointing at several others, including my old friend Anna Rain. "You ten, plus Zoe Dawn and myself, will form the second team."

"And I will lead the first team. She wants me dead, so I will be the perfect distraction," Jax said, pointing once again at the map. "First team will invade from this entry point. We need to pull as many guards away from their posts as we can. No one needs to die if it can be avoided, but when Tallisa reveals herself, she is all mine."

"What about Tatum?" Alex asked. She sat next to Dax on a mound of rocks a few feet from the rest of the group.

"Tatum is a misguided old friend of mine," Jax responded, folding his arms over his chest. "I would like the chance to speak with him after this is all over."

Boring. I left the crowd and found my seat on the ship. I really hoped they would hurry.

Not long afterward, Alex and Dax entered the bridge and quieted when they saw me. Dax was still wary of me after my fire show in the field, and Alex did not understand my sudden change of heart. They would adjust once I was gone.

"Malcolm needs to run through their plan with you," Alex said, sitting on the edge of her chair. She slid me a guarded look.

"They just need to follow my lead." I ignored her sideways stare, fanning my face with my hand as I stretched out my legs. "It will be easy. Stop worrying so much, Alex."

Malcolm stormed onto the bridge and threw me a fierce glare before collapsing onto his chair. It squeaked under the weight, and I snickered from the sound. There was so much that amused me right now. Anna Rain and several others arrived shortly after him and gathered in the remaining seats on the bridge.

"Alex, if you are still planning on joining your father's team, you will need to leave now." Malcolm swiveled in his chair, but his gaze fell on me.

"Just grabbing my belongings," Alex answered, stuffing her hand in her pack and pulling out Kia Lynn's necklace. She held it toward me. "You might want to hold on to this for her."

I did not want the responsibility, but the unsuspicious direction would be to take the jewelry. My fingers curled around it. "A good luck charm is just what I need." I flashed Alex a smile, pulled the chain over my head, and patted the tiny horse against my chest.

Alex stared quietly at me for a moment. "I will see you soon, sister."

When I did not respond, she left quietly with Dax following after like a lost puppy dog. Those two were too much.

The cool touch of the silver against my chest reminded me of Kia Lynn and our bond. Her memory tugged at my heart, and when the void slithered against my mind, I forced it back. I did want more of what it was offering, but I also wanted control of my body, and this dark entity seemed to be consuming me from the inside out. It pressed against my barrier, but I held it firmly.

Kia Lynn was my top priority. Then I would allow the darkness to guide me on my next adventure.

It relaxed and agreed. As if I needed it to give me permission...

The ship was already zipping above the terrain and within a few moments was settling onto an open road, littered with rusty vehicles from the ancient years. Just like on the coast, the structures still stood, although they did not appear as steady as most. There had been damage here, aside from the stars' collision. The cracks across most of the buildings indicated many earth shakes, but the giant pieces crumbling to the sides, as well as strewn out in all directions, told the edges of a story we would probably never hear in its entirety.

"Our entry point is not too far from here," Malcolm told us, strapping on his gear and weapons. "Zoe Dawn, you are our leader. We are waiting for your instruction." He handed me two more anaman weapons.

"What is Jax's signal?" I asked, tucking the weapons away in each of my boots.

"You would know this if you had stuck around earlier," Malcolm replied, his jaw clenching. He turned toward the small group. "Once Jax attacks, Eshah will fire into the sky. We will circle around from the other side and infiltrate from the back."

Expanded Chaos

Everyone nodded and I rolled my shoulders, uninterested in his plan. I would still lead, whether Malcolm liked it or not. My fire was far more powerful than any of their weapons.

The sun was rising higher in the sky, beating hard against my hair and drenching me in perspiration. Human bodies were fragile.

The thought fluttered through my mind as if it were me, but I knew the void was mocking my body. It wanted an anaman host. Preferably Alex. For some reason, it believed I was lesser than my sister. As the elemental of water, she could control this world. *But I could burn the whole planet to a crisp*, I argued in my mind. The void laughed, and I cringed.

I ran my arm across my forehead, then wiped my palm across my shirt. All the distraction inside my mind and the group had left me behind.

Refocusing on the task at hand, I once again pushed away the void and sprinted to catch up with the others. Anna Rain slowed to walk beside me.

"Are you well, Zoe Dawn?" she asked, clutching one of the larger anaman weapons in her right hand and pointing it at the ground.

"Yes, of course." My skin was prickling with a growing heat, and it suddenly occurred to me that the sun causing me to sweat was the least of my concerns. "Why do you ask?"

"You look flushed." She reached over with her left hand and pressed her palm to my cheek. Flinching, she stepped back from me. "You are burning up. Zoe Dawn, what is wrong?"

The void laughed again. I swallowed back a ball of rising terror, realizing I never had any control over it. It was going to burn everything down to find the time machine.

I panted as my flame simmered just under the surface of my skin. "Anna Rain, focus. I will be fine." I wiped more perspiration from my chin as it dripped down my cheeks. "This is all part of my plan to keep us safe."

She did not look convinced but nodded before moving to the front of the team. Malcolm waved at me, but I shook my head. I was going in last. If the void wanted to start fires, I was not going to have a dozen people between me and the doorway. I needed to keep some control.

"What are you?" I asked, my voice barely a whisper.

It was silent for several breaths, then it spoke. *I am the in-between*, it replied in my head. *The tear in the heavens has set me free from the shackles of never-ending darkness.*

Expanded Chaos

My eyes locked on Malcolm and the rest of the team. They were growing farther ahead as I slowed my pace. "Why do you need me?"

A temporary situation.

It seemed to enjoy how uncomfortable I had become as it slithered like a snake through my body.

"What do you mean temporary?" I asked, my voice growing louder as fear knotted inside my stomach.

Soon. Soon. You will know soon.

With those words, the voice dissipated and my mind cleared. I pressed against my heat, begging it to cool until I really needed it, but the temperature continued to rise. I was leading everyone right into the fire.

The team disappeared around the next corner. I lurched forward, racing to catch them again, but when I rounded the corner at full speed, they were already gone. I tore up the pathway and slid to a stop when I caught Malcolm's stature creeping up another route. Now I wish I had paid attention.

I slipped on the loose pebbles and grabbed on to the side of a structure to steady myself. The wall crumbled in my hands, and I jumped away as the rest of the building rumbled and shook from the pressure. Shooting past it, I did not look back as it crashed to the ground and blew dust and debris at my back.

This was a mistake! I screamed in my head. The void was quiet, but I knew it was there. I wanted it out of me now. Turning my attention to another building, I raced full throttle toward it. If I could not force it out of my body while I was conscious, I would not give it a choice to use me against my family and friends.

I closed my eyes as I drew nearer to the structure, then shrieked when I was struck in the side. As I pried open my eyes, the sun tumbled around the sky as I bowled and slid to a stop on my back. I drew in a shaky breath and heaved myself up to my elbows. Kia Lynn was on her hands and knees, glowering at me.

"Have you lost your mind, sister?" she asked between shaky breaths.

I vigorously nodded. My quivering hands curled into fists. "Yes, I have. And if you do not knock me unconscious, I will not be able to stop my inferno." I rolled to a sitting position.

"Then let it burn," Kia Lynn said, holding her hand out to help me up. "Mama needs to be stopped."

I smacked her hand away, trembling from the terror clawing through me. "Listen to me! You do not understand. There is something in my head. A demon—" I choked on my next words and without thought, rose to my feet like a feather in the wind.

Expanded Chaos

Kia Lynn took several startled steps back. "How?"

Fire erupted across my entire body, and the void took control of my mind, silencing me. I walked past Kia Lynn. The color had drained from her face, but I could do nothing but watch the horror consume her expression.

I was a ball of fire, and the unsuspecting people ahead of me were my next victims.

CHAPTER TWENTY-FOUR
All for Nothing

ALEX

Tallisa's people swarmed inside the amusement park. I was floored when I saw the masses just beyond the iron gates. Somehow, my tyrant of an aunt had convinced them all to follow her.

The California Adventure side of the Disneyland Park was their base, and it was flooded with humans and anamans, mixed and full of both kinds. She had an army that far surpassed our numbers, and I did not believe we were prepared to stop them.

"The numbers don't matter," Dad argued. "If we take them by surprise, we can still secure the time machine."

"And Henry," I reminded him.

"Yes, of course. He's the only one who can repair the tear between our dimensions." Dad nodded as if it were obvious.

"*And* he is family. Don't forget that reason to save him." My irritation with the whole operation was bubbling to the surface.

Mom stepped between me and Dad. "Lose the attitude, Alex. We are not your enemies."

I bit down on my bottom lip to stop myself from saying another word. She was right, but so was I.

"We stun them one by one," Dad said, instructing those of us who were closest to him. "There are only twelve patrolling outside the gates. We take them first and lock them in one of these outside buildings. Then we attack. They will be down the twelve guards and we are only here to subdue, not kill. I don't think I have to say this, but I am going to anyway—children are to be left alone. Any person who is not a threat, we do not engage. We distract and allow Zoe Dawn and her team to rescue Henry and find the time machine. Any questions?"

Silence greeted him. He nodded when no one spoke, then directed the first seven to sneak around the front.

"You stay here," he said to me, patting my shoulder as he circled around me. "When we enter their camp, I need you to have my back."

"Yes, Dad," I replied as he disappeared around the corner. I pressed my back against the small structure we were hunkered behind and watched as half the team left.

After connecting with the vast ocean, I knew my elemental powers ran far deeper than I had originally believed. With a snap of my fingers, I could drown every person in the vicinity of the old theme park. If Dad knew what I could do, having his back would turn into me finishing this off, once and for all.

But I would wait for my moment.

Several minutes later, everyone returned and Dad held up his fist. "This is it. Remember to stay true to yourself and our people. We are here to create peace, by eliminating only those who threaten our very existence. If Tallisa or Tatum are captured, please take them to holding, back at the ship. I will deal with them both myself."

He waved his front line forward, then beckoned for me and Mom to follow him as he crept toward the entrance. Partial letters of the Disney California Adventure sign still graced the entryway's roof with the sun beating down on them, reminding me that we were doing this at the worst possible time of day. But time is what we did not have, not when the portal was growing above our heads.

We pushed through, and I heard the screams before I saw the crowd running. I followed Dad, who weaved through the hordes and pushed toward the building that held Uncle Henry. The team ahead of him continued to stun anyone who threatened our advancements.

Expanded Chaos

Then I saw her. Standing at the end of the road, near the old water fountain. Beatle. She was still alive. My heart raced with anticipation. She was a ferocious fighter but an innocent by nature. I would not allow anyone to hurt her.

Her attention zeroed in on me as we neared, and she shifted one of her feet back, preparing to pounce. I should have known Tallisa would instruct her to find me first. She bobbed back and forth on her toes, waiting patiently for me to draw nearer.

I slowed to a crawl and brought my thumbs to my fingers, rubbing across each one and focusing on the water deep within the dirt below us. With my mind, I pulled it up to the fountain. It burst through the old pipes and shot high in the sky before showering Beatle. The girl shrieked and threw out her fists, trying to fight the water as it continued to pour on her.

Digging my heels into the pavement, I concentrated on the drops of water and swirled them around Beatle's body, cocooning her in a thick sheet of ice from her feet to her shoulders. She fought against it, screaming and cursing until her arms and hands could no longer move. Her gaze shot to me. A roar of anger burst across her lips.

"I will deal with you later," I said to her, then searched the panicked crowd for my parents.

They had left me. I twirled around and saw Eshah pointing one of her large anaman weapons toward the sky. This was it. Zoe Dawn had better not fail us now.

The shot echoed through the crowd, and people ripped past me, running for shelter. I watched them tear around the rock structure that used to be the river rapids ride I had loved so much. As I watched their receding backs, Tallisa stepped into view. Her smile stretched across her face the moment our eyes met.

"D-do not l-l-leave me here!" Beatle screamed, thrashing her head around.

I threw her a sideways glance. "Be careful, Beatle. Too much of that and you are going to give yourself severe whiplash." I patted the ice, and she snapped her teeth at me. "I promise to return for you. And then you and I will talk. There is no reason for us to be enemies."

"An en-n-nemy of my f-f-father's is an en-n-nemy of mine!" she screamed as I walked away.

Tallisa slapped her knee, laughing at my exchange with Beatle. I stopped in my tracks and whirled around to face the blonde Down's syndrome girl.

"Who's your father?" I asked, keeping one eye on her and the other on the soldiers barreling down the crossroad toward us.

Beatle cracked a smile, revealing a perfectly straight

row of white teeth.

We were out of time. I whirled around and raced after Tallisa who had disappeared behind the rock structure. When I circled around the bend, Tallisa waved at me from up ahead and skipped as if we were playing a game. My feet lifted off the ground, and my energy exploded around me. I shot toward her at lightning speed.

Tallisa glanced back in surprise at my quick advancement and held up her arms in defense when I plowed in to her. We rolled, but I remained levitated. I recovered well before she skidded to a stop.

Tatum stepped out of the shadows and helped Tallisa to her feet. She brushed her clothes off and turned toward me with raised brows. I didn't miss the terror in her expression before she squashed it away with a sneer.

"I can see you have come into your own. Took you long enough," she said, with a hint of sarcasm laced in her tone.

Tatum snickered. I snapped my fingers and his eyes widened as ice sealed his lips shut.

"We've danced before." My gaze sharpened on him, and I only had to think about the ice forming. "Do you really want to challenge me again?"

He wiped at the ice and broke it with his knuckle. "It is too late, Alex. Unless you plan on freezing all of us to the ground, we will be leaving. Your parents have already been stopped from rescuing Henry. It is over."

I cocked my head to the side, then smiled. "This battle between us" —I pointed at myself and then at them— "is just beginning."

Water trickled up through the cracks in the pavement, and Tatum leapt backward trying to escape the flood. He threw me a stony look of disdain when he fell back against a stone wall.

Tallisa slinked a few steps to the side and pressed against the nearest structure, then snuck around the corner as I remained focused on her comrade. She had no problem leaving him behind. A true coward.

Tatum watched her leave him, seemingly not surprised by it. He threw me one last glance over his shoulder, then sprinted toward the wharf with the water trailing right behind him. I drifted after him. As he neared the next fork in the road, he shot to the right and headed in the direction of Henry and the others.

I stopped and glanced back toward where Tallisa had disappeared. Tatum could be Dad's problem. I really only wanted my aunt.

Still hovering an inch off the ground, I turned to the right and followed after Tallisa through a rundown building. Her footsteps echoed against the broken floor, giving me an idea of which direction she was heading. As I started to close in on her, the running stopped and silence greeted me. I slowed, searching every nook and cranny until I was back in the open.

I twirled in a circle and then planted my feet back on the ground.

"Looking for me?" Tallisa asked.

I whipped around and flinched, stumbling backward as a sharp pain exploded on my hip and flashed like lightning through my nervous system. I crumbled to the ground, grabbing my hip. A flood of hot tears ran down my cheeks as I scooted away from my aunt. She was holding an anaman weapon.

"You just had to save your pathetic uncle, didn't you?" Tallisa snarled, following me as I crawled back inside the building. "I knew you would be foolish enough to come. So predictable. I planned on finishing you off, but that would take away from the pleasure of knowing you imploded with the rest of your family here on your new Earth." She spat at me, then lifted her foot and stomped down on the side of my chest.

I gasped for air as my lungs screamed from the shock ripping through them. She smiled as I writhed in agony and pointed her anaman weapon at my head. I leaned to the side and coughed against the broken floor. My throat felt like it was on fire. One eye remained glued to Tallisa and I tried to push farther away from her at the same time, but my arms gave out on me. I collapsed forward.

"What makes you think you will still be leaving?" I asked as I drew in a sharp breath and twisted back to face her.

"I always win in the end, Alexandria." She jabbed her weapon against my skull. "You lose. Again. All you had to do was complete five days of torture back in our dimension, and this would have been over long before now." Her smile returned, but I noticed sweat dripping down her face and a slight quiver in her hand that was not holding the weapon.

She was scared. Maybe the ones who survived still had a fighting chance.

"This is all your fault." She leaned closer and sneered at me. "Everything these people have to suffer through is because you chose to run instead of face your fate."

"Finish me," I begged, falling to my back. I was exhausted from this fight, and I would do anything at this point to protect my new home. "Then save the people of this world. It is yours. Please."

"No!" she screamed at me, her lips drawing back into a snarl as she tightened her hold on the weapon. "You do not get to be a martyr. You are nothing. Do you—"

Expanded Chaos

An explosion ripped through the building, and the sound of Tallisa's body impacting the already-broken wall behind her reverberated alongside the blast. The world went silent as a cloud of dust blew above me. I rolled to my side as the wall crumbled from the impact, and a crack in the ceiling spread out like a lightning bolt. I cringed when large chunks of plaster scattered around me.

I yanked my legs into my chest and swung to my knees before crawling to my feet. My hip screamed with excruciating pain, but I took a step forward, limping once again to the outdoors. In the corner of my eye, I noticed Tallisa crawling after me. The weapon was gone. Her red hair was covered in dust, and a large gash colored her forehead red with blood.

I doubted I looked any better.

My gaze shifted to the sky and focused on a ball of smoke rising from the direction of the entrance. Wiping away the grime from my eyes and face, my thoughts turned to the dirt right under my feet. With a wave of my hand, I pulled more water from it, forming a river that shot toward Henry's building.

I ripped Tallisa up from the ground and threw her into it with a strength I did not know I possessed. Her head dipped under the surface. I reached in and held her above water by her hair as I levitated next to the invisible edges.

She sputtered out water, then cried out in pain, but I ignored her. My leg was burning from the wound she had inflicted, and my family was probably dead. She no longer mattered.

When we circled around the old river rapids ride, smoke filled the air in every direction and flames licked the sky as they raged up ahead. They were coming from the building Henry had been held in.

I dropped Tallisa into the water, stunned by what I was seeing. She gasped for air when her head bobbed above the water, then she sank back in. I turned to her in horror, unable to compute what was happening. Everyone was gone, and it was her fault.

I watched her hold her breath, then resurface and gasp for air. And again. She couldn't escape my water. I was in charge, and in this moment, I needed her to take her last breath.

Instead, I hauled her out of the river, lifted it with my mind, and hurled it all at the fire. The flames sizzled, but it had not stopped the inferno.

Tallisa crumbled to the pavement, drawing in one deep breath after another. She looked like a drowned cat with her auburn hair plastered against her face. I stepped around her and raised my arms, pulling the moisture from the air and forming a storm above the burning building. The rain poured from the cloud, just as Kia Lynn sprinted from the crumbling structure. Her face was covered in soot and a cloud of smoke followed her.

I waved. Kia Lynn blinked, then wiped her eyes before refocusing on me.

"Alex!" she screamed, tearing toward me. "Zoe Dawn. It was Zoe Dawn." Her eyes widened as she neared me and pointed. "*Mama, stop!*"

Searing hot pain sliced through my upper back. I flailed my arms to reach behind me, but they became leaden and fell back to my sides. The world spun on its side, and I tilted with it and smashed headfirst into the broken cement. White speckles invaded my eyesight. I rolled to my back and tried to focus on Tallisa who was holding both my daggers. They were dripping with blood. My blood.

Kia Lynn rammed into her mother, and I heard the daggers clang to the pavement. The sky rotated above me as the storm clouds disappeared and the sunshine returned. Except there was nothing sunny about my circumstances.

As the agony rolled through me, I squeaked out a cry for help. My throat thickened with sobs and I wept against the hard ground, feeling the torment rage through every cell in my body. I cried out again and this time my voice returned as my screams filled the air. I lifted my hands upward for someone to help me, but no one came.

Kia Lynn was screaming at her mother, but I could not see either of them. I had to help myself.

Tears poured from my eyes, and I wiped at my face as I pushed upward to roll to my knees. My legs shook, and I tumbled back to my side, desperate breaths rolling through me like the waves of the ocean. My life was draining from my body. This was it, the end Tallisa had wanted.

Closing my eyes, I wrapped my arms around my chest and focused on the ocean I had left earlier. The beautiful water elementals. I relaxed into their protective embrace. Their whispers soothed the turmoil raging in my mind and body, making it easy to release myself to them. I exhaled one last time and welcomed the melodic calling of Earth's waters.

CHAPTER TWENTY-FIVE
Crushing the Rip

KIA LYNN

"*Mama, you are a demon!*" I screamed at the one woman I had once believed was an angel. I held her down by her wrists, unable to budge to help Alex. "I believed in you, Mama." A few tears slipped from my eyes and ran down to my chin as my throat thickened with sobs. "You were my idol. My person. The only one I believed could never do any harm. But I was wrong."

Mama's eyes closed, and she stopped thrashing against my hold. "Life trauma changes a person. I did everything I could to survive, and I really believed sacrificing this world and my daughter was the right thing to do to keep others from following after me."

Alex groaned, and from the corner of my eye, I saw her curl into a ball. My lower lip trembled. First Zoe Dawn and now Alex. I could not face the world without those two.

I slammed Mama's hands against the ground. "You

have torn my heart to shreds," I cried. My entire body shook with anger. "I hate you, Mama. I hate you, and I hope your worst nightmares haunt you for the rest of your days."

A flash of hurt washed down her expression. I ignored it and leapt off her, collapsing in a heap next to Alex. I brushed her soaking wet hair away from her face.

"Alex, stay with me. Please do not go." I peered over her side. Blood was seeping out from two long wounds in her back.

Mama rubbed her wrists and rose to her feet. "You chose her over me. You have no one else to blame but yourself. This" —she waved her hand around at all the destruction— "is all your fault."

She turned her back on me and strolled away as if she hadn't just ripped out my heart. A calloused woman. Her traumas had created a monster.

As she rounded the corner, two small whirlwinds followed her, colliding with one another as if they were two small children playing in the wind. I squinted at them, but the sound of nearing footsteps brought me back to Alex.

"Kia Lynn, is that you?" Malcolm asked from behind me.

I did not look but nodded in reply.

His arms circled around Alex, and he drew her into his arms. "The others are leaving. We have Henry and the time machine. Come, Kia Lynn. We must hurry for Alex's sake."

I closed my eyes, driving away the demons gnawing at my mind and heart. She had walked away. As if I was nothing to her. I gulped back the grief and rose to my feet, slowly opening my eyes to follow Malcolm and the others.

The distance grew between us, and I trudged past the building that had exploded after Zoe Dawn entered it. I could not bring myself to look. The agony writhing in my heart was too much for me to bear.

Up ahead, a mound of broken ice stood in the middle of the path. For a brief moment, I envisioned Alex using her ice to keep enemies entrapped. Clearly that had only been a temporary help. The shattered ice was of no use to us now.

When I rounded the corner, my gaze fell on Malcolm who stood on the other end with his back toward me. There was no one else around, and it looked like he was no longer holding Alex. I wanted them to leave me behind. Disneyland was now empty and destroyed, and Mama had abandoned me once again. All my childhood dreams had gone up in smoke.

Malcolm glanced over his shoulder and then shifted to the side. Zoe Dawn stepped out from the shadows and raised her hand to greet me. I froze. It was not possible. I had seen her vanish inside the building and then watched it exploded soon after. How could she be standing there, unharmed?

I peeled my foot from the ground and stepped forward, then leapt into a sprint, racing into Zoe Dawn's arms.

"I saw you turn into a giant ball of fire," I said, rocking on my feet as I hugged her close. My elation was mixed with a weight on my heart. "Then the building exploded. How are you here?"

"I will explain, but first we need to hurry," Zoe Dawn replied, prying my arms from her neck. "Malcolm's team was fast and had Henry moved from the building before I even arrived. The time machine was hidden near their small ship. Jax just left with it."

"What—"

"Not now, Kia Lynn." Malcolm grabbed each of our shoulders and dragged us through the entryway. "Tallisa escaped, along with several of her armed guards. They will not lie low for long, and if they have a tracking device, we will be sitting ducks out in the open."

The cruiser was still parked in front with its side door

open. Dax poked his head through.

"Let's go. Alex is strapped in, and Jax is on the line. He says they are ready to leave. Should they pick us up here?"

"Tell him we are on our way to my ship," Malcolm hollered back, hauling us at a sprint toward the cruiser.

I collapsed on the first seat I came to. Alex was lying face down on one of the beds, with a restraint across her back. Her shirt was pulled up, and two blood-soaked cloths were taped to her back where the daggers had sliced through her. And her breathing was shallow and shaky. Mama had done that, and I would never be able to erase the memory.

Zoe Dawn sat beside me. Her hand slid over and covered mine. "That was not me, sister. A demon had possessed me, and I was trying to stop it."

"What happened when you entered the building?" I asked, not daring to look her in the eyes.

The cruiser was flying across the land, and I could already see the ships up ahead.

"I do not remember much," Zoe Dawn said, patting my hand before pulling back. She leaned back and crossed her ankle over her knee. "When the fire surrounded me, it was as if I was sitting back within myself, watching the events unfold. I no longer had any control. But when I entered the building, a force stronger than the demon inside me yanked it clean from me. The result was the explosion."

"How? How would that even happen?" None of her explanation made sense to me. A demon.

Malcolm glanced back at us. "There were protection runes engraved into the paneling of the building. Tallisa knows more about this entity than us, as she was prepared for it, but she was not counting on a fireball coming through that door." His fingers flew over the monitor as we neared his ship. The bay door opened, and he eased the cruiser inside. "That was her one miscalculation and our one saving grace as ironic as it sounds. It was lucky we had already retrieved Henry, but her ship was unsalvageable."

"She has another one." I sprang to my feet and unclasped Alex's restraint. "It is a smaller vessel, but she still has a ride."

Malcolm heaved Alex into his arms. "She does not have the time machine."

"That will not stop her," I told him, following as he raced to the medical station.

"Kia Lynn, we will deal with your mother after we repair the portal." He set Alex down inside the medical bed and closed the glass covering. "We have used this way too many times in the past few days." He turned toward me after Alex's scan began. "Promise me you will not run off again. Promise me we will not have to use this station again for a very long time."

I rubbed my temples from a growing headache pounding against my skull. "I will not run off again, but I cannot promise that my mother will not retaliate." My arms dropped to my sides, and I fell into Malcolm's arms. I could no longer hold back as my sobs rose in waves. "She chose herself and her friends over me. And then she tried to murder Alex right in front of me. I thought she loved me."

Malcolm's arms circled around me and crushed me against him. "There are those who lose the ability to love. Too much trauma and heartache. They seal away their hearts, even from those who are the most loyal." His hands swept down my hair. "You have a visitor. I will give you two some privacy."

He stepped away, and I turned to face Rafael in the doorway. He slipped inside after Malcolm left.

"I have missed you, Kia Lynn," Rafael said, running his thumb across my forehead and tucking my hair behind my ears.

I inhaled deeply as my hand found his. I pulled it up to my chest and pressed his palm against my skin. "I choose you, Rafael. You have been my one shining light through all this darkness. When this is all over, I want you to be my mate."

A smile blossomed across his face, then he cupped my chin in his hand and pulled me closer. His full lips sealed over mine, and I melted into his embrace. His arms wrapped around my waist, and for the first time since Zion, I felt a sense of peace wash over me.

"It is time to buckle up," Malcolm's voice sounded from the ceiling, echoing through the corridor.

I leaned back and Rafael planted a kiss on my nose, before leading me out of the room.

When we returned to the bridge, Malcolm was preparing the ship to make the trip out of our atmosphere. Jax and Adina had left with Henry and the time machine, expecting us to follow to assist in keeping Mama far away while they repaired the rip between the two universes.

None of their words made sense, but Malcolm reassured us we would understand soon enough.

I closed my eyes when turbulence shook the vessel. My fingers dug into the armrests of my chair and every muscle in my body tensed from the shaking. It lasted for what seemed like ages, and then the noise suddenly stopped. I pried one eye open. There were stars for as far as I could see. My jaw dropped open, along with my other eye. It was dark but stunning. After all the stories of the anamans' view of Mother Gaia, I would finally be able to see her from afar as well.

Up ahead was a massive ship, wider and taller than any building I had ever seen. This was Alex's ship that she had told me about, and it was just floating up here, unaffected by the pull of the planet.

"Wow!" Dax exclaimed, his feet bouncing against the floor. "Alex was not kidding."

"It is spectacular," Aly said, swiveling in her chair and looking at Zoe Dawn. "How are you feeling, sister?"

Zoe Dawn was staring, her eyes unblinking. A smile stretched across her cheeks. "I am in love."

Malcolm chuckled. "This is the ultimate exploration, but you have to learn a few important safety rules before venturing out this far."

"Sign me up," Zoe Dawn said, never once taking her eyes off the stars. "This is all I have dreamed of and more."

Covyn had not said much since I had arrived on the ship. She had not been with the others, and she seemed strangely quiet. Her gaze drifted from Zoe Dawn and back to the window, but she remained silent. Zoe Dawn's flair for exciting adventures might not be all that Covyn had signed up for and worry tugged at my thoughts. Finding love with someone who shared a similar view was not an easy task in this world.

Dax undid his restraints. "May I be excused? I would like to be with Alex."

Malcolm's entire body shook as he burst with laughter. I had never seen him so jovial. It was as if he was releasing a load of tension alongside his laughter. He turned toward Dax. "You are a grown man. As long as we are not zipping around, you may do whatever you please, but thank you for your courteous nature. It is more than I have received from the three elementals."

He glanced our way and he winked at me.

Dax rose and saluted Malcolm before racing from the room.

My attention returned to the larger ship. We circled around it and stopped on the other side. A glimmer of a dark void flickered up ahead. It waved like a cloth in the wind, slowly spreading across our view as if it were wiping away the stars.

Another small ship was closer to the void, but there was nothing happening. The large screen in front of Malcolm flickered, and Jax's image sprang into view.

"Henry was not as coherent as we would have liked," Jax said, running his hand over his bald head. "But he has been healing in the medical station, and we just pulled him out." He shifted out of the way so we could see the room behind him.

The time machine was propped up in the middle, and Henry was kneeling to the side of it. He looked our way, then shook his head. The sores around his wrist were lighter, but still shone against his pale skin.

"The repair to the portal could take hours, days, or a just a few minutes," he grumbled, fiddling with a lever. "I really won't know until I am able to power this on. No matter what, I will not leave until I fix this."

"Where is Alex?" Adina called from the other side of the room. Her back was toward us as she worked on another machine.

Malcolm's gaze shot to Adina and then he bowed his head. "She is recovering in the medical station from Tallisa's handiwork."

Adina whirled around. "What did she do?"

"Mama stabbed Alex with two daggers." My voice shook. How would they ever forgive me for running off to find my barbaric mother?

Adina's hand fluttered up to her mouth, and the other reached out for the wall to hold her steady.

I undid my restraints and rose to my feet. "The wounds are in her back. Adina, I am so sorry for what my mother has done. If I had only known—"

"How could you have known?" Jax shook his head as he stepped into view again. The lines around his eyes had deepened with worry. "She was supposed to be your loving mother, not a spiteful monster. We are sorry she subjected you to any heartbreak. Will Alex's healing be successful?"

"Yes, Jax." Malcolm chin lifted and he glanced my way. "She lost a lot of blood, but I have programmed the medical station to give her a blood transfusion and then to repair any damage. Dax is with her now, and I will check on her soon. She is in good hands."

"We believe you," Jax replied with a slight nod.

Adina was no longer in the room or she had moved to another side. She was either not as trusting as Jax or she could not handle the pressure of waiting to be with Alex again. I sank back into my chair. I understood her pain. The sorrow of Mama's betrayal was crushing me, and I wanted nothing more than to curl into a ball and forget I ever saw her again.

Zoe Dawn reached for my hand. "Together we are stronger," she whispered, rubbing her other thumb against her fingers. "We connect with Alex and Mother Gaia now and assist Henry."

The sorrow in my mind blocked my elemental gift,

but when Zoe Dawn's hand encircled mine, a fresh wave of energy crashed over me. Her fire and my air circled through the ship like an invisible force, searching for its missing piece. When it reached Alex, the euphoria spread from my fingers to my toes.

Zoe Dawn was right. Our destinies had not changed and now that we were together again, it was time to turn our attention to saving our world.

Silence filled both ships as the others watched Henry work and we connected internally, focusing on Mother Gaia next. Henry moved around the machine, jamming his hand into one space and pulling wires from another. Then just as the flow of Mother Gaia's essence collided with the three of us, he clapped his hands. A burst of light enveloped the void and slowly began to crush it.

"Done!" he exclaimed, jumping to his feet. His fingers flew along something I could not see, then the machine buzzed to life. "Just adding the coordinates and voila, it should start closing now." His finger dropped down on a hidden portion of the machine.

"Look, it has already started closing," Covyn said, speaking up for the first time since we entered the ship. "How did your machine do that if it wasn't turned on?"

White sparks outlined the dark void. All eyes turned to me and Zoe Dawn.

"We are only helping," Zoe Dawn whispered, returning her concentration to our connection. "Let us focus."

The darkness shrank more, but something white suddenly pressed against it. Malcolm's breath came in short.

"What is that?" Covyn asked, scrambling to clasp together her safety belts.

Zoe Dawn and I ignored the commotion, keeping our attention on the dazzling glimmer flowing around the void.

"It looks like another ship," Malcolm replied. "Do you see that, Jax?"

"Yes, it is a vessel from my dimension." Jax's hands squeezed into fists. "Henry, can you stop them?"

"If they keep pushing against the portal, it will rip them apart." Henry glanced our way. "And we will be caught in their explosion."

"Move away," Jax commanded as his gaze landed on Malcolm. "Both ships need to move away."

Malcolm did not question him. He eased the ship back. The large vessel did the same, but it took them much longer to build up speed. Before long, we could barely see their ship.

The void continued to shrink as the white light and

the vessel both continued to press against it. I glanced away from it and looked at Henry.

"We need to do it together, Henry," I said. My fingers squeezed Zoe Dawn's hand as I leaned forward. "Focus the energy of your machine around the edges."

He nodded and pulled down on a lever. "Okay, Kia Lynn. I have it," Henry finally said after several silent breaths.

The white sparks grew in diameter and snapped at the darkness, and the others gasped. They must have finally noticed the intensity of our magic. It was growing into a force much stronger than what we experienced with Mother Gaia back in Zion. It flowed through us, around us, and swam through the empty space intent on eliminating the darkness.

The void shimmered once more, then crushed upon itself from the massive strength of our combined energy. The sparks dissipated as well until they both vanished completely. I released a withheld breath. A deep sense of relief flowed down my entire body, and Zoe Dawn flashed me a wide smile. We had done it.

Despite all the pain that awaited me down on the surface, I continued to thrive and evolve. Unlike Mama. Her rejection was tearing me up inside, but without her I was still a goddess—a fierce mystic, intertwined with the elemental magic of our world. I was a legacy and nothing Mama could throw at me would take that truth away from me.

We had done something she could not do. Our two universes might be forever connected, but we had stopped the destructive collision and saved our world.

CHAPTER TWENTY-SIX
Sapphire Spirit Tribe

ZOE DAWN

Malcolm turned the ship to face Mother Gaia. Kia Lynn clapped a hand over her mouth at the view, and I reached over and gave her a big sideways hug, squishing our cheeks together. A rush of pride swept through me. The Earth's beauty was astounding from the stars' viewpoint. No wonder the anaman had been attracted to Her.

I released Kia Lynn, reached the other direction, and curled my fingers over Covyn's hand. She jumped from my touch.

"Easy there," I said, laughing from her startled expression. "I just want to hold your hand."

She flexed her fingers and leaned toward me. Her fingers wrapped within mine, and she finally smiled. "Do you still want to introduce me to your mum?"

My lips twitched at the thought. Mum's words had stung, and she had been nasty before we left the village, but Covyn was still the only woman I wanted. All the annoyance I had been feeling earlier had disappeared with the dark entity. It wanted me to despise everyone.

The question remained. Where had it gone?

"Of course I do." I squeezed her hand. "This time we will make it official, no matter what."

Her smile lit up her entire face, and she pulled my hand toward her lips and kissed it. "No matter what," she repeated as her eyes sparkled with joy.

The ride through our atmosphere was bumpy, but once we were through, the ship zoomed toward the black mountains. I could see their peaks rise up against the horizon and I sighed with happiness from the sight.

Before long we were hovering just above the familiar trees and modest structures. Malcolm settled the ship near the village center, like he had done before. As we were unloading, Jax and his team landed next to us.

I peeked in to see Alex, with Kia Lynn right beside me. "How is she?"

Dax twisted around. "She's waking. We will be right behind you. I'm just giving her a moment to gain her bearings."

Kia Lynn rubbed his shoulder, then leaned in and planted a kiss on his cheek. "Thank you for taking care of her."

"She is my whole world," he replied, leaning his face against Kia Lynn's head.

I placed my hand on top of the glass shell, then reached out for Kia Lynn. "We can give her some of our energy. It is the least we could do for all she has done for us. Not to mention, she is our sister."

Kia Lynn grasped my hand and slipped her other one on top of the shell as well. The euphoria was unreal, a sensation so intense it nearly took my breath away. Mother Gaia flowed through us and into Alex, pouring Her healing love throughout Alex's body. Our light flooded the room and Dax had to close his eyes when it became too bright for him to bear.

When it was done, Alex's eyes fluttered open, and her hands pressed against the glass. She turned our way and a relaxed smile rose on her lips. To the end of our days, we would always remain sisters.

We left Dax to help Alex out of the medical station. When we exited the ship, Adina tore out of her bay door and in through ours, not stopping to speak to any of us. Jax was not too far behind her, his large feet pounding hard against the metal.

"*Zoe Dawn!*" Mum hollered, waving her arm erratically as she shuffled toward me.

Warmth filled my chest when I saw her. Despite her

angry words, I had missed her dearly. I leapt to the dirt and raced into her arms. She folded me into her embrace.

"I will fight them all," she said, her breath hot against my cheek. Her entire body was shaking. "I regret ever agreeing to their arrangement. They do not have any right to take you away. We will return all our crops before I ever let them lay a hand on you."

"What are you saying, Mum?" I asked, pulling away from her.

I saw them before she answered. My expression sobered and I battled the urge to recoil. Lindon was sauntering through the crowd with dozens of other men and women following behind him. They exuded a confidence of superiority with their heads held high, while looking down their noses at the villagers surrounding them.

A silver object sparkled in each of their right hands, holding it against their left shoulder. My eyes narrowed at the threat. They were weapons I had never seen before. Lindon's gaze was glued to me.

"Zoe Dawn, we have returned to collect you," Lindon announced, waving his arm for everyone's attention. "We are not of the Black Mountain People, but your crops grow in your village because of our trade with your Doyen. Honor the agreement, or we will take you by force."

Malcolm stepped in between me and Lindon. "Excuse me. Who are you?"

I shifted slightly, so I could still see Lindon.

His gaze traveled up and down Malcolm's large stature. "I am Zoe Dawn's chosen mate. The Doyen agreed to this union."

"Did she actually choose you?" Malcolm asked, folding his arms over his chest.

"This matter is not your concern." Lindon sneered and then turned his attention to me.

Malcolm curled his hand over my shoulder. "Zoe Dawn is my concern. And the crops have grown because of her and the other's elemental connection to Mother Gaia. *They* have healed our lands. Not you. Your claim on her has no value here. Take your people and leave in peace."

Lindon did not budge, but the edges of his lips quirked up in amusement. "You are mistaken, old man. We are the reason these crops have flourished and in the coming days, our people are destined to transcend with Mother Gaia. You will remain with the broken world you see before you."

"You are the mistaken one," I hissed, bitterness filling my mouth. I licked my lips and scowled at him. "We have already healed the lands. This talk of transcendence is preposterous."

A few of Lindon's people chuckled and he shot them a look that quieted them quickly. His eyes turned back to me. "You have been brainwashed by your people, Zoe Dawn. You know this already. It is not something I need to explain to you as it is an inner knowing you have been pondering for many years. Am I correct?"

Every muscle in my body froze. How did he know this?

My expression must have answered his question as a wide smile spread across his face. "It is settled then." His gaze swept over the growing crowd of villagers and his voice rose so they could all hear. "The elementals are a myth, stories we have passed along from generation to generation to instill hope." He raised his weapon and pointed it at Malcolm. "I insist on Zoe Dawn accompanying me back to my home."

"Why?" Alex asked as she stepped from the ship. "Why her?"

Lindon's jaw twitched, but when he focused on Alex, his eyes widened. "It is you."

"It is me, who?" Alex strode up to my side and wrapped her arm protectively around my shoulders.

"It is the woman from the painting," Lindon said,

turning toward his people, then pointing at Alex with his weapon. "Do you recognize her? She is an ancient one, but not from our tribe."

I leaned in close to Alex. "They are an amusing bunch. How do they know you are an ancient one?"

"Beats me," she replied. Her mom and dad joined us, and Jax wrapped his hand over hers.

"If you have something to say to my daughter, you best be keeping it respectful." Jax's other hand tightened into a fist. "Malcolm asked you to leave in peace. Why are you still here?"

Lindon regarded Jax with a thoughtful stare, then his gaze snapped back to me. He pulled the neck of his shirt down, revealing his chest and what appeared to be the kenaz rune in the same place as mine. "I did not want it to come to this, but you have forced my hand." He jabbed his finger against the marking. "You were marked with this rune by your birth parents, a symbol of our ancestral torch for those who are descendants of the Sapphire Spirit Tribe." He turned in a circle, showing everyone who could see. "She is one of us," he shouted to the crowd. "A child stolen by the Doyen to fulfill the wishes of a barren woman."

My heart dropped to my stomach. I focused my attention on Mum. The color in her face had drained, leaving only an ashen hue.

"Is this true?" I asked her through clenched teeth.

She swallowed hard and turned her gaze to meet mine. "I did not know, Zoe Dawn. The Doyen promised me a child, but they never said you were stolen."

My whole world crashed down on me. I gasped for air and stumbled backward. Alex's long arms wrapped around my waist to hold me up. I had never fit in to this world. My home was a lie—a filthy secret.

My gaze searched the crowd and met Kia Lynn's. Her stunned expression slowly melted into a crimson fury, and I knew she would never betray me. Throughout my life, only she had accepted me and my eccentricities. My family was Kia Lynn, Alex, Covyn, and all my new friends. The Sapphire Spirit Tribe could take a hike right off a tall cliff for all I cared.

"This does not change anything," I said, pushing Alex's arms away and standing up straight. "I belong to no one. My answer is still no. Leave now and never return."

Lindon pointed his weapon at Malcolm, who had taken a step closer. "It is not an option to leave without her. She is needed by her real family, and our union was foreordained long before her birth. Long before this ridiculous elemental story." He pointed at his kenaz rune again. "Zoe Dawn, we were meant to be together."

"My path is not controlled by anyone but myself!" I shouted, my fury simmering just below my skin. If he was not careful, I would no longer be able to hold back the flame.

Kia Lynn jumped forward and wrapped me in her arms, hauling me backward into Malcolm's ship. I watched in horror as Rafael threw himself at the nearest intruder, knocking him to the ground and kneeing him in the side. Lightning struck the tallest peak and everyone turned to look at the storm clouds raging over the tips of the mountain, blowing a torrent of rain toward us. They were trying to protect me. Terror overtook my heart, knowing this would not end well for them.

Lindon glanced at the darkening clouds and lifted his weapon above the crowd. "So be it," he replied with an inquisitive tilt of his head.

"No, please," I cried, holding out my hand toward the pale man.

Kia Lynn dug in her heels and continued to pull be away from him.

As a fist fight ensued around Lindon and the winds and rains ripped at the vegetation near the edges of the village center, he pressed the trigger on his weapon. I shrieked at him and yanked myself free of Kia Lynn's grasp.

A high-pitched screech echoed around me. Malcolm tumbled to the ground, unconscious before he struck the dirt. Kia Lynn's arms fell away from me and she slid to the ground. I reached down and stopped her head from smacking into the ground as her entire body shook uncontrollably. Many others around me fell to the hard dirt, writhing like dying insects. I turned and saw Alex lying on the ground, staring at me with pain in her eyes. Blood oozed from her nose and her eyes fluttered close.

I pressed my palms into my ears to drown out Lindon's weapon. "Stop it!" I screamed over the noise, collapsing to my knees. "You are killing them."

Lindon marched forward and grabbed my arm, hauling me back to my feet. His fingers around my wrist tightened as he dragged me through the swarm of bodies and toward the village's northern entrance. My flesh was an inferno, but I could not push my fire out. The noise was suppressing it. I dug in my heels and pulled on his vice grip, but he only tightened it more.

"The longer we are here, the more they will suffer," Lindon hissed in my ear. My heat had not seemed to bother him. "Your fight is over."

I glanced back at my family and friends, lying on the ground either unconscious or screaming from the agony.

My body felt leaden from the sight. I submitted, willingly following him up the pathway, until we came upon their vessel. It was nothing like Jax's or Malcolm's. It glittered from the sun's rays, a silver that seemed to blend in with the terrain. Alex had mentioned this technology—a bend in perception.

"Who are you people?" I asked, tugging at his hold on me once more.

"I have told you already," Lindon replied, the noise quieting as he yanked me inside the ship. "And you are one of us. Please stop resisting."

I balled my free hand into a fist, swung out, and knocked him in the jaw. His head swung to one side and his arms flew backward, releasing his hold on me. I whirled around and sprinted away. My feet pounded against the strange-sounding material as I launched myself out of the vessel. Back in the sun, I raced toward the village. Halfway down, I remembered the anaman weapons that were in my boots. I slowed and leaned over, my fingers skimming over the ends of the firearms.

The screeching noise brought me to a dead stop. I collapsed to the ground and fell to my back, staring up at the wispy clouds. My screams filled the air, trying to drown out the beating against my head. I pressed my fingers against my ears as I stretched my body and arched my back. The only thought I had was how easily they could halt me in my tracks. Their weapon continued to hold my fire hostage, as my mind could not conjure my flame.

The clouds above quivered, and I blinked at them to make sure the movement wasn't in my head. Lindon bent over me.

"You are making this much harder than it needs to be," he said, grabbing ahold of my elbow. His fingernails dug into my flesh. "When you arrive to your true home, all will make sense, and you will wonder why you fought against me for so long."

My gaze never left the shifting clouds. With my free hand, I pointed at the sky, and his noisemaker quieted as he turned to look. The sky was filling with a massive anaman ship similar to Jax's in high orbit, but this one was flatter and wider. It broke through the atmosphere, pushing the clouds out of the way as they rolled across the sky. Soon it filled most of my view, and the shadows grew longer once the sun slipped behind it.

I shivered from the sudden chill. "What is that?" I asked, picking myself off the ground and wiping the dirt from my clothes.

Lindon stood in silence as many of his people gathered around us. The stillness beat against me, and for the first time, I had this overwhelming feeling that I had to leave with Lindon. Not because of the terror snaking through my insides… but what if this was all happening for a reason? My birth parents, whom I did not know existed until today, were alive and waiting for me.

And now an anaman vessel had invaded our space. We needed every Earth-living human and anaman to bond together and prepare for whatever fight was being brought to us.

"We need to leave, now," someone yelled from the ship. "The anaman ships are returning from the outer planets."

Lindon held out his hand for me to take. I glanced at the enormous ship in the sky one last time, then twisted to see my fellow villagers lying unconscious on the ground where we had left them.

"We cannot save everyone," Lindon whispered in my ear. His hand settled on my shoulder. "These are not your people. We are."

I shook my head. "I do not belong to just one tribe. Never mistake my willingness to go with you as a submission to that notion." I drew in a long breath, then turned to face him. "We are on equal grounds, Lindon. I will not accept anything less, and when the time is right, I will return to save them all."

His lips pursed, then he nodded. "Agreed."

Once again, he held out his hand. This time I took it and followed him to his vessel. The bay door closed on my village, and I turned to face it, sorrow shredding my insides. I silently said my good-byes, praying to Mother Gaia that they would be safe. With my fingers, I traced my kenaz rune, lifted my fingers to my lips and kissed them, then held them toward the sky.

Until we meet again, sisters.

The *Chaos Awakened* adventure continues!

NikiLivingston.com

Releasing February 4, 2021

A missing link to their elemental magic has been hidden from them, and now that the power of three has been forced apart, it will take an energy far greater than they can imagine to unite the elementals once again.

Alex had no choice but to stay behind, alone. Whispers of a painting increase her unease, but saving her father and sisters is the mission at the forefront of her mind.

Between the rogue riders, the black void, and a battle with the anaman fleet, she is second-guessing all that brought her to this dimension.

Every which way Kia Lynn turns, another person reveals their revulsion for her mother, but deep inside, she holds onto hope of gaining Tallisa's love. The longing weighs heavily on her heart, bringing with it self-doubt in her abilities. It has proven to be safer to play small and live in the shadows of those far more powerful than her.

A new family awaits Zoe Dawn. Leaving with Lindon had not been her plan, but with the anaman fleet hovering in the skies, she had to make a choice. Live now, fight later. When a handsome, sapphire-eyed man reveals her potential, she realizes there has to be a much better approach to end the battle she knows is ahead.

Unbeknown to the three elementals, a final transcendence must ignite across the lands of Earth, but this time, it will require more than the power of three. A lower vibration still tethers them to their old behaviors, and in order to complete their destinies, they must release their attachments before the final one awakens.

ACKNOWLEDGMENTS

I dove into this series fully expecting one outcome and by the time I finished *Expanded Chaos*, my characters had veered off onto a completely different path. Congratulations to all my readers for making it to the end of book two. Soon you will partake in the final tale of the *Chaos Awakened Saga*!

Thank you to my editor, Angie, and her staff at Novel Nurse Editing. Your skills are quite magical and fit in well with this Dystopian Fantasy! I appreciate all the work you have done to help me mold this story and complete this masterpiece. I know it was a bumpy ride, but you helped me make it to the end and I am so grateful for your guidance and feedback.

I want to give a big round of applause for Niki Ellis Design. I adore the *Expanded Chaos* book cover and appreciate all the intricate details you brought to life to showcase this enchanting tale. Thank you for your patience with me and all my requests!

Thank you to my family and friends for your support. As always, you all have my back and I truly appreciate the love you shower upon me, especially on the days I did not deserve it.

A big thank you to my advanced readers. I really love the advice and constructive criticism. It helped build the final version of the story and I would not have been able to do that without your words of encouragement.

Finally, thank you to all my readers. You are the reason I continue on this writing journey. I love the thrill of the story, but most of all, I am absolutely delighted when they make another person smile. Thank you for making it possible for me to do that for you!

ABOUT THE AUTHOR

 International Bestselling Author Niki Livingston writes tales of epic and dystopian fantasy worlds filled with magic, mysticism, and mystery.

When she's not busy writing enchanting stories of diverse women rising in their power and strength, she spends her time walking her rescue puppy, quieting her mind with meditation and yoga, diving into the newest books of Veronica Roth and Anne Bishop, and binge-watching Game of Thrones, The Mandalorian, and The 100.

For all her latest releases and updates, subscribe to Niki Livingston's newsletter!

www.NikiLivingston.com

www.ingramcontent.com/pod-product-compliance
Lightning Source LLC
Chambersburg PA
CBHW051946240626
47153CB00005B/1651